BLOOD FOR THE MASSES

OTHER BOOKS BY B. L. MORGAN

BLOOD AND RAIN
BLOOD ON CELLULOID
NIGHT KNUCKLES

BLOOD FOR THE MASSES

B. L. MORGAN

SPEAKING VOLUMES, LLC

NAPLES, FLORIDA

2011

BLOOD FOR THE MASSES

ISBN 978-1-61232-020-5

Library of Congress Control Number: 2011920002

This book as well as every other I write is always dedicated to my wife Judi.
Without you, I have no idea where I would be.
Without you, all of this would mean nothing.

This is also a special dedication to my Dad.
The best parts of J.D. come from you. The worst parts, well, I should have
listened when I didn't. Then maybe I wouldn't have to know what I do.

PROLOGUE
1966
Vietnam

We moved through the jungle like shadows.

Five of us, Special Forces, seek and destroy specialists.

Spread out along the trail we moved as silent as all the rest of the animals in this hot rain forest. The undergrowth was thick, but we didn't use our machetes to chop our way through. That would make too much noise.

The heat beat down on us from all sides. The thick undergrowth and trees stopped any breezes that might be blowing out in the open spaces.

We avoid open spaces.

Our target was a prisoner of war (POW) camp that was around a half mile away.

The ground was moist and squished beneath our boots.

Mosquitoes flew in rings around our heads. When they land and bite we brush them off. Even a slap can give us away. Just one slap from any one of us, can get us all killed.

It is dark in the forest, almost as dark as night. The trees are so lush with thick green leaves that not much sunlight makes it down to ground level.

We remain alert by reminding ourselves any creak or pop or snap or any sound at all could be made by someone with a rifle pointed at our heads.

The clearing is just ahead and below us. It is still midday. We communicate using sign language.

Our faces are painted with black and green stripes and blotches to mimic the foliage and shadows we move through.

It's a dead heat we move through out here in the jungle.

There is no breeze, no wind and no relief.

Just heat.

We carry light weapons. M-16's with crosshair scopes and plastic explosives with radio controlled detonators.

The report is that there is a Lieutenant Colonial Ray Sharp in this POW camp. We either bring him out alive or level the whole place.

I'd rather just level the whole place and take whatever POW's back with us that we find still alive. Our orders are to get Lieutenant Colonial Ray Sharp. They don't give a shit about the rest of the men held in the camp. The Lieutenant Colonial is a relative of some congressman back in Washington. So his family has clout. He is important. The rest of us are just meat for the grinder.

We set up observation posts in the trees back away from the perimeter of the POW camp. Far enough away so they won't see us, but close enough where we can watch them.

From up high in my perch in my tree, I can look down on the entire camp. I watch through hooded binoculars.

The camp is made up of bamboo and wood huts in a rough semicircle. Around that is a wide space, wide enough for jeeps to be driven around the edge of the camp. Around that is a high barbed wire fence. Two guards walk the fence. They smoke cigarettes and appear to be half asleep.

Inside the semicircle of huts are bamboo cages sitting on the ground. Anywhere between ten and thirty men are stuffed into five cages. The cages do not look to be large enough for the men to be able to stand up. They are probably only tall enough for the men to move around on hands and knees.

A soldier walks by the cages swinging a stick.

He says something and spits on one of the prisoners. He jabs the stick at the prisoner and laughs when the prisoner scurries away on all fours.

"Now, there's a son of a bitch that's just got to die," I say silently to myself.

The afternoon wears on.

The hours pass slowly.

The bugs keep me company buzzing around my head. The other men are too far away in their own perches so we converse using sign language. I take a long slow count of how many soldiers I see individually around the camp. From watching them go through their normal duties for the day I estimate there to be around twenty five soldiers in the camp.

A lizard, looking something like a gecko, crawls out off a limb and onto the back of my hand.

"What's up?" I ask him in a whisper. He rolls his eyes at me. "Thanks for inviting me to your home," I tell him.

"You belong here. You're green and cold blooded, just like this place." I catch my own reflection in the lenses of my binoculars. My face with its black and green stripes blends in with the tree trunk behind me.

"Well, what-a-ya know," I tell the lizard. "Maybe I belong here too."

Down in the camp near the largest building there's some activity going on. What looks like a square nailed together is in reality the entrance to a tunnel. The end rises up and a large man, much larger than the Viet Cong soldiers, emerges from below.

From my perch even with the binoculars, I can't make out any details about the man's appearance. His size alone identifies him as a non-oriental.

A Viet Cong officer comes out of the tunnel behind the large man. The two are friendly. They pass a bottle back and forth as they walk to where the cages sit in the dust.

The large man pulls out what appears to be a machete. He walks around the cages inspecting the men inside. The officer and the large man talk and laugh gesturing toward the prisoners. The large man keeps slapping the blade of the machete against the bamboo bars of the cages. He stops and points to one of the prisoners, then moves to another spot and does the same to another prisoner. He says something to the officer.

The officer shouts and four soldiers run up.

They drag the two prisoners out of their cages.

The two American soldiers stand bowed over from being in the small cages for so long.

Other Viet Cong soldiers are gathering around. They form a large circle around the pair of prisoners. The large man walks back and forth in front of the prisoners. He has a soldier give him his canteen. He lets the prisoners drink from it.

What the hell is going on? I ask myself. My question was not long in being answered.

The prisoners were separated. With rifles pointed at their heads each was handed a machete. The large man motioned the two toward each other to fight.

The jungle seemed to get suddenly hotter, if that was possible, as I watched the two POWs. They stood frozen; looking at each other for a moment that seemed like it went on forever.

The large man shouted something at the two prisoners. One of the POWs shouted something back and threw down the machete. It looked like he gave the large man the finger.

The large man laughed and snatched away a soldier's rifle. He fired four shots into the prisoner's chest. The prisoner went down in a spray of his own blood.

His body was dragged away.

The large man went back to the cages and pointed to another prisoner. This one was hauled out of his cage screaming.

When the prisoner was handed the machete he immediately charged the other POW slashing and shouting curses as he came at him. He had the look of someone who'd lost touch with his sanity. He came in with wild cuts and slashes meant to dismember and disembowel.

The other POW calmly side-stepped and back-peddled from his attacker. When the crazy prisoner missed a particularly vicious stroke and threw himself off balance, the other stepped forward. He thrust his machete through the crazy prisoner's throat.

With no change of facial expression, he pulled his blade free and watched as the other prisoner on his hands and knees coughed his life's blood out in the dirt.

The large man took the machete away from the victorious prisoner. He clapped him on the shoulder. It seemed almost like a congratulations.

At gunpoint the prisoner was forced down through the trapdoor into the tunnel beneath the ground.

The large man gave something to the officer and followed the others down into the earth.

We stayed in our perches until night came. What we had witnessed made no difference to our mission. We came to get Lieutenant Colonial Ray Sharp. That is what we were going to do.

Night came.

Under the cover of darkness we cut holes in the fence and cut the throats of the sentries walking the perimeter.

Using stealth tactics we planted plastic explosives under all the huts.

The plan was to distract the guards at the cages by blowing up the huts. Then kill them from the other direction before they knew where we were coming from.

The plan worked like a charm. Except for one detail, we didn't plan on the true viciousness of the Viet Cong.

We detonated the explosives set beneath the huts and one after another all of the buildings in the compound went up in balls of flame. What few men survived the explosions could be heard screaming as they roasted inside the huts. The smell of burning wood and burning flesh was in the air.

Confusion reigned among the guards at the cages. But before we could take advantage of the confusion, one of the guards emptied his rifle into the cages. The other guards followed his example and started shooting the helpless prisoners.

The guards made easy targets in the open middle of the compound. We took them out as quick as we could, but there weren't too many of the prisoners left alive by then.

We hadn't lost even one man from our five man Special Forces unit.

One of our guys threw a hand grenade down into the entrance to the tunnel that we'd seen the large man come out of and go into. After doing a mop up on the compound to make sure no soldiers were still alive, we started looking for Lieutenant Colonial Ray Sharp.

Two American soldiers were still alive. One had a sucking chest wound. We gave him some atropine and made him comfortable. He wouldn't last long. The other had been shot through the legs. His wounds were extremely painful but if he could make it to a morning helicopter pick up, he just might make it back home alive.

There was no Lieutenant Colonial Ray Sharp among the dead in the cages.

We searched the entire compound. He was not there. Our surviving rescued soldier was still conscious and we questioned him about Lieutenant Colonial Ray Sharp.

Ray Sharp was the one the large man had taken down into the tunnel.

Our NCO in command was Staff Sergeant Robert Olson. The son of a bitch hated me with a passion ever since I'd started fucking a Vietnamese nurse who dropped him. One night after I'd given the nurse a two hour American internal meat massage, I asked her why she stopped seeing Olson.

She told me, "He no got long dong like you. Not enough for me."

So naturally, I told just about everybody on base about Sergeant Olson's shrunken member.

That might have been why he sent me down into that hole to see if Lieutenant Colonial Ray Sharp was down there. Going down into the tunnels in Vietnam was usually a suicide mission. The tunnels were small, tight cramped spaces with all kinds of twists and turns. A Viet Cong soldier could be hiding around any of the corners and you wouldn't know it until you're nose to nose with him.

I looked down into the pitch blackness and realized this might be the last time I'd ever be above ground. What the hell, I thought, you got to die sometime. Let's get this over with. With my flashlight in my left hand and my M-16 in my right I went down into the earth.

With the flashlights beam cutting through the dusty darkness I saw right away that this was a different kind of tunnel than the ones I'd encountered before. Usually there's a ladder leading down to a roughly level crawlway that was too small to stand up in.

I walked down on stone stairs. The ceiling was high enough so I'd have to reach up over my head and stretch up to touch it. Going down, I passed the spot where the grenade had detonated on the stairs. Except for a few chips of stone knocked loose, there had been no damage done to the tunnel. In fact, the tunnel going down seemed to have enlarged so much that I was starting to feel like I was in the darkened stairway of a large building.

I wasn't counting my steps as I went down, but after a while of moving steadily downward, I realized I had to be a long way under the ground. Somewhere between seventy and ninety steps is what I must have taken before the stairway came to an end and I stepped on level ground.

Going so deep into earth was disorienting. My mind couldn't quite get a grip on it. Up above was a rain forest. That meant the ground was almost a swamp. I shined the flashlight around me. On both sides were brick walls. The bricks were of varying sizes, mortared together. The bricks were cold and lightly moist to the touch. The ceiling was a good ten feet from the floor.

In front about thirty paces was a large steel door. I went to the door expecting it to be locked.

It was not.

I opened the door onto a scene that could have come right out of Dante's Inferno. There were no living people here. But there sure were a lot of dead ones.

It was a huge chamber that I stepped into.

Estimating the chambers size would be hard because of the surprise of finding an opening of this size down here. The floor of this chamber covered roughly the same area as a high school football field. The height of the chamber was impossible to judge. It was so high that the ceiling was lost in blackness.

This was an ancient temple of some sort. The floor was obsidian black, polished to a highly reflective sheen. Torches burned from pedestals all around a central ceremonial alter. The ceremonial alter had a large stone slab platform that a man was strapped to. His chest had been ripped open. When I moved closer I saw his chest cavity was vacant. His heart and lungs had been pulled out. This man was Oriental, definitely not Lieutenant Colonial Ray Sharp.

There were two piles of similarly mutilated dead men and women, one on each side of the ceremonial altar. I estimate there were around thirty bodies. None fit Ray Sharp's description.

In back of the ceremonial alter was a huge stone statue of a hellish looking god of some pagan religion that I'd never heard of and didn't want to. The statue had the body of a man, except for having six arms. The two arms extending from its midsection ended in lobster pinchers.

The head of the stone idol was that of an elephant, except it had the horns of a bull sticking out of its forehead. It must have been a trick of the light caused by the flickering torches, but the idol's eyes seemed to be following me when I moved around the room.

In between the stone alter, where the man with the ripped open chest lay and the elephant god statue, there stood upright an oval of stone. Strange hieroglyphs were carved into it that reminded me of astrological signs, but they were in no language I'd ever seen before. The oval formed a standing upright ring, large enough for a man to step through its center easily.

I had no idea what that oval might be for and I really didn't want to know.

The uneven flames of the torches cast dancing shadows all around me. I checked the walls for exits and entrances. The only door I found was the one I came in through.

While I was checking the wall behind the elephant god, a weird high pitched hum started to gradually fill the chamber. Strange stroboscopic lights bounced around from in front of the statue. I came out and saw that the hieroglyphic symbols on the oval were glowing and pulsating.

Standing in front of the sacrificial alter I looked into the glowing oval. The air inside the oval looked like it was congealing. It was shimmering like jelly and the center of the oval was getting darker. The darkness spread out from the center of the oval until I was looking at a pure black void. The high pitched hum had now turned into a scream.

An intense feeling of vertigo seized me. I was dizzy. I couldn't tell what was up and what was down. As I looked into the oval I realized that it was some sort of a gateway. I could see an enormous gulf of space through the oval. Stars blinked in the distance. The screaming sound was the shrill screaming of the never ending nothingness that waited beyond the door of the stone oval.

Something in the far distance of the vast emptiness was coming forward. Looking at that void, I felt sick to my stomach. I felt like I was falling from a great height. The doorway into the void was drawing me toward it. I could feel myself being pulled. It was not like wind at my back. It was like magnetism. It was as though my entire body was metal and the oval was a powerful magnet drawing me in.

The thing inside the void was looming larger. I could just make out the outline of it and I didn't like what I saw.

Size was impossible to judge but it looked to have a woman's body covered by gray flowing robes. The head was what was disturbing. It appeared to be a mass of squirming snakes. Looking at her made me feel chilled to the bone.

The thought passed through my slow moving mind that this is Medusa. To look in her face meant being turned to stone.

I tried to pull my gaze away but my mind seemed in a fog and my body refused my mind's commands. A strange lethargy filled all of my limbs. It was like I was standing in rapidly solidifying cement.

To my right one of the torches suddenly flared high like it had burned down to a more volatile section of whatever fed its flame. Unconsciously, my eyes shifted in that direction.

With the unconscious shifting of my eyes, the spell was broken. I stumbled to the side and fell to my knees on the polished obsidian floor. My legs were stiff like I'd been outside in the freezing cold for a long time.

The screeching from the void beyond the stone oval was getting louder. It was vibrating into my bones. The thing that I'd seen on the other side of the gate must be getting closer now. I didn't know if it was the Medusa that I'd heard about in grade school from Greek Mythology or if it was one of the Harpy's from Hell. All I knew was that I didn't want to be here when whatever it was came though that gateway.

I had two grenades on my belt. One of them should do the trick, I thought. With my back to the sacrificial alter that still held its final victim I pulled one of the grenades loose from my belt. Aiming more from memory than anything else, I pulled the pin and flung the grenade backward over my shoulder, hopefully into the oval. I took four steps to the side and dove for the ground.

The grenade exploded behind me and sent a shower of stones raining down. The shrill screaming hum coming from the oval stopped almost immediately.

I got up and ran to the door and flung it open, went through and slammed it shut behind me. I had never even taken a glance at the stone oval ever since the flaring up of the torch had distracted me on an animal level. Whatever had been on the other side of that gateway, I didn't want to face it.

After climbing around fifteen of the stone stairs I stopped and pulled my remaining grenade off my belt. I pulled the pin and threw it at the door and ran for all I was worth up the stairs. The explosion below me came a few seconds later.

When I came out into the open air Sergeant Olson was waiting for me.

"All right Private Dark," he said, "Report!"

"Nothing to report," I told him. There was no way I was telling him the truth. "The tunnel came up in the jungle. No one was there."

"Then what was that explosion we heard?"

"Just sealing the tunnel," I told him. "I wouldn't want anyone creeping up behind us when we leave."

He considered this.

He said, "I think you're lying."

"Then go check it out yourself," I told him, "If you've got the balls to do it."

He never went down the stairs.

I didn't figure he would.

I've tried to forget what I saw that night.

PART I

Not drunk is he, who from the floor
Can rise alone and still drink more.
>   -T.L. Peacock, The Misfortunes of Elphin

"This is the hurtin' game.
It's all about hurtin'."
>   -George Foreman

Here's to you, as good as you are
And here's to me, as bad as I am.
>   -Old Scotch Toast

"I'm gonna hit you so hard and so fast
You're gonna think someone's pattin' for a dance."
>   -Bob L. Morgan Sr.

"I'm gonna kill him!"
>   -George Foreman on Muhammad Ali
>   before they fought

CHAPTER 1
East St. Louis, Illinois
April 1st
April Fools

Well, here it is April Fool's Day and I'm walking the streets again in the rain. If they were going to name a holiday for me, they should have at least thrown me a parade. I don't see no damn parade, and I bet there's no surprise party waiting for me at home.

Its eight o'clock, on Friday night and my woman Julia just kicked me out. Well, actually she just suggested I leave. But ain't that the same damn thing.

Julia's daughter Felicia, was going to be staying over at a friend's house for the weekend, so I figured I'd go on over and tonight would be the night. For the last few months, I'd been hanging around Julia like a dog hangs around a lean steak.

I'd only gotten some long kisses and feels of her ass through the fabric of her dress, so I was long overdue to be parking my Johnson where it would be snug and warm and well cared for.

I got a little bit too handy and Julia didn't like it. She said I was going too fast.

That was when I asked her, "So when the fuck am I going to be fuckin' you anyway?"

Julia's chocolate face went a bit darker and I didn't have the good sense to shut up right then. I went on with, "You know, if you don't use that pussy pretty soon, it just might dry up and clamp shut and you might not be able to get it open when you do want to put something in there."

The expression on Julia's face told me that I'd scored a direct hit.

I thought I was doing kinda good, until that slap of hers landed. I didn't know Bruce Lee could move that fast, much less a well-built black woman. That slap rang my bells but good.

That was when Julia suggested I leave.

Since I figured I'd be wearing that hand print on my jaw till the next day and I didn't want to be fist fighting with a woman that I was still hoping to be doing the horizontal tango with some day, I left.

* * *

The rain was cold and bitter. It felt like buck shot was being thrown into my face. The streets were wet and cold. My spirits were low. My bank account was lower.

Bank account, what back account?

I had a hundred and fifty dollars in my pocket and that was it.

I hadn't taken any jobs for the last few months because I was trying to straighten myself out. I was going to walk the straight and narrow, and be a solid citizen, the kind of man that Julia could love and spend her life with. Not to mention the kind of guy she would spread her thighs for.

What's that got me?

I'm sober, broke and pissed off. I got a hard-on that won't go away and I got nowhere to put it. A car came down the street from behind me. I glanced over my shoulder as it passed by. The car hit a puddle and showered me with dirty stinking water.

If I would have had my .38 with me that I haven't carried for two months now, I would have shot that bastard through his back window.

Happy April Fool's Day.

* * *

I went to Johnny's Bar and Grill. I was just tired of wandering the streets, and staring at cracked sidewalks.

Johnny saw me as I came through the door. "Hey, speak of the devil," he yelled. "Here's his second cousin."

"His first cousin," I told Johnny and plopped down on a bar stool in front of him.

"You off the wagon?" He asked.

"I think it ran over me," I told him.

He poured me a Schlitz from the tap.

I tasted it and grimaced. "This stuff tastes like piss water." I told Johnny. "Man, you know I can't stand Schlitz. Why you give me that shit for?"

"Cause you're a sorry mother-fucker," he answered. "I'm low on Bud and Schlitz is cheap. You came walkin' in here like your dog died. Hell, you ain't got no dog. A dog wouldn't hang around you. Would it make you feel any better if I tell you I'll give you that beer for free?"

"I get all my beer here for free," I said.

"See, you feel better already, don't you?" Johnny grinned at me.

That was my best friend trying to cheer me up.

There were about ten people in Johnny's that night. Most were quiet drunks, hiding in the shadows. Drinking down the poison of their choice, they were trying to hide from themselves as much as anyone else.

Johnny waved at the air between us, "Woo!" He said. "Damn, you smell like the devil too."

"I just got a sewage shower," I told Johnny and the smell I was giving off did tell me that the heavy rains we'd been getting lately were making the sewers back up again into the streets.

"I told ya to quit hangin' around with those golden shower chicks," Johnny said getting a Miller High Life for one of his customers.

"Why can't you give me one of those?" I asked Johnny and pointed at the Miller that was going to a table in a dark corner.

"Cause you're a cheap mother-fucker who don't pay for shit," he said and sat twelve ounces of Miller in a bottle in front of me.

I drained the glass of Schlitz in one drink and twisted off the cap from the Miller.

Laughter came from the corner table where the Miller had gone.

"You are off the wagon," Johnny said.

"In a big way bro," I told him.

Johnny looked at the TV mounted over the bar. A rerun of the *Dukes of Hazard* was on. The Duke boys were in another car chase where everybody's car gets trashed but theirs.

"I didn't know you were in to those southern country faggots," I told Johnny. "Don't you know Bo and Luke been given each other the sausage since they quit gigging frogs when they was about twelve."

"I hope Bo and Luke are giving each other the business," Johnny said. "About fifteen minutes ago, I became a lifelong fan when Daisy Duke bent over in front of the screen. Them shorts she's got on are so small I think I saw Ohio through the crack in her ass."

He went on about the *Dukes of Hazard* for a few more minutes, but Daisy wasn't coming back.

"You low on money?" Johnny asked.

"You could say that," I told him. "I think the cockroaches in this neighborhood got more cash than I do."

Johnny went into his shirt pocket and produced a business card that he handed to me. It read: *Sherman Oakes, Pugilistic Trainer. We Create Champions.* There was a phone number and the address of a gym near downtown St Louis.

"The guy stopped in and said he wanted to get hold of you," Johnny said. "He said it would be worth your trouble to call him."

I put the card in my pocket. "You never know," I told him.

"Another thing," Johnny said. "Some cute little half Oriental, half Caucasian chic came in here a couple of times the last few days. She's been asking about you."

"What's her name?"

Johnny thought hard and with his California Raisin face, he looked like he was either contemplating the mysteries of the universe or he was just constipated. "Hell, I can't quite remember. Sherry, Teri, Mary," he said. "One of those -ery names. Anyway, she wants to talk to you."

"Get her name if she stops in again," I told Johnny.

"Do I look like your fuckin' secretary?" Johnny asked.

"You look like my bitch," I told him.

"Fuck you," he said. "If she stops in, I'll give her your address and phone number. But, I do want to warn you about black women that get cheated on. Cause I know you got something with Julia."

"What's that?" I asked.

"If a black woman loves ya, she'll cut your nuts off."

"I'll keep that in mind," I told Johnny.

"You do that," Johnny said. "Cause we only get one set and you can't glue them back on."

*   *   *

It was about midnight when I decided it was time for me to go. I'd spent the last couple of hours staring at the bubbles in my beer, staring at Johnny, staring at the TV then starting the circle of staring all over again.

I couldn't even remember what was on the TV it was so lame. Johnny was telling me some joke I wasn't listening to. He finished up with, "So she told the young guy, well honey, I'll keep an eye out for you." He slapped the bar and laughed like a wild man.

I didn't laugh. I didn't know what the hell the joke had been about. Johnny saw me looking at him with my sober expression.

"God damn man," he said. "The joke wasn't that fuckin' bad."

I looked at Johnny, then at the TV.

Johnny said, "You are one sorry-ass son of a bitch."

"Thanks bro, I needed that," I told him.

"Damn man," he said to me, "What the fuck is wrong with you. You ought to at least tell me to go fuck myself."

"All right," I said. "Go fuck yourself."

Johnny made a dismissive gesture with his hand and snorted in disgust. He said, "That's just words bro. Ya got no passion!" When he said the "P" in passion, spit flew from his mouth that I had to duck away from.

"What's the matter?" Johnny asked. "Julia got ya by the balls."

I thought about that one for a second.

"The problem is," I told Johnny in a genuine buddy to buddy moment of pure male bonding, "Is that Julia doesn't get me by the balls at all. If you know what I mean."

Johnny looked serious. He leaned forward over the bar and whispered, "You mean you ain't fucked that broad yet."

"No," I answered.

Johnny slapped the bar and cut loose with high pitched loud laughing that had everyone in the bar looking at us.

"I should come over this goddamned bar and jerk all the fuckin' hair out of your head," I told Johnny, who was doubled over laughing.

"I'd still get more pussy than you," Johnny said in between laughs, "Even if I was bald and ugly."

I got off the bar stool. "I'm getting the fuck out of here," I told him. "You already got the ugly part down pat." I walked to the door.

Johnny yelled after me, "Sorry man, but I just couldn't help myself. That is some sorry shit."

I opened the door and gave Johnny the finger.

"Oh yeah," Johnny yelled. "One other thing, don't spank that monkey too hard. He ain't done nothing to you."

I stepped out into the rain with the sound of his and a few other people's laughter ringing behind me. That's my best friend, Johnny. He really knows how to cheer me up.

CHAPTER 2
Julio

There was an all-night liquor store about two blocks from Johnny's Bar and Grill. I walked in that direction. It was after midnight on a Friday night. I should have been playing Hop-along Cassidy with some neighborhood Pocahontas about this time. But I was just out walking along in the rain because I couldn't think of anything better to do.

This rain was cold as hell, too. It seems like when it rains hard, even I have enough sense to stay out of it as much as possible. But this drizzly, drowsy type shit that was coming down tends to fool you into believing it ain't as cold as it is.

You walk outside. A couple of drops hit you. It's no big deal. Hell, it ain't no monsoon we're talking about here. It's just a light shower.

So, you figure you can walk around for a while and be none the worse for it.

Then a drop hits you on the back of the neck. That's the first sign you get that you should have just stayed home. Before you know it, you step in a puddle and your left foot's soaked inside your shoe. You squish every time you take a step, like you're wearing a sponge instead of a shoe on that foot.

The drops keep hitting the back of your neck and keep running down your back until your shirt is soaked and you have a river of water running right down your back and into the crack of your ass. That water don't get no warmer either on its journey from your neck to your asshole.

I stepped through the door to Quicker Liquor.

This was a small liquor store with only three aisles of assorted mind wasters. Without so much as a glance behind the cash register I headed for the middle aisle, the one where the whiskey was.

Cheap whiskey was what I was after. I only had around one hundred and fifty dollars to my name. I figured I better make it last for at least a couple days.

On the middle shelf were Walkers and Southern Comfort and Jim Beam. I like those brands, but tonight they were a bit too expensive for my budget. I needed cheap, with a capital C.

On the bottom shelf, the one where you have to bend all the way down, practically to the floor, were the cheapest brands. McCormick's whiskey was the cheapest at three-fifty a quart. I knew McCormick's tasted like shit, but if you drink it fast enough, you never even notice the taste.

I took my quart of McCormick's to the counter.

"Say Vato! You look like hell tonight," a scratchy Chicano accented voice said to me from across the counter.

I looked into the blood shot eyes of Julio "Padre," Paez, a longtime acquaintance of mine, from back in the days when I was still a licensed prize fighter.

"I feel like hell," I told him.

"Yeah," he went on. "You look like a fur ball my cat spit up."

Tonight, everybody just had to try to make me feel better. I looked at Julio's battered face. He had old scar tissue over both eyes and both his ears were misshapen from absorbing hooks.

I smiled at Julio. He was an O.K. guy who never meant anyone any harm.

"You don't look like you've won any beauty contests lately," I told him.

He laughed and said, "My wife tells me she likes the rough look. The uglier I get, the more she loves me."

*   *   *

Julio "Padre," Paez had once been a professional boxer. The last I heard he wasn't taking prizefights anymore. His wife didn't like him coming home so beat up, he was scaring their kids. He had been making some extra money being a sparring partner. Sometimes you get just as beat up from sparring as you do from actual fights. But since you wear head gear, your face doesn't look as bad.

Julio got the nickname "Padre," when he was eighteen years old in his fourth professional prizefight. At the time Julio had three wins, zero losses and the local press was taking notice of him.

He was a fiery Mexican warrior who wasn't afraid of taking two punches to land one. Julio wasn't a big puncher, but he was fast enough with his hands that if he landed a good shot and the opponent backed up he would attack instantly. Julio would keep punching in quick bursts until the referee would stop the fight before the opponent had a chance to counter attack.

In his fourth fight, Julio went up against Sam Letterman. Sam was a trial horse with a solid chin and one hell of a straight right cross. He also cut real easy and had a record of five wins and five losses. All his losses were due to cuts.

Julio waded into Sam like Sam was beef stew and he hadn't eaten for a week. Julio landed a good left hook in the first round and when Sam backed up he attacked wildly. There was no way Julio was going to listen to his corner's instructions and just wait for a cut to develop. He wanted Sam out of there, and he wanted him out now.

Julio came in firing haymakers with both hands. Sam covered up and slipped and dodged the incoming punches. He fired one punch back. It was a compact, short, overhand right to the point of Julio's chin.

Julio froze, like he'd forgotten something in the dressing room and was trying to remember what it was. It seemed like he also locked eyes with some guy in the fifteenth row. Julio crashed face forward, stiff as a board, into the canvas.

The referee counted Julio out and he was carried, still unconscious, to the dressing room.

In the dressing room Julio regained consciousness as suddenly as he went out. He sat up and shouted, "Jesus Christ the Lord is my savior, I have been touched by an angel and seen the face of God!"

Julio told everyone there that he had been taken by three angels on a journey where he'd met Jesus and God himself. God told him that man was not a viscous animal by nature and that he needed to spread the word that we should all be kind to each other and that God does exist and loves us.

Of course, no one listened to Julio.

He preached on street corners and in parks. He handed out bibles every-where he went, and never took any money for giving the good word. Julio said being the messenger was reward enough.

He continued his boxing career and received the nickname "Padre" for trying to give the good word to the other boxers around him. Julio told everyone, when he found God, he found peace of mind.

Unfortunately, he also lost his killer instinct.

Now, whenever Julio hurt an opponent, he backed off and let the guy recover. Frequently Julio took some bad beatings from guys he'd let off the hook. Boxing is a brutal business. If you're not willing to be brutal, you have no business being in it.

Julio "Padre," Paez became just an opponent, just a name for rising fighters to have as a "W" on their records.

A few years later, Julio married one of the neighborhood Mexican girls and in two years she gave birth to two babies. Maybe there is a happy ending for Julio after all.

*   *   *

We talked for a few minutes about people we knew from around the neighborhood. It always surprised me how many people I'd grown up with that I was outliving. That was just one more thing I was not going to think about.

I asked Julio if he was taking any more sparring partner jobs.

"Yeah I am," he answered me. "For a while, I couldn't hardly get no work at all in the gyms. Lately it seems I've been in demand. Some of the trainers have even been calling me up."

"Really?" I told Julio, "I didn't think there was ever a shortage of guys that didn't mind getting smacked up-side the head."

"Me neither," he answered. "But hey, as long as they're paying me, I don't ask too many questions. Gotta feed those babies and god bless their souls, most of the trainers have been telling their guys to go easy on me. That makes the work a little easier on you."

CHAPTER 3
Women in Need

Back at my apartment I peeled off my wet clothes and threw them in a corner on top of the other dirty clothes there. I reminded myself that I'd better pick up the pile and throw them into a closet before Wednesday. Otherwise Rosa was going to jump on me for leaving a pile of dirty clothes out.

It doesn't make sense to me that I pay a woman to come and clean my place who gives me hell if I leave a mess for her to clean up. But I'm not sure why I do anything anymore.

I switched on the TV and sat down on the couch in my jockey shorts cradling my friend McCormick.

I took a long gulp from my friend. The whiskey burned as it went down. I focused my eyes as well as I could on the TV screen.

A movie I'd seen a few times before was just starting. I didn't really want to see this bullshit again but what the fuck else was I going to do. It was named *The Fall of The House of Usher*. Vincent Price was the only actor I recognized in the movie. I didn't really want to watch it, but I didn't want to use the energy to get off the couch to change the channel either. So, I guess I was going to suffer through this piece of shit one more time.

I took a couple more deep hits from McCormick. The burning in my throat went away and I didn't really care what was on the TV anyway.

The story was that this young sweet thing, who wore dresses too tight to breath in, was Vincent's sister. She and her fiancé came for a visit to the family castle to announce they were getting married. She acts like she's sick and half stoned all the time. Vincent tells her fiancé she can never leave the castle again.

Think again Vince! If that was my girl, I'd have put my boot so far up your ass you'd be puking leather.

I was deeply into this movie. I wanted to kick Vincent Price's ass. I wanted to kick the fiancé's ass for being such a fucking idiot and not getting his girl the hell out of there. I wanted to fuck Vincent Price's sister because, well hell, just because I wanted to. I hadn't been fucked for a good long time and even if at this part of the movie she did look like one of the zombies from *Night of The Living Dead*. I would have given her the high hard one anyway.

She looked like she needed it almost as bad as I did.

The phone rang beside me. It jarred me out of the TV screen and I almost spilled my bottle of whiskey on myself.

I leaned over and picked up the receiver from the end table. "Yeah, what-a-ya-want?" I said into the phone. I think I slurred the words into the mouth piece, but I couldn't be sure since I was riding a pretty good buzz by that time.

The voice that came back at me was definitely feminine. The voice had a smooth, silky quality. It was very controlled. The words this voice spoke were carefully chosen and spoken clearly as though they were from a script.

"May I speak to Mr. John Dark please?"

"That's who you've got."

"Good," she said. "I received your phone number from your associate, Mr. Johnny Davis."

I instantly had a mental picture of a nice looking lady executive in a tight fitting woman's business suit, the kind of woman who sits behind a desk and makes decisions, the kind of woman who wears glasses and looks intelligent. You know she knows things that other women don't know. I was thinking I know a guy who could make use of some of that knowledge you have, and maybe teach you a few new tricks at the same time.

"Good old Johnny," I said to the lady at the other end of the line. I was trying as hard as I could to not sound as drunk as I was rapidly becoming aware that I was. "Who am I talking to?" I asked.

"Let me apologize for not introducing myself," she said. "My name is Sherry St. Clair. I would like to hire you."

The words sprang into my mind, I hope this is for stud service, and a cash register was ringing in my head too. I was badly in need of making some cash.

"What type of work?" I asked.

"I am in need of a body guard," Sherry said. "Since your altercation at Dottie's Body Shop, you are rather famous with the dancers."

What happed at Dottie's was that a young pro middleweight caused some trouble and I wiped the floor up with him. That happened some months back. I was surprised anyone remembered anything about it.

She went on, "I need someone who can handle himself in an ugly situation and you certainly fit that bill. I mainly need someone to be with me from home to work, then from work to home. The building I live in has good security, so I'm not worried about my safety at home."

"All right," I said. "We need to talk about money."

"Would five hundred a week be sufficient?" She asked.

You're damn right it would be, I thought. Just being a few bucks away from needing to sell your blood to the Blood Bank for twenty dollars a pint will make you take this kind of a paycheck real fast.

What I said was, "In advance?"

"Of course," she answered.

"Do you need me tonight?"

"Not necessary," she answered. "One of the guards at Pattie's Kitten House, the club I work at, is going to escort us home. I share an apartment in The Blaine Building with two other girls. Could you meet with me at five P.M. tomorrow, at our apartment? We can finalize all the arrangements before I start my shift at six."

"I'll be there," I told her.

She gave me her address and phone number and hung up.

Well, at least my money problems appeared to be over for a short while. I knew the club Sherry said she worked in. Pattie's Kitten House was an upscale Gentleman's club. I'd never been in it. The cover charge was twenty dollars and the drinks had to be outrageously high. That place was far outside of me being able to afford a night of fun there.

I also knew where the Blaine Building was. It was right in the middle of the high rent skyscrapers of downtown St. Louis. I didn't know what the rent was for an apartment there, but I bet it wasn't cheap. This lady had to have a lot of money to be living there. She could have paid me anything I would have asked for.

I should have asked for more.

*   *   *

By the time I got back to the movie, Usher's Mansion was collapsing in on itself. I couldn't remember if Vincent Price had gotten his ass kicked or not. Well, he deserved it.

The walls of The House of Usher were falling down. It was about time too. This movie made you feel like you were going to die of old age before it was over.

The thought hit me that I really might want to clean myself up a bit before I went to Sherry St. Clair's apartment tomorrow. For five hundred dollars a week, she could hire two bodyguards and if I showed up looking like a skid row bum my new good fortune might be over as quick as she could say, "I've reconsidered our arrangement."

I looked at the whiskey bottle I had cradled in my arms like a lover.

McCormick's, this stuff really was shit. It tasted like shit. It was making me feel like shit.

It must be shit.

I went to the window and opened it. A wet wind blew in at me. It was cold and wet on my skin, kind of like the devil was laughing in my face and I was being showered by the spit flying from his lips.

Maybe that's the message I thought. I've been trying to live like a good man and it just doesn't fit me.

It's like I'm a dog trying to take a crap in a litter box. That kind of shit is OK when you're a cat, but when you're a dog, you just look kind of ignorant standing in that fucking box. Dogs just squat and shit wherever the feeling hits them.

Well, I'm not a good man. I'm that mother fucker that your mother warned you about. Guys like me are the reasons parents can't sleep when their daughters come home late from dates. That's me.

The eyes looking at you from the pitch black alley.

I threw my bottle of whiskey across the alley and shattered it on the facing wall. Some drunk, two floors below, called me a mother fucker.

That's what I am.

I'm going back to enjoying it.

CHAPTER 4
Cats and Making Cash

Julia's head lay on my chest. As she breathed she was making little moaning, purring noises and her nails worked at my chest making one of my nipples go erect.

"Yeah, I like that," I told her and she snuggled closer. She started kissing my neck and took little gentle bites with her teeth. The sensation sent goose bumps up and down my neck. The kind of goose bumps I liked.

"Yeah," I murmured and pulled her head even closer to my neck. She pulled back. "Come on baby," I whispered. "It's all right."

Now her hands on my chest felt like needles that were sticking into my flesh.

"Christ, take it easy," I said.

Her mouth pulled away from my neck and I heard a low growl.

I opened my eyes. A furry grey and white striped feline face was inches from my face.

"What the fuck?" I yelled and flung a large calico cat off of my chest and over the back of my couch.

The cat took a line of skin off my chest before I could get him out of my arms.

The cat landed on his feet. They always do. He assumed a low slung stance on the floor that meant he was ready to fight.

This was one hell of a way to wake up. A few seconds before, I thought I was about to be raped by my favorite tigress. Instead, I find all I've got on top of me is a confused alley tom cat who was probably about to try to fuck me in the ear.

I got up and came around the couch. The window was open. That must have been how he'd gotten in.

I waved my arms at the cat and yelled, "Get the fuck out of here!"

The cat backed up a step and a low rumbling growl came out of his throat. He hissed like a big angry lizard. All of his muscles were tensed to spring.

I made like I was going to charge the cat. Then, I thought better of that. I felt the line of blood on my chest from the one claw he'd gotten to me before I'd flung him. I looked at my bare ankles and legs imagining what they would look like after a serious bout with this miniature knife fighter.

I pointed at the large calico cat and said, "I'll be back, you little mother fucker, and you better be gone."

Maybe he'll head back out the open window I thought, and went to the bathroom.

I took a hot, steaming shower. It did me a lot of good. Loosened me up, real nice.

After shaving, combing my hair and dressing in the bedroom, I came back into the living room.

The cat was gone.

The little mother fucker was smarter than I had thought. He knew better than to mess with me twice in one day.

I closed the window and left.

* * *

Coming out of the stairway's door into the morning sunlight, the light scratched into my eyes like a cat's claws. The rain was a fading memory, like the dreams from last night. I was blinded for a moment in the brightness of the new day.

"John Dark," a man's voice with a slight British accent said to me. "How do you do?"

I was still as blind as a bat under a sunlamp, so I put my right hand up to shade the sun from my eyes. A little old guy who had on a faded plaid pork pie hat and looked a lot like a cab driver was standing in front of me with his right hand thrust out in front of him.

"I'm Sherman Oaks," he said.

I looked at his hand in the air between us and didn't take it. "So, what does that mean to me?" I said, even if the name did ring a bell. This was the guy whose card Johnny had given me last night.

"All right," he said in a peculiar British - PT Barnum style of speaking. "We'll get right to the point with no pleasantries. I handle Roy Wilson, the young gentleman who you had an altercation with some months back. I want to hire you for one sparring session to help rebuild some of his confidence."

"First of all, Sherman," I said. "Roy ain't no gentleman. He's an asshole. He got what he deserved that night. If putting him on his ass, when he was going to beat up on some people who couldn't stop him, has hurt this punk's feelings or ruined his confidence, then too fucking bad! I don't put on the gloves any more. I'm retired."

"Mr. Dark, all I'm asking is for you to do one round with him." The more I listened to this guy's voice, the more he reminded me of Roddy McDowell, only older, with a more weather beaten face. "Just do one round," he continued. "Tell him that he's a great athlete and that you got lucky that night. Think of what that will do for this young man's career to have the doubts removed that have been there since the night the two of you met."

"I don't give a fuck about his career," I told Sherman Oaks.

He fished into his pocket and came out with a large roll of twenties. "I will pay you well," he said.

"Now you're speaking my language."

"One hundred dollars," Sherman said, "For one round."

"Forget it," I told him. I knew I was going to be making five hundred dollars tonight so I had a bit of room to negotiate.

I said, "Three hundred, take it or leave it, for three minutes of sparring."

He thought for a moment. "All right," Sherman said, "paid when you arrive at the gym and are ready to go."

I smiled, "Sure thing."

*   *   *

After Sherman Oaks told me where he was having Roy Wilson work out today, I went back up to my apartment to dig out what I could find of my boxing gear.

I hadn't touched any of this stuff for a couple of years so I figured my boxing shoes, hand wraps, mouth piece, cup and trunks would be in the back of the closet under a lot of other stuff.

When I opened the door to my apartment the big calico tom cat was sitting in the middle of the floor staring at me. I started for him and he darted across the floor into my bedroom and under the bed.

I spoke to the cat. "I really don't have time to play with you right now," I told him. I walked over and opened the window again. "Leave while I'm gone," I yelled, "And I won't snap your little fucking neck." If he understood what I said, he chose to ignore me.

My gear was in the closet where I'd dropped it at least two years before. Everything smelled musty, but it hadn't rotted to the point of being useless.

I made sure the shoes didn't have any spiders or cockroaches in them. I washed my old mouthpiece out and checked to see that no small bugs were living in the crevices that my teeth fit into. Then I put all my gear and something extra as insurance into a paper bag and headed back out to the street.

My heart was already starting to pound in my chest as I walked to my car. I'd forgotten what this feeling was like. When you have a street fight you don't know it's going to happen. So you just react to the situation and dive in. Before you know it, it's over.

But, going into an organized fight, you know what's ahead of you. Your mind has more time to imagine all the terrible things that can happen in just a short time ahead.

I told myself. "This is only a sparring session. No one is supposed to get serious when you're only sparring." Another part of my brain said back, "Yeah right, so when has anything ever happened the way it's supposed to."

CHAPTER 5
Dancing and Knuckle Dusting

I pulled my tan Olds Delta Eighty Eight into the parking lot of The East Side Gym. It was about eleven o'clock. Breakfast was long overdue and I was hungry as hell.

The thought ran through my mind that I could just go and get breakfast then come back. The truth was, the chances of me coming back at all if I left now would not be high.

The East Side Gym was a half block up from the riverfront in a warehousing district. It looked like a small warehouse itself that hadn't been able to make it at that business and was sold and converted into a gym. People talk about the atmosphere that a boxing gymnasium can have. Places where the sweat and grime of champions learning their craft can inspire the young fighters coming after them to train harder, run longer, and listen closer to their trainers to absorb everything the older champions left behind.

Well, The East Side Gym didn't have any of that. It was an ugly discolored white building on the outside with a spray painted stenciled sign over the door identifying what it was.

The inside was just a big room where six hanging heavy bags were being banged on. There were four places where speed bag platforms were bolted to walls. All the speed bags were being slapped around. There were two rings set up on mats level with the floor. Both of the rings had pairs of boxers flailing away at each other inside of them. I noted with some satisfaction that neither pair of boxers showed any skill at all. They were just banging away at each other. You don't learn much training like that.

A bell rang and the two pairs sparring left the rings and were replaced by two new pairs. One of the boxers sparring was Julio Paez. The guy they had him in with was none other than Roy Wilson.

I spotted Sherman Oaks standing on the other side of the squared circle, leaning into the ring saying something in Roy's ear.

Just past the two boxing rings was a weight training area where muscle heads were pumping up and flexing for each other. The bell rang and the sparring started up again. I was walking around the rings to where Sherman Oaks was when a strange sight caught my eye.

One of the muscle heads in the weight area was using a weight bar with no weights on it. In exaggerated slowness he was mimicking sword fighting slashes. The bar had to weight at least thirty pounds but he handled it with ease and controlled the bar with admirable skill.

The guy with the bar had long brown hair that came down to his shoulders. He was roughly around six foot two and probably weighed around two twenty. There wasn't an ounce of fat on him.

I couldn't put my finger on it but something about the guy just didn't seem right. He just did not seem to belong here. He caught me looking at him and his eyes flashed me a challenge that if I didn't know better, I would of taken for a death threat.

* * *

Sherman Oaks had his back to me when I walked up to him. He never took his eyes off of his fighter in the ring.

"Didn't think you'd show up," he said to me.

"You got my money?" I asked.

"Of course," he answered. "If I pay you now, you're not going to duck out the back door are you?"

"No chance of that," I told Sherman. In fact, the idea had gone through my mind.

Sherman shouted to Roy, "Move and jab the rest of the round. Practice defense the rest of the way."

He turned to me. "No, I don't think you are the kind to run."

I smiled at him. "Not likely," I said.

Sherman reached into his pocket and brought out the same roll of bills I'd seen on the street. He counted out three hundred dollars in twenties and handed them to me.

I stashed the money in my pocket.

* * *

In the locker room as I was changing from street clothes to my boxing gear, some of the training fighters wandered in and out. There was a full length mirror at the end of the aisle that I was changing in. I could see the difference between them and me.

They were lean, and hard, and young, and fast with corded muscles, and hard steely eyes. I only had the hard eyes. My body was soft. I hadn't even worked out for a couple of years. I knew I was not prepared for this. So, what in the hell was I doing here? I asked myself.

Just making a couple of bucks was my answer and knowing the risks involved, that was not a good enough reason. The truth was I was here because I couldn't stomach the thought of ever backing down from a fight. I'm getting too god dammed old for that attitude, but I just can't seem to out-grow it.

I changed into my stuff. My cup, my trunks, my socks and shoes, put my mouthpiece in and wrapped my hands. On the way out, I shadow boxed for about thirty seconds in the full length mirror. Even in that short period of time, I caught myself doing lots of things wrong.

I'd shoot a left jab and my left hand would drop when I brought it back. That invited a counter right. I wasn't stepping in when I threw the jab. That was decreasing my reach. I kept seeing my elbows wind-milling out when I threw a left hook or a right cross. Doing that can get your ribs broke by a good body puncher.

Roy Wilson was an excellent body puncher.

Damn, this sparring session is going to be real fun, I said to myself. Just like going to the dentist.

As I finished my shadow boxing Julio Paez walked in. "Hey John," he said to me and took off his sparring gloves and helped me put them on. "I think Roy loves you man."

"What makes you say that?" I asked him as I pushed my hands past the elastic wrist bands of the gloves.

"Roy was being kind of lazy today," Julio said and laughed. "Until Sherman told him he'd be sparring with you. Then he tried to take my head off."

"Thanks Julio," I told him. "That's just what I needed to hear."

Julio followed me to the ring, but I was the only one who climbed between the ropes. The first thing you learn in this business is that the ring can be one of the loneliest places on Earth. It's only you and that guy that's trying to rip your head off, because you can't rely on the referee to keep you from getting killed.

We didn't even have a referee today.

Roy Wilson was standing in the far corner with his back to me. Sherman Oaks was talking to him.

I banged my gloves together to get the feel of them on my hands. They were tight and sweaty from Julio using them.

They felt good. I never did like starting with cold gloves on my hands.

Sherman looked at me over Roy's shoulder. "No cheap shots," he shouted. "OK."

"Just as long as he doesn't," I said through my mouthpiece. I didn't know how long I'd be able to stick to that.

Sherman shoved in Roy's mouth piece and Roy turned around and faced me.

Our eyes met for a second then he jerked his gaze away. Roy was biting down so hard on his mouthpiece that his lips were white.

Without any ceremony, the bell rang.

Skipping to the center of the ring, I did something that was uncharacteristic for me to do. I extended my left hand to touch gloves. It was a show of friendly good sportsmanship.

Roy leaped forward past my extended glove and threw a wild left hook.

Without thinking, I stepped inside it and Roy's hook went behind my head. I shoved him backward and was grateful as hell that my reflexes weren't so dulled that I couldn't avoid that first hook. If he would have landed that one, my head would have been bouncing among the muscle-heads and their weights.

Roy backpedaled and moved to his own left in a circle away from me. He flicked out a few fake left jabs that missed by at least a foot. Roy was moving far faster than he needed to.

That right hand shot that I'd landed on Roy at Dottie's Body Shop must still be giving him all kinds of nightmares. Roy wasn't letting me get anywhere near him.

So I moved toward Roy slowly and carefully. If Roy wanted to run out the three minutes that would be fine by me. Sherman paid me three hundred dollars for three minutes of sparring. If his boy wanted to do it as a three minute track meet, that was okay. I'll just follow him around for three minutes.

Roy probably had no idea how far out of shape I was. I didn't want to show him.

While giving Roy some shoulder and head feints, I moved toward him gradually. He was falling for almost every one of my feints by jerking away from the anticipated punch. While Roy was out of position, I didn't take advantage of him on purpose.

I didn't want to engage Roy in a shootout. All I wanted to do was get through these three minutes as painlessly as possible.

Everything was going along just fine. I was sliding around and feeling a little bit of a rhythm to my feints and half thrown punches. Roy seemed to be cooperating. He was moving around, making serious faces, throwing punches not intended to land and posing.

He threw a series of left jabs and slightly pulled back his right to throw a punch I knew wouldn't even be close to my head and ripped a left hook instead.

That one caught me clean.

I was now convinced that Roy Wilson definitely could punch. The left hook smashed into my teeth. Fireflies buzzed in front of my face. The bells of St. Michael's church were ringing all around my head. I didn't like the song those bells were playing. It seemed like all the bones in my legs vanished at once and I was having one hell-of-a-time just staying on my feet.

I stumbled forward and Roy let loose with a series of left hooks to my right side. Roy was close to me so I grabbed onto him like a horny high school quarterback going after his cheerleader girlfriend.

"Get loose! Get loose!" I heard someone yelling and turned my head and saw Sherman Oaks shouting at Roy. "Get loose, damn it. Make him pay."

There were quite a few onlookers now. The one that caught my eye was the one that stood in back of Sherman. It was that big muscle-head that had been doing the slashing movements with the weight bar. He had a kind of a half-smile on his face as he watched me get pummeled. The look in his eyes, I can only describe it as hunger.

I got Roy's arm under my armpit and locked it to my side. Roy was trying hard to shove me away because I was too close to him for him to get off another powerful punch. I had a hold on Roy like a politician grips a taxpayer's money. I wasn't letting go till I was ready.

After about fifteen seconds, that felt like three hours, my legs came back and my vision cleared up. When Roy shoved to get me off of him, I went with it.

Roy leaped after me with a wide right hand that I easily avoided.

Sherman yelled from ringside, "Use your speed! Use your speed!"

Roy circled, dancing lightly on his toes. He came in with a quick jab-right-left hook All of them landed. When I tried a counter right to the left hook, Roy was gone and I ate two more left jabs for my trouble.

Roy was in a rhythm.

Sherman yelled, "That's right, use your speed, he can't handle your speed!"

Why don't you just shut the fuck up, I thought. Because the truth was, he was right. When Roy used his quickness and basic boxing technique, he was too fast for me. Way too fast.

Well, I thought, I'm just going to minimize the exchanges. Maybe I can last these three minutes out.

Roy snapped a jab in my face. When he tried to follow it up with a combination, I picked off those punches with my gloves or slipped them with head movement.

Roy tried the exact same sequence again. Jab followed by a right-left-right, with the same results. I ate the jab and avoided all the rest of the punches.

When a man is only trying to avoid punches, he's hard to hit with anything other than the fastest punch. A properly thrown jab is too quick to react to before it hits you. I knew I could avoid everything that Roy threw except for that jab. Roy knew it too.

After I had eaten about five jabs and avoided somewhere around fifteen power punches Roy was getting frustrated. I was beginning to get a little winded, even if I wasn't letting it show. This round seemed like it had already lasted far too long. I was beginning to wonder when the hell the bell was going to ring.

Roy decided that now was the time to make everything personal. He dropped his hands and while standing halfway across the ring from me he yelled, "You ain't nothing but a bitch! Quit running and fight me, you faggot!"

I smiled at Roy.

Sherman must have sensed something. He shouted, "Roy, don't!"

Roy Wilson launched himself at me in a wild and uncontrolled attack. He was throwing bombs meant to kill.

The gloves come off now, I said to myself.

I backed off and slipped a few of the wild hooks. Roy was cursing at me the whole time he was attacking, calling me all kinds of names that weren't in the dictionary.

Suddenly I stopped and moved into Roy and we were nose to nose.

I grabbed Roy behind the head with my right glove.

"Let go of me, bitch!" He yelled and went to shove me off.

He gave me the little bit of room I wanted. I stomped down on his toes with the heel of my foot. The crunch of breaking toes was loud enough to be heard at ringside.

"No!" Sherman shouted.

I smashed my forehead into Roy's nose and heard it snap. My knee, I slammed into Roy's crotch. With his cup on, that didn't do much damage. But, he instinctively dropped his hands.

Using my right glove I drove Roy's face into my left elbow. Blood flew in a spray from Roy's crushed nose and gashed right eyebrow.

Roy fell away from me. I felt like kicking him on his way down but didn't. Roy lay on his side blood running from his ruined nose and busted lips. He spit out a few bloody teeth.

I turned and walked away toward the corner and ducked out between the ropes.

Sherman Oaks was looking at me in white faced shock. I spit my mouthpiece out.

"Your boy sure is one hell-of-a-fighter," I told him. "A real fucking contender." I spit back into the ring where Roy was still crawling around on his hands and knees.

CHAPTER 6
Muscle-heads & Meat-heads

Julio met me at the door to the locker room. He helped me pull the gloves off my hands.

"Damn John," Julio said, "You are one bad mother fucker."

"He ain't nothin' but a boy," I told Julio. "Anybody could've slapped him down."

"Maybe so, but you made it look like fun." He slapped me on the shoulder and walked back into the gym.

The adrenalin from our short bout was wearing off now. I walked the rest of the way to my locker and looked at myself in the full length mirror. The right side of my torso had large red splotches up and down it. A few of the larger spots looked like they would be purple by tonight.

My ribs on that side felt tender. It was starting to hurt just to breath.

While I gingerly started to change from my gear to my street clothes, the muscle-head who was doing the slashing movements entered the locker room. He walked straight toward me. The way this guy moved reminded me of the lions and tigers I'd seen on Marlon Perkins' *Wild Kingdom*. He moved like he was balanced and gave the impression of a coiled spring.

The muscle-head stopped in front of me just as I pulled up my trousers and was buckling and zipping up.

"You are a good fighter." He said. His words were stiff. He had some kind of a foreign accent that I couldn't identify, something between German and Russian. "A good boxer? No! A good fighter? Yes!"

He looked at me. His eyes moved up and down my body like the way I look at a woman who I want to do the horizontal tango with. He reached toward my chest with his left hand.

I backhanded his hand to the side before he touched me. "Back off faggot Frank! I don't go for none of that guy on guy shit."

He looked at me with a puzzled expression on his face. Then he put his palms out toward me to show there was no threat. He stepped back and opened up a locker that was full of clothes and other things.

He grinned while looking into the locker at something. The grin looked totally evil. He looked at me again while rummaging through the locker. His eyes were intense. They bore into my skull.

"You think I want to have sex with you." He spit the words out like vinegar. "If I wanted to, you could not stop me." He laughed a loud laugh and I felt almost sick to my stomach.

"Not fucking likely, Chuck!" I said to whoever this big asshole was. "You go shoving something at me and I'll rip it off and feed it to ya."

Our eyes locked.

"You are mine." He snarled at me.

I had my shoes and socks and shirt on by then. "Bring it on, Faggot Frank!" I said and motioned the muscle-head toward me. I wanted to bust this idiot's head wide open.

He smiled at this.

The door to the locker room banged open. Into the room strode two tall lean mean looking black fighters.

The instant they saw me, the one in front thrust his finger out and pointed at me. "Yo, Motha-fucka!" He yelled. "Sherman wants his money back and we're comin' to take it. Sherman told you no cheap shots. You threw about a dozen and a half."

The muscle-head was between me and the two blacks.

I reached into the paper bag that I'd put my gear back into and grabbed onto the insurance I brought with me, my .38 caliber revolver.

This is my gun of choice. It's small and maneuverable but has enough weight so I feel like I have something in my hand I can grip onto and it packs a big punch.

"You and Sherman can both kiss my ass," I shouted back at him. "I ain't giving shit back."

They were coming at me fast when they reached where the muscle-head was. He stopped the first black cold with an open palm blow to the chest that sent him stumbling backward into his buddy behind him. The two went down in a tangle of arms and legs.

"Hey bitch!" The first one yelled at the muscle-head. "You don't have shit to do with this. But we'll fuck you up too."

The muscle-head calmly reached into his locker and pulled out what looked like a short wide bladed sword. The kind you'd see in an old *Hercules* movie.

"He is mine." He snarled at them. "I say when he will be harmed."

The black in back yelled, "You think that Ginsu knife gonna scare us? You're full of shit. We'll kick your fuckin' ass for ya!" The second man in line was talking shit, but the first man in line didn't look too eager to be charging that big blade.

I figured it was about time to end the meeting of this social club. I pulled my .38 out and showed it to them.

"Back the fuck off!" I told all of them. "I'm leaving now! If any of you follow me, I'll shoot a hole in you that you can stick your fist through."

I motioned them off to the side with my gun.

They stepped aside.

At the door I told them, "It'd be better for all of you if I never see any of you again."

The muscle-head smiled at me. "I am Caesar Lanista," he slowly hissed at me. "Remember my name. You will see me again."

I walked out through the gym with my gun in my hand. There were a lot of mean looks thrown my way, but no one tried to stop me.

It was just another nice day for making new friends.

CHAPTER 7
Tacos for Tom

It was almost twelve o'clock noon. I was dying for something to eat. I drove down the streets of St. Louis and every time I turned the steering wheel my right side screamed to the rest of my body for mercy. Where Roy used my torso for a heavy bag hurt all the way to the bone.

But you know what?

I felt good.

That boy was a world class middleweight, rated in the top ten by at least one of the known sanctioning bodies. And I just beat the fuck right out of him.

Yeah I fouled him. But so fucking what? That kid's got somewhere around twenty years less wear and tear on him than I do. He should have been ready for me to do anything. If he wasn't, then too fucking bad.

I drove through the take-out line in a Jack in the Box and ordered five giant tacos with extra Picante sauce. I was in a spicy mood, so I figured why not have my mouth on fire too.

The voice that came out of the speaker when I gave my order was one of those sultry Spanish sounding voices. I had an instant vision of Sophia Loren or maybe Rita Moreno, the way she looked in *West Side Story*. So when she said, "Is there anything else I can get for you?"

I came back with, "Yeah, you can get yourself naked and we'll become best friends and get real close, real fast."

She giggled over the microphone, which surprised the hell out of me. When the words were spilling out of my mouth faster than my brain was working, I figured I'd soon be wearing these tacos. I was too far away in my car to soon be wearing a hand print like I'd got the night before.

The way she giggled it almost sounded like she actually liked what I'd said to her.

"Come to the second window, lover," her voice purred at me through the speaker.

Well, what do you know, I thought. Maybe this will be my lucky day. Hey, as much as I've tried to, I haven't fucked Julia yet. So what she won't know won't hurt her anyway. Maybe I'll be throwing the bone to someone tonight.

I drove up to the second window.

Through the opening a large head with a bush of bleached blond hair was thrust out at me.

"Hi lover," it said to me. It had on heavy black eye make-up, huge fake lashes batting at me and ruby red lipstick. The most important feature on this face though, was the mustache and goatee that he wore.

"We can be real good friends," he purred at me and winked.

"Not fucking likely," I told this cross-dressing nightmare.

He handed me my bag of tacos and deliberately brushed my hand as I took it. I jerked my hand back as though I'd been electric shocked.

"Ooooh, so tense," he purred at me. "My number is in the bag. I can calm you down."

"Fuck off," I said and squealed my tires getting out of there.

This might be my lucky day but that wasn't the kind of luck I was looking for.

I drove back to my apartment, taking McKinley Bridge. For a Saturday, the traffic wasn't all that bad. On the way to my place I listened to K-SHE on the radio. They were blasting out some ear-ringing rock songs.

Ted Nugent told me about Wang Dang Sweet Poon Tang and Nazareth told me that Love Hurts. As I was turning off the car's ignition Blue Oyster Cult was telling me, Don't Fear the Reaper.

Well I don't. The Reaper is going to get you in the end no matter what you do. So what's the use of worrying about it?

In my apartment I dropped the bag of tacos on my coffee table and took a long hot shower. As I inspected my bruises closer in the shower, I was definitely aware of the fact that I was getting too damn old to be doing this shit anymore.

My right side was already turning purple. My shoulders, elbows, and knees hurt from being moved faster than they wanted to go. Even my arms had large purple and blue welts and blotches from blocking punches.

This had only been for something less than three minutes, one round.

If I had just finished up a ten rounder in a semi-main event, I guess I'd be heading for the emergency room right now.

I stayed in the shower until the water was starting to come out cool.

In the bedroom it occurred to me that I hadn't seen that cat that was here earlier. While I was putting on a pair of boxer shorts and a tee-shirt I heard some scratching coming from the front room.

In the front room the cat was there underneath the open window. He was on top of a thick magazine. The cat was squatting and was taking a dump on the magazine.

I didn't rush at the cat screaming and yelling and waving my arms. I figure, there really are sometimes when everyone needs a little peace and quiet to work by.

So I left him alone to finish his business and I went and finished dressing.

Sitting on the couch, I took my tacos out of the bag.

The cat came and sat looking at me from across the room. I looked at the cat then looked at the pile of shit he'd left on the magazine under the open window.

"I guess you're not all that dumb after all." I told the cat. He had to go, but at least he didn't just do it on the floor like most animals would have. And, he'd dragged the magazine close to a place where I could get rid of it.

"Not bad at all," I told him. "I guess I better get rid of it before Rosa shows up."

I went over and picked up the magazine by its edges, keeping it flat out so the shit stayed in the middle of its cover.

The magazine was an old Playboy the cat must have dragged out from under my bed. Marilyn Monroe was on the cover. Now her face was covered in a pile of cat shit. That was probably the cat's way of telling me his opinion of Marilyn's film career.

I couldn't agree more. It was a case of great tits making up for no talent.

"Good shot," I told the cat. "You gave her the old brown-eyed kiss."

I dropped the magazine and crap out the window. Some drunk in the alley yelled something up at me.

I yelled, "Fuck you, there's more where that came from." You'd think they'd learn not to hang out under my window with all the bullshit I throw out.

I sat back on the couch.

The cat was still sitting in the same spot. He looked at me. I looked at him.

I unwrapped a taco.

"If I try to chase you out of here," I said to the cat. "You're just gonna run under my bed, right?"

The cat blinked at me. He gave a quiet meow.

"I'll take that as a yes."

I took a few bites of the taco.

"We've got to come to some kind of an agreement," I told him.

He looked interested. Well, at least he didn't fall asleep.

"Look, I'll let you stay. But, you've got to eat any other critters that come in here. You know like mice, rats, ants, flies, hell cockroaches, too. You got to eat them all. Think you can handle that?"

The cat looked at me. He blinked. He made a motion with his mouth like a silent meow.

"OK, then," I told him. "We got a deal."

I finished off the first taco. That sucker was hotter than hell. I started on the second one and unwrapped the third.

"Another thing," I told the cat. "No bringing home your friends with you. I don't want to come in to no fifteen tom cats running around here acting crazy. Now, if you bring home a woman cat," his ears perked up when I said this. "That, I can understand. Every Tom wants pussy. I know that. Just don't make her scream too loud."

The tom cat looked like he was grinning. I decided right then I was going to call him, Tom. I've always hated animal names life Fluffy or Tiger or

Snowball or some shit like that. If I was going to do that I'd call him Shit-head or Fuckhead or Asshole or well, the list goes on and on.

Tom would do just fine.

I unwrapped a taco and laid it on its wrapper on the floor between us. Tom sniffed at it.

"Go ahead," I told him. "Just don't get the shits from that picante sauce, all right."

Tom took a little bite and shook his head from the spiciness of the pican-te. Then he sneezed.

"Yeah, I know," I told him. "That goes for the both of us."

CHAPTER 8
Doormen and Babes of All Flavors

I stretched out on the couch and dozed until it was almost four o'clock. When I woke up, Tom was laying on my stomach.

"You're not all bad," I told him and scratched the top of his head. He made that motor sound that cats make then jumped down.

After I cleaned up a little bit and got ready to go over to Sherry St. Clair's for tonight's body guard stint, I laid another old Playboy magazine under the window for Tom.

A playmate grinned at the both of us from the cover of the magazine.

"Hey Tom," I told the cat. "You give her a big butt-hole beard for me too."

He meowed.

I took that as a yes.

*   *   *

At five o'clock I was standing in front of the Blaine Building.

This was one of those steel and glass structures that looked like it belongs in a science fiction flick that takes place in the far distant future where computers rule the Earth. The Blaine Building didn't look like an apartment building. It looked like where the CIA Headquarters should be.

Sherry St. Clair lived here.

At the big glass front doors a doorman of sorts stood with his arms crossed. He had the build of an old time movie *Tarzan* and wore a three piece, black, pinstriped suit that liked a little too small for him. His face had the look of a prize fighter who never met a punch he didn't want to eat. This wasn't the prettiest boy in the world.

He halted me with an upraised palm. "What's your business here?" He asked.

"I'm here to see Miss Sherry St. Clair in apartment five-twenty." I told him. "I'm expected."

"She called down," he answered. The doorman's voice was a hoarse raspy whisper. He sounded like he'd been hit one too many times in the throat.

"You're her new bodyguard?" He shook his head. "You don't look so tough to me." He opened the big glass door.

I smiled at him and answered, "Good, keep thinking that fuckhead. You might live longer." I went through the door, to the elevator, and punched the up button.

While waiting for the elevator, I looked around to get a feel for the security set up.

Where I stood was actually just the entrance to a long hallway with what looked to be office doors on both sides.

There was no reception desk, just a couple of chairs and a fake plant near the glass doors. The wanna-be tough guy was outside the doors. He was now smoking a cigarette.

I spotted a camera mounted from the ceiling. It was pointed toward the glass doors.

Assuming that all the other entrances to the building were locked and that the windows were secure, this wasn't a bad set up. Not fool proof, but not bad either. I was not going to do an inspection of the entire building. I was hired to guard Sherry St. Clair from home to work, then from work to home. That's what I was going to do.

The elevator came. I took it up to the fifth floor, then found five-twenty and knocked.

The door was answered almost instantly.

I was expected.

The woman that answered the door was a bright bouncy blond. Her eyes sparkled. She seemed to be holding back a giggle and looked like she was almost bouncing up and down even though she was standing still.

Just looking at her made me feel like grinning.

"You must be John Dark," she said and licked her lips, which gave me a twitch in the crotch.

"That's me."

"Sherry," she called over her shoulder. "Your boy's here. Come on in and sit down." She indicated a couch that was occupied by a black girl with skin as dark as coal.

I came into a room that was like an art deco display. The couch was a large wraparound model. No pictures were on the walls. The coffee tables and end tables were solid black, as was the couch and the entertainment center that their TV played from. A Lazy Boy chair was also black. The thick shag carpet was pure white. It was a room of sharp contrasts. Everything was either pure white or pure black.

The color scheme was hard on the eye balls.

"I'm Bobbie," the bouncing blond said followed by an air headed giggle. "That's Terry." She pointed to the black girl on the couch, who was so into the soap opera that she was watching that she waved her red fingernails at me and never took her eyes from the screen.

These two girls didn't have enough clothes on between them to cover a small poodle. Considering how little bare female flesh I'd seen lately, I wasn't gonna complain.

I sat down on the black couch. Terry was almost invisible against the couch since she was wearing black panties and a black bra. What I did see of her, I liked. Terry was a short stocky black girl with large almond eyes and thick lips. She had all the right curves in all the right places.

Bobbie disappeared through a door into another part of the apartment. I was left there to look at a woman who never took her eyes off the TV screen and was moving her lips to the dialogue the actors were speaking.

A few minutes later Bobbie came bouncing back in. "Sherry will be out in just a minute or two," she said. "Do you want anything to drink?"

I did, but I said, "No, that's all right." I wanted to keep my head clear for tonight. It was my first night on this job. I wanted to be on my best behavior.

I sat and waited and true to Bobbie's word, in a few minutes the door to the other part of the apartment swung open and in walked a startlingly beautiful Asian woman.

To say I was surprised is a huge understatement. This was not the woman I had envisioned from our phone conversion. This woman was small, compact and moved with the sureness and strength of a ballerina. She was dressed in a full length evening dress, complete with high-heeled shoes and sparkling silver earrings. She had jet black hair and small finely cut features.

I stood up.

She walked to me and thrust her hand out for a hand shake. I was surprised at the strength of her small hand.

She said, "I am Sherry St. Clair. Please to make your acquaintance, Mr. Dark."

There was not a trace of an Asian accent. This was the clear, precise, perfectly paced voice that I had heard over the phone the night before.

I answered her with, "And I am pleased to meet you."

She smiled at me and I found myself looking deeply into her liquid black eyes.

"You are surprised at my appearance?"

"Pleasantly surprised," I told her.

"My name throws many people off. My father is French, Jean Claude St. Clair. My mother is Japanese. Her maiden name was Myong Tokuyama."

"A nice combination," I told Sherry. It was hard to take my eyes off of her.

She looked at the two girls.

Bobbie was stretched out on the Lazy Boy. Terry was curled up on the couch. They both looked like big lazy cats. Both of them had their gaze glued to the soap opera.

Sherry shook her head, "That thing will destroy the minds of the youth of this country," she said. Neither girl heard her.

She slapped her hands together twice.

Sherry raised her voice. "Time to get ready to go to work," she told them.

Bobbie stirred from her funk and bounced into the other room.

Terry said, "I'll get ready when *As the World Turns* is over."

Sherry slapped her hands together again, making a loud pop. "You will get ready now!" She said her voice an octave higher. "And you will not say anything or you will find yourself back on the streets that I pulled you off of."

Terry sprang up from the couch and locked eyes with Sherry. She looked like she was going to launch herself at Sherry. Then she changed her mind.

"You see what I must put up with," Sherry told me with an even voice. She motioned me to sit back down on the couch.

Sherry sat beside me.

She said, "Now we will discuss my particular situation."

CHAPTER 9
An Unwanted Lift

With the two girls gone, Sherry turned the television off with a remote control. She asked if I wanted anything to drink. Again, I said, "No, thank you." It seemed like everyone wanted me to get a buzz going today.

I was tempted, but figured, I better not.

Sherry turned to me and looked into my eyes with her big dark Asian eyes.

"Normally," she said, "I am never worried about any man who takes an interest in me. Sometimes, I am flattered. But I have no romantic interest in any man, at all." Sherry paused for effect.

I guess she was trying to send a message to me to not try for the quick feel-en and fuck-en with her. Well, we'll see about that.

I said, "With the kind of work you are in, you can't very well blame some men for wanting more than just the show."

"I do not perform!" Sherry said sharply. "I am the manager for the evening shift at Pattie's Kitten House."

"Sorry," I told Sherry, "I stand corrected."

"A perfectly reasonable assumption," she went on, "Some men do make advances. Even if I do not disrobe for pay in front of them, they assume that if I am there, I am available."

"And you are not?" I said.

"Certainly not," she answered.

I was wondering just what might make Sherry available to a man. I was hoping she wasn't a lesbian. The expression on my face must have asked the question that was in my mind.

"For a man to have me," she said. "He must prove himself worthy. No man has."

Yeah, I thought, this one would be a tough nut to crack, but a nice one to crack your nuts on.

"What is it that's worrying you?" I asked Sherry.

She took in a deep breath.

"A man came into Pattie's Kitten House about a week ago," Sherry began. "It was strange the way he was looking at the girls. He went from stage to stage. We have four stages where the girls dance. He appeared to be inspecting them."

I must have raised an eyebrow.

Sherry, said, "It wasn't the way you are thinking. Men come in the club to watch the girls. They have lust in their eyes, hunger, even sometimes, a kind of reverence. What I saw from this man had none of that. He was coldly inspecting the girls. It was like he had a mental checklist that he was marking off when he looked at them. It was like he was looking at cattle or livestock of some sort."

"Really?" I asked.

"Oh, yes," Sherry said, "It was very weird. I was watching him from behind a one-way mirror when he first arrived.

"It was obvious that he was unnerving the dancers. The girls mostly just ignore the men and go through their dance routines. ut this man was scary. They could not ignore him.

"After he had some words with one particular girl, who you will meet tonight, I thought it was time that I take security with me and ask this man to leave. Of course, I would refund his cover charge and money for any drink not yet consumed. Customer relations are important to us."

"Of course," I said.

"To put it bluntly," Sherry went on, "The expelling of this customer from the club did not go as planned. I don't remember any of the details, probably because I was knocked unconscious. I had two security guards with me and both of them are still in the hospital with injuries. I woke up in the back seat of a car with the man while someone else was driving. I have been carrying a small can of mace on a keychain for so long I had practically forgotten about it.

"At a stoplight I spotted a police car. So I maced the man in the back seat with me and jumped out of the car and flagged down the police. By the time

I was able to tell the police I had been kidnapped, the car with the man who had taken me was gone."

"I see," I said as I rubbed my chin with my thumb and first finger and looked toward the wall with an expression on my face that I hoped made it seem like I was considering all that Sherry had just told me. Actually, all I was thinking was that this was just a nervous chick that was going to pay me five hundred dollars a week for being a glorified taxi ride. The chance that this guy was going to come after Sherry again was practically nil. Whoever the hell this guy was, he grabbed Sherry on the spur of the moment. He wasn't going to do it again.

Looking back to Sherry and letting my gaze wander over the smooth light coffee with lots of cream skin just above her breasts the thought did come to me, if I did put the clutch on this woman, I probably would be back for seconds. This lady was tasty.

I was not going to ask Sherry why she had waited a week after the incident to hire me. I didn't want Sherry to even have the thought that my presence was unnecessary.

She went on. "I believe I am being followed. I think I saw him twice in the last two days. That is why I called you."

Sherry went into her purse and pulled out a roll of bills. She counted out five hundred dollars in twenties. She looked in my eyes and put the bills in my hand and closed my fingers around them, holding my hand in both of hers.

"The way this man went through our bouncers," Sherry said, "I know he is extremely dangerous. Will this money buy my protection?"

I smiled at her.

"If he fucks with you," I told her, "He'll be fucking dead!" I put the money in my pocket and opened my jacket and showed Sherry the .38 in my holster.

"Will you hesitate to use that?" Sherry asked.

"'Hesitate' ain't in my dictionary," I told her. "I'll enjoy it."

CHAPTER 10
What Wet Dreams are Made of

When the girls came out from changing they had on blue jeans, tennis shoes and sweat shirts. Each of them was carrying a gym bag packed with costumes. They looked like the kind of girls I was trying to fuck back when I was in high school.

You can be sure they gave a lot of the guys that go into Pattie's Kitten House a whole lot of wet dreams.

I escorted Sherry, Terry, and Bobbie down to where my car was parked.

While I was unlocking my Olds Delta Eighty-Eight Sherry stood with her hands on her hips. "Is this your car?" She asked her lip curling.

"Yeah," I tell her and opened the door. "Hey, it's a classic."

Sherry looked in at the weather worn seats. "I bet it is." She said.

Terry and Bobbie looked in at the back seat, littered with my empty bottles, McDonalds and Jack-in-the-Box fast food containers.

"I'll arrange for another car tomorrow," Sherry told the girls.

Arrogant broad, I thought and held the door for her to get in.

"Hope I don't catch nothing from these seats," Terry said.

"Just get in," Sherry told her.

*   *   *

I dropped the girls and Sherry off at the front door of Pattie's Kitten House and parked around back in a fenced in customers parking lot. The doorman, an ex-pro linebacker with the Cardinals, phoned the man at the gate to the parking lot. He let me park for no charge and slipped a VIP card under my windshield wiper. They were charging five bucks a pop, so the customers could walk around front and pay a twenty dollar cover charge, then order drinks that were at least three times the price you'd pay anywhere else. It's a nice racket if you can make it work.

Here, they were making it work. Pattie's Kitten House was smack dab in the middle of the downtown high rent business district. They had to be bringing in some serious bucks to be operating down here. It was somewhere around five thirty in the afternoon and the parking lot for Pattie's Kitten House was already half full.

I wanted to see what was so good inside this club that the guys were paying such high prices to get in.

The ex-linebacker at the door was named Ron Martin. He was a big corn-fed country boy who developed a like for the city life while he was playing football. A busted knee ended his football career. He stayed on in the area doing body guard and bouncer work.

At six-five and two hundred and eighty solid in shape pounds, his size alone was enough to deter just about anyone from causing trouble at a club he was bouncing at. He met me at the door and told me anything I wanted to drink was complementary as long as it had no alcohol in it. That sounded good to me. I pretty much wanted to stay straight anyway.

I walked into the club.

*   *   *

Just inside the door I was met by a sweet looking brunette who was wearing a tuxedo jacket, high heels, stockings and garters, a fur bikini and cat ears on her head.

"May I take your jacket?" She asked.

"I better keep it on," I told her and flashed open the jacket so she saw my holstered Thirty-Eight. Today seemed to be my day for showing everyone my gun.

"Your boss knows about me." I told her and brushed on past. Glancing back I saw that the coat-girl had a large black cat-tail sticking out into the air from between the folds of the tuxedo jacket at her ass. Cute, real cute, I thought. The guys do come here to see some pussy. So they're going to throw it at them a few different ways.

The other waitresses moving among the tables and the customers were dressed just like her. The colors of the fur for the bikini's or the ears or the tails might be a little different, but the uniforms were pretty much the same. They had this cat theme down pretty good.

I'm not complaining none either. These were some healthy felines roaming around here with their tails in the air. Who knows, I may become a cat lover yet, or at least a cat fucker if nothing else.

As soon as I sat at a table a purrrrrrfectly tasty waitress appeared at the table. I ordered a coke and watched her tail bounce as she walked away. Watching tails could become habit forming.

The lighting was subdued but not overly dark. I guess they had to give the guys at least enough light to check out the girls. There was more than one room. How many, I didn't know. I didn't really want to stroll around looking like a tourist. All of the lights had a faint tint of red to it. It gave the skin a slightly flushed look. I could give a shit less what the guy's skin looked like to the girls. I wasn't looking at the guys.

I must have walked in between sets because the three stages I could see were bare.

In the corner of the room a glass enclosed Deejay put on a disco record, something by the Bee Gees. A heavy base beat and high harmonized vocals. I could really give a shit less about disco music. I'm more of a heavy metal man myself. But it was good music for a woman to be dropping her duds to.

From a door in back of the stage closest to me a woman appeared. She was tall, had long black hair and was dressed like an Indian maiden. Looking at her made me feel like going west right then and there. This woman was built like every young Indian scout's wet dream. She had long smooth legs, a flat stomach and small round perfect sized breasts, perfect for sucking. I saw all this and hell, she hadn't even dropped any clothes yet.

I watched her from my table as she moved to the music and realized it's been way too long since I've been fucked. I had a hard-on that could break bricks. She untied a string that held up a little Indian mini-skirt and flung the skirt back toward the wall. Seeing this made me feel like someone squeezed my dick from under the table.

And that face of hers was like the face of an angel's. Almond shaped dark eyes. Large ruby red lips. She must have seen the effect she was having on me because she locked eyes with me and licked her lips. I swear if I hadn't of had a pair of pants on, my dick would've flipped the table over.

I took a long drink of a coke that had magically appeared from nowhere and put the sweating glass to my forehead. I had to cool down fast.

I looked around the room, got up and took a walk. Walking wasn't easy at that moment either. The song went on, and I went to the bar. The bartended smiled at me as I took a stool.

"She's a hot one, ain't she," he said. His name tag read Joe.

"Really," I answered with a grin. "I hadn't noticed."

We both laughed.

"You want to see a real good one," he said. "Take a look at that little bit of Chung King." He pointed at a stage at the far side of the room. The woman over there was definitely tasty. I did have to admit that.

"Shit!" I said.

"What?" Joe asked.

"You really don't want to know," I told him.

That was Sushi on the stage over there, my best friend's girlfriend. And a little while back Johnny told me she promised him she would quit dancing. He couldn't handle knowing she was taking her clothes off in front of a roomful of guys every night.

Sometimes, promises don't mean much.

I drank my coke and slung the shit with Joe for a while, then took a stroll around the club. I guess I was going to end up looking like the tourist that I didn't want to look like after all. Oh well, big fucking deal.

Guys come here to see female skin and even though I got in for free, why should I act like I'm any different.

I strolled into another of the rooms in time to see the last song of the three song set that Terry and Bobbie were doing. They were doing a tandem dance routine that was damn close to being pornographic and not soft core porn either. They were undressing each other and rubbing on each other and the contrast of Bobbie's almost white skin on Terry's almost black skin was close to being hypnotic.

Terry saw me watching them and smiled at me and winked. I figured I'd better get some air and headed in that direction. Over the bar I saw a clock and noticed that two hours had passed. Damn, why does time seem to run by in these places?

I was just a few steps away from the front door when someone grabbed my arm.

It was Sushi. She smiled at me.

"What do you want?" I asked and her smile faded a little.

"Johnny does not need to know," she said. "Please do not tell him you saw me here."

"Am I supposed to lie for you too?" I asked.

"I need to make money," Sushi said.

"We all do," I told her.

"But I need more than he can give me." She said. "I don't want to hurt him."

Sherry St. Claire appeared beside us. "I see you have met Sushi," she said. "I was going to introduce you later. She is the young lady who had words with the man who kidnapped me."

So our personal matter was put on the back burner for the moment. The three of us took a table and Sushi ran through what happened between her and the guy.

The man had stared at her during her entire routine and approached her at the end of it saying he wanted a private performance.

"I don't do that," Sushi said. "This is a show and that is all. He went to grab me and I shoved him and kicked him. I must have caught him off guard. That's when Sherry and the guards showed up. You know the rest."

"What does he look like?" I asked Sushi.

"Tall," she said. "But, just about everyone looks tall to me. Brown hair, light skin and really stocky built. Even through this guy's clothes, you could tell he had really big muscles."

"Anything about his face you remember?" I asked.

"He looked very hard." Sushi said. "His face was like a statue's. No expression at all."

*　*　*

I talked to the two of them for a little while making mental notes to be on the look-out for a muscle-bound guy with brown hair and a shitty outlook on life. I knew if I hit the health clubs and gymnasiums I could spot a thousand men who fit that description in an hour.

I still needed some air, so I told Sherry I'd be back at the end of her shift and headed for the door again.

Sushi again grabbed me by the arm before I made it outside. For a place that people pay a lot to get into, I was having a hell of a time getting out.

"Please," she said to me, her eyes pleading. "Do not tell Johnny."

I shook her arm off. The expression on her face was almost like I'd struck her. "Look," I told her. "I won't lie for you. If Johnny doesn't ask me, I won't tell him I saw you here. But if he does ask, I will tell him."

Then I walked out the door. Just what the fuck did I tell that woman anyway, I asked myself? I didn't want to be in the middle of Johnny and Sushi's shit. It wasn't my fucking problem. I don't want to be a part of their *Peyton Place* romantic soap opera.

Damn! I should have said, "No, I won't tell him. If you suck my dick like the Chung King Tongue Fu Ball Master Bitch that we both know that you are, I won't."

Shit! But the truth of it is I knew I never would betray a friend. I may lie, cheat, steal and kill, but there's some things I don't do.

Go after a friend's woman? No way!

*　*　*

Around back in the parking lot I was fumbling for my car keys when I heard a squeal and a female voice yell, "Let go of me, you bastard!"

I recognized the voice. It was Terry.

Another voice that I knew was Bobbie yelled, "Leave her alone!"
"Back off you dike bitch!" A man shouted back.

CHAPTER 11
Rocking and Rolling

I followed the voices to the center aisle of the parking lot. Bobbie and Terry were there, with a lot more clothes on than they'd had on in the club. A tall black man in a black leather jacket had Terry by the hair with his left hand. He was drawing back his right fist to punch at Bobbie, who looked to me to be a bit out of his sight range.

Where the hell were the security guards now?

I walked up directly in front of him. He was struggling with Terry so much that at first he didn't notice me.

"Hey mother fucker!" I yelled at him. "Let her go!"

He froze, then slowly turned his eyes on me with an intense glare intended to scare the hell out of me. I smiled at him. He must think he's some kind of bad ass, I thought.

"Get the fuck out of my face white boy!" He yelled. "Before I bust a cap in yo' ass."

Bust a cap? That almost made me laugh, somebody's been listening to too much gangster rap. I'd have bet he didn't even have a gun. Otherwise he'd have already pulled it.

I laughed and said, "Like this fuck-head," and jerked my .38 out of its holster. I was getting tired of showing my gun and not doing anything with it, so I aimed a few inches to the left of his feet and squeezed the trigger blasting up a spray of concrete.

Terry and Bobbie both screamed and the guy jumped about three feet in the air. He let go of Terry's hair when he jumped and backpedaled about ten feet. I followed him.

"What the fuck's wrong with you?" He yelled at me and his voice had raised enough octaves so that it sounded higher than Terry's or Bobbie's.

"I'm in the mood to kill something," I told him. "And you're available."

The sound of running footsteps came from behind me. Here comes the cavalry, I thought.

Someone yelled. "You two, hold it right there!" The security guards were on the way.

Ron Martin was the first one to arrive, followed close behind by the parking lot gateman.

Bobbie and Terry were hugging each other. Terry was sobbing and Bobbie was telling her she was going to be all right and was cuddling her like her mother. I could sure use some cuddling like that.

Ron grabbed the guy by the arm and twisted it up behind his back. "Let go of me, motha-fucka!" The guy yelled. "That's the crazy son-of-a-bitch you should be grabbin'. He's got a gun, man."

"When I got here," I told Ron. "Mr. Nice Guy here had a hand full of Terry's hair. He don't look like no hair dresser, so I made him let go." I still had my pistol in my hand. I showed it to Ron then holstered it.

Terry spoke up now. "Mike was pimping me out when I lived on the streets. He owes me some money. He called me at the club and said for old time's sake he wanted to pay me and tell me good-bye. He was gonna drag me off when Mr. Dark stopped him."

"You be a lying bitch!" Mike shouted at Terry.

There was a white Cadillac about five feet from where Ron held Mike. He grabbed the back of Mike's head with his right hand then tripped him, and running forward rammed his head into the Cadillac's door. Mike's head made a loud "Bwopp!" into the metal and left a dent.

Ron let Mike slide to the ground. He left a smear of blood down the side of the car.

"Damn Mikey," Ron said to the prone form on the ground. "Now why'd you have to go messing with this here car," He kicked Mike a good one in the ribs. Mike's ass made a squishy wet sound, like he shit his pants.

Terry and Bobbie started walking back toward the club.

Ron picked up Mike by his belt at his waist like a gym bag. He said, "Dark, if you don't have nothing to do, we're gonna play a game of wallyball with this boy's head in the back room. You can get in on this if you want."

"I'll take a pass," I answered. "Think I'll go down and get me a couple White Castles."

Watching Ron carry Mike away, I could tell Mike was sure going to have a rock and roll night. All the rocks were going up-side his head and he'd be rolling around the floor.

*   *   *

I ate four White Castles and watched the families come in and go out of the swinging metal and glass doors. Couples with kids–I don't have any kids, as far as I know.

Rug rats, why do people want them anyway? They just fuck up everything. Make noise, make messes, and get in the way all the time.

I was taking the final bite of my burger when a little girl in line with a man hugged his leg and said, "Daddy, I love you."

He answered her back stroking her head, "I love you too." His face glowed when he said it.

Hell, I just don't understand that shit.

*   *   *

The thought of going by and playing Johnny a game of chess went through my mind but for some weird reason I'd feel strange if I did. I almost felt like I was betraying my friend already by just not telling him that Sushi was still dropping her duds for dudes.

I had no idea why I should be feeling awkward. It wasn't like I was fucking Johnny's girl or anything like that. I wouldn't even consider doing anything like that, even if Sushi did look like she could do some major league boning.

So, I drove around for a while, going nowhere in particular. After a while, I got bored with that. Before I knew it, I was driving back to Pattie's Kitten House.

*　　*　　*

The place was the same as when I'd left it. Sweet looking women on the stages enticing guys into giving them their money for nothing more than a lingering look or smile. While strolling around the club I saw Terry and Bobbie going through their routine on another stage.

With their white and black limbs all entwined on the stage they reminded me of a hot fudge sundae. I wouldn't mind finding out if they melt on your tongue too.

When they saw me, Bobbie waved and Terry gave me a come-on-over flip of her head. I did go on over. I watched them and near the end of their set Terry leaned out to where I was and whispered, "Follow us when we're done. I want to thank you the right way."

My nuts jumped in my underwear when she said that.

The music ended and Bobbie and Terry blew kisses to all of the guys, about six of them, that were seated at the stage. Then they exited through a door at the rear of the stage.

The door was left ajar.

I went through it, and before it shut behind me, glanced at the guys outside who wished they were where I was. Too fucking bad boys, some guys get it, and some don't.

I was about to get it.

Hooray for me, and to hell with you.

The girls were just a little bit up the hallway from me.

They waved me on and I followed them around a corner to a door where their names were on a hanging sign with stars beside each. They opened the door and we entered a rather large dressing room. Well, at least it was larger than the dressing room where I'd taught Dallas what private investigating was all about.

Terry was in front of me and Bobbie slid around behind me. Bobbie closed the door.

In her high valley-girl voice Bobbie said, "Sherry doesn't like us bringing no customers back here, even if we do like them. But after what you did, you're not just a customer."

Terry slid up close to me. Her lips were on my neck. Her breath was warm. "Mike would've got me out of here if it weren't for you. He'd of pumped me full of junk and used me again."

She unbuckled and unzipped my pants and felt around inside, grasping my dick. Bobbie slid up close to me from behind. She pushed my pants and underwear down to my knees. She reached around front and cupped my balls with one of her hands and squeezed lightly.

Terry kissed me on the neck then kneeled down in front of me. She took my erection in her hand and stroked it. "Uh huh!" She said. "You do sho' like this salt and pepper now, don't ya."

With that, she slid her lips over my dick and took its entire length into her mouth. As I watched Terry swallow the whole of my manhood in one swoop, it hit me that Terry could go to work as a sword-swallower: "The Amazing Terry and Her Incredible Expanding Throat Muscles, able to swallow entire sides of beef in a single gulp."

It was feeling good. That mouth of hers was slick and hot and she didn't nick me once with her teeth. This girl knew what her jaws were made for and it wasn't for singing.

I grabbed the back of her head and pumped in and out a few times real deep. She took it like a champ and just smiled at me as good as she could with her jaws full.

Then the door banged open.

"Oh shit," Bobbie said and let go of my balls.

"You know I don't allow you to do that here!" It was Sherry St. Clair. She didn't look none too amused.

Terry gave me one last good slide deep into her throat. Then with a smack she pulled her lips from my dick running her tongue once over the head.

"We'll finish this later at the apartment," she breathed at me.

Sherry came around to the front of me–me, with my trousers around my knees and my dick sticking straight out in front like a flag pole.

"Do you have anything to say for yourself?" She asked.

"Yeah," I said, "Why don't you pick up where Terry left off?"

Sherry stifled a laugh and her gaze moved down my front to my erect member. "Put that thing away," she said with a smirk on her face.

I pulled my pants up and took my dick in my hand and looked in Sherry's eyes. "Do I seem worthy?" I asked her.

She blushed a bright red, cleared her throat then said, "We'll see."

The girls were giggling and changing costumes.

I buckled and zipped up and stepped out the door. The door swung open behind me. Sherry looked at me.

"The one thing that pisses me off about this," she said to them while looking through the crack at me, "Is that you started without me".

Sherry smiled. The door swung shut.

Yeah, I thought, this is going to end up being one hell-of-a good night.

*   *   *

I walked back out through the door at the rear of the stage and went past a cute red head that had her butt in the air and an expression like she was constipated on her face. The eyes of the men at the stage followed me as I went down the stairs. I took a few steps then stopped and straightened my jacket.

Nodding my head at them I said, "Just showing them what I'm famous for. You can check me out at your local triple X rated theaters in Long Dong Rides 'Em Again. Oh yeah, leave the kiddies at home."

I went to the bar.

"Give me an orange juice," I said to the bartender. "I need to build up some vitamins."

Joe brought me the glass of juice. "I saw you follow those two backstage," he said. "Knowing them, you better drink a lot of this."

I took a drink of the juice and saw Sushi in her street clothes walking toward me. I gave her a look that said, "Now what the fuck do you want?"

"I know you are not my friend tonight," she said. "But could you just give me a ride to Johnny's after you take Sherry to her place. My car won't start."

"I don't know, I..."

She cut me off, "I will tell Johnny tonight. It is only right that I do."

"I'll run you by," I told her.

CHAPTER 12
Face Down on the Pavement

On the way to The Blaine Building it was agreed that I'd drop the girls and Sherry off at the front door, run Sushi to Johnny's then come back for the after midnight delight. I had four fine looking women in my car. One of them I was getting rid of. Two of them I was definitely going to be throwing the bone to in as many creative ways as we could come up with. The other one well, we'll see.

Sherry was sitting in the front seat across from me, giving me sly sideways glances and half smiles. There was a real possibility here that my three-way could become a four-way. One Black, one White, one Japanese-French, a sexual smorgasbord.

You damn right I was getting rid of Sushi as fast as I could. Shit, she'd be lucky if I didn't kick her ass into the street at the first stoplight.

*   *   *

As I drove across town Terry was playing with my neck from the back seat. She was kissing me on the back of the neck and was leaning over and sticking her tongue in my ear, every now and then she would run her hand down into my shirt and feel of the hairs on my chest. I was glad I'd just cleaned the wax out of my ears a few days earlier. I didn't want her to be sucking something out of my ear that'd be big enough to blow bubbles with.

We got to The Blaine Building and I pulled up behind a delivery van parked at the curb in front of the glass doors. The doorman that came out was a different guy than the man I'd met earlier. He was the same type though. Thick neck, thick arms, thick head.

I got out of my door and opened the rear door. Terry bounded out and grabbed me in a bear hug. I didn't mind the hug from this sweet black bear so I pulled her to me.

"Get yo' white ass back here fast," she whispered in my ear. Then her lips were on mine and her tongue was in my mouth and either our tongues were dancing or wrestling. It didn't matter which, we were doing a grappling session, right there in the street.

"John!" Sherry shouted and I came up for air. I thought that Sherry was just ticked off about my public display of horniness.

A fist smashed me in the side of the head rocking me to the side and sending the lights around me spinning in crazy circles. I staggered. Strong arms looped around me, pinning my arms to my sides.

My vision cleared for an instant. I looked into the grinning face of the muscle head from the East Side Gym. "I told you we would meet again," he said and laughed.

I snapped a kick at his crotch. He stepped to the side and my foot connected with the back of his thigh. "Good try," he said in that weird semi-Eastern European accent of his.

The girls were screaming. At least three other guys had come out of the van and were after them.

I stomped on the guy's toes behind me with the heel of my shoe. He didn't even grunt. It felt like he had steel toe boots on.

"Enough playing!" Caesar Lanista said. He drew back and blasted me with a hard overhand right. I tried to roll with it, but was held too damn tight.

Stars exploded in my head. I sagged. He reached under my jacket and pulled my gun from my holster and threw it across the street.

"I will let you live for now," Caesar said. "I will come back to kill you, man to man, to enjoy it more."

Then another punch hit me, and then another. Whether they were uppercuts or crosses or hooks, I don't know. I don't even know if he hit me with ten more punches or just those two. After the two shots, I was out.

*　　*　　*

I woke up face down on the pavement. A siren was going off and getting louder. I didn't know where I was or how I'd gotten there. Flashing lights were coming from a distance.

When I tried to sit up someone said, "Stay down, an ambulance is coming." Whoever it was put his hand on my back.

I rolled over and knocked the guys hand out of the way.

"Get the fuck off of me!" I yelled at him and he backed off.

I stood up and the world was still doing flip flops so I sat on the hood of my car until the earthquake in my head stopped.

All four of the ladies that were with me were gone and it was a sure bet they weren't sitting upstairs waiting for me to finish my nap.

CHAPTER 13
Police & Lawyers

The ambulance arrived about fifteen seconds before the two police cars did. I told the EMTs to fuck off. I was up and on my feet so I didn't need them.

The St. Louis Police didn't take to the "FUCK OFF!" I threw at them as easily as the EMTs did. Before I got much more out, they had me bent over the hood of a squad car with my hands cuffed behind my back.

When a big ugly cop who said he was Sergeant O'Malley frisked me he found I had on my empty holster. He looked through my wallet and after he saw my driver's license said, "All right Dark, why are you wearing that holster?"

"I keep my tissues in there," I told him. "For times when little balls of shit like you show up."

He leaned down toward my cuffed hands, sniffing. I knew he was smelling for burnt gun powder that would leave an odor for a few hours on the hands of anyone who'd fired a pistol.

His face was a few inches from my hands and my ass, so I ripped off a loud fart. It must have just about burned the hair off his mustache. O'Malley got a good whiff of that one.

The three other cops laughed.

I laughed too, I just couldn't help it.

"You slimy bastard!" O'Malley yelled, shaking his head and fanning the air in front of his face to clear the stench, then he upper-cutted me between the legs into my balls.

Pain shot through me. My legs sagged. I slid down the side of the car to my familiar place on the ground.

"Get him in the car," O'Malley shouted and the other patrolmen bundled me into the back seat.

*   *   *

At the Police Department I discovered that the guy who found me on the ground was a criminal attorney. He saw when O'Malley slugged me in the nuts and followed the police cars to the station. His name was Anthony Steller.

If it wasn't for him, I probably would have gotten my head beat soft that night.

O'Malley wasn't in the mood to play around with me. After I eat those White Castle burgers I let loose with gas bombs that are damn near deadly. His brain must have been close to rotten after the way I'd fumigated his face.

I was thrown on the cold cement floor of an interrogation room and left there.

After a while O'Malley came in with another cop and started grilling me about a dead guy they found in the stairwell of The Blaine Building. That must have been the real door man. His throat had been cut.

A young white female had also been thrown out of the back of a delivery van a few blocks from The Blaine Building. She was identified as Bobbie Chambers. Her throat also was cut.

What a shame, I thought. She never even got a chance to know what the John Dark dick can do for a woman, or two or three at a time.

All joking aside, she seemed like a good kid, especially when she was holding my balls.

I told O'Malley and his buddy what I knew, that the guy who took the girls was Caesar Lanista. O'Malley told me I was lying. That was when the door swung inward and my attorney, who I didn't even know I had, came to the rescue.

Anthony Steller strode into the interrogation room like he had the deed to the entire Police Department.

"Hello Jonathan," he said to me. I nodded to him like we were old friends even though I didn't know who the hell he was.

"Have you charged Mr. Dark with anything?" He asked and looked into O'Malley's eyes, then into the other cop's eyes.

"Aaaaaa, we're holding him, pending questioning," O'Malley started and was cut off.

"Which is against his Constitutional Rights and I also noticed back on the street, Mr. Dark was arrested without any attempt at making his full rights known to him, which is also, illegal!"

"We haven't arrested him," the other cop squeaked out. O'Malley gave him a "you shit-head" look.

"Then Mr. Dark is being detained without due process of law, in violation of Civil Statutes!" He paused for effect.

The cops looked at each other and didn't say a word.

"Take the cuffs off my client now or I'll be in the Mayor's office first thing in the morning and you'll be in the unemployment line, if you're not in one of your own jail cells for assault!" Anthony Steller, my new friend, said calmly. "We are leaving."

The police did as they were told.

As I left the room O'Malley said under his breath, "I'll be watching you. You'll mess up, and I'll be there."

I gave him the finger.

As soon as we were out the front door of the Police Department, Anthony Steller shook his head and laughed. "You need to be more careful," he said. "They could have just arrested you for public profanity."

"Fuck them," I said and that made the attorney laugh some more.

He gave me his card. "Keep it. You'll probably need me," he said.

"And what do I owe you for helping me out?" I asked.

"Don't worry about it for now." He said. "I know who you are. When I need you, I'll let you know."

He trotted down the steps to his Ferrari parked at the curb.

*   *   *

I took a taxi to Johnny's Bar and Grill. The Police had impounded my car to go over it thoroughly for clues to who kidnapped Sherry, Terry and Sushi and murdered Bobbie. I'd told them his name, but they'd tear my car apart anyway.

PART II

Hail Caesar! We who are about to die, Salute thee!
                         -Salutation of Roman Gladiators

A wonderful stream is the River Time,
As it runs through the Realm Of Tears,…
                         -B.F. Taylor, The Long Ago

There are Gates, that should never be opened.
There are Doors, that can never be closed.
                         -The Walker In Darkness

CHAPTER 14
Old Gods & Gates

It was after hours at Johnny's. The closed sign was lit, but the front door was unlocked when I tried it. I went in. The place was totally dark except for one table where Johnny and his grandmother Jeanette and a guy who I'd never met before sat around a table that had a glowing bluish sphere in the center of it.

I went to the table and Jeanette motioned me to sit in the remaining chair. When I went to tell them about the kidnapping she silenced me with an upraised hand. "We know about the abductions and the many deaths caused by this man who is out of his place," Jeanette told me in her deep Cajun accent.

Hell, I'd only known about one killing Caesar was connected with. That was Bobbie. I knew Jeanette didn't exaggerate. So, Caesar Lanista must be a busy boy.

I sat down.

Waves of bluish ethereal light washed over the faces of the three staring into the globe. The pulsating sphere almost seemed to have a life of its own as clouds of swirling light danced within the glass before us at the center of the table.

"Friendly Loa, spirits who watch over us from birth to death, show us the way. Show us the path to the one who violates the order."

I looked into the glass too. At first I didn't see anything, just swirling swimming colors, bluish in shade mixing around inside the ball. Then they seemed to coalesce, the colors and lines converged and I saw.

It was like I was drawn into the glass, my entire field of vision, my entire mind. I became eyes without a face. I could see all around me. I was gliding down dark, torch lit corridors. The walls were of uneven brick. They were slick with moisture and slime and moss.

I had the feeling I was far underground. I didn't know why I felt that, I just did. Like the weight of tons of Earth was pressing down upon the tunnel I was gliding through.

Flying down the dank corridors I knew I wasn't really there but I was feeling everything as though I was. The chill of the air on my face, the smell of the mold on the walls, all of this I could feel more than see. I knew my consciousness was being given a piggy-back ride by whatever it was that Jeanette had called to her crystal.

I glided silently down the depressing halls until an opening was ahead. Into a vast open chamber, I floated above a stone alter where there stood warriors in ancient garments that I couldn't identify. I drifted over the top of it all.

Several people along with Sherry, Terry and Sushi were being held in chains. They were being lined up in front of a huge standing stone oval that had weird symbols and hieroglyphs carved into it.

Behind the stone oval was a statue that stood at least nine feet tall. The body was that of a muscular man except that it had six arms. The two arms in the center ended in a sea creature's claws.

The head of this thing was like an elephant's except that it had bull's horns sticking out of its forehead. I saw all of this with a growing sense of dread and deja vu.

Caesar Lanista was striding back and forth in front of his captives. He had a short sword in his hand. Impatiently he was slapping his leg with it. Finally he stepped in front of a young white man and barked some orders.

The man was grabbed and dragged screaming to an upraised stone slab.

Another prisoner yelled something at Lanista and I realized that while I could see and feel what was around me, I could hear nothing. All was silence.

The captive that shouted at Lanista turned so that I saw his face. It was Julio "Padre" Paez. What the hell was he doing there?

Caesar strode to Julio and back handed him, knocking him to the floor. Then he walked back to the stone slab where the white man was being held down. He waved his short sword in the air and looked to be shouting some sort of an invocation to the idol behind the oval.

He waved the sword around his head, standing over the screaming white man.

Out of the air around me came the shout, "Look, oh look what they've done to the Temple I built to my forgotten goddess. This is an abomination! Oh, Isis please, strike them down!"

Lanista looked up into the air. It seemed like he looked directly into my eyes.

"Be silent!" Jeanette ordered. "He can hear you."

Lanista laughed and the crystal went dark and like waking suddenly I was sitting back in my chair in Johnny's place.

Johnny was on his feet. "Where the hell are they?" He shouted to the guy I'd seen before. "We need to get over there and mess those mother fuckers up and get my woman back."

The guy Johnny talked to was a chubby middle-aged man who wore a business suit and a worried expression. "I can tell you where they were." He said to Johnny. "But it is already too late. They are leaving as we speak."

Jeannette got up from the table and switched on the overhead lights. "He is correct. I can feel them departing."

"We'll catch them on the way out." I said.

Jeanette put her hand on Johnny's shoulder. "Sit back down. You have time. Listen to what this man has to tell you."

"Yeah," Johnny said. "You best tell me how you knew about all this or I'm gonna be jumping in your ass."

"Isis gave me the gift of foresight and far seeing. That is how I saw what was happening tonight from a distance and knew this was done by the man who stole my temple from me," the man explained.

Jeanette turned to me. "As Johnny was closing up, this man came looking for my help. He uses different tools, but he is like me: One whose soul is close to the spirits while he still is in this life. I knew he was on his way to me from the moment he started seeking assistance. It is the way we are. We know these things about each other."

"You don't have to tell me," I said to Jeanette. "I've seen you do some weird shit."

The chubby guy spoke again. "My name is Paul Brady. I am the Grand Master of The Masonic Temple in Cahokia. I practice transcendental meditation and while in a trance the wise and wonderful Isis spoke to me. She showed me the secret passage down to the tunnels that lead to an old Indian temple far below ground. I converted the temple to a worship place for Isis and built the sacred gate to her world from her instructions. After doing a secret ceremony, the gate opened and Caesar Lanista came through. I welcomed him with open arms, believing him to be a messenger of Isis."

"He brought some of his warriors through and I welcomed then as well, until he brought Asmodius, the Lord of the Pit. He stands now immobile, in the form of stone."

"When I saw Asmodius I tried to make them leave my temple and barely escaped with my life."

"Well, why don't we just get the goddamn history of the fucking world while we're at it," Johnny said. "We're standing around jacking-off while Sushi is being carried off to god knows where." He leaned over the table toward Paul Brady. "Tell me where the hell that place is we just saw or I'm going to bust you upside your fucking head!"

The look on Johnny's face told me he wasn't joking.

"All right," he answered and gave Johnny and me directions to where his Temple of Isis below the Masonic Temple was. He finished with, "Just remember, to get to them now you'll have to travel through the gate to another world."

"I'll walk through the fires of hell to get Sushi back," Johnny said. "Are you with me?" He asked and it was the first thing he'd said to me tonight. The look he gave me was like he was pissed off at me too.

"You know I am," I told him. "We got to get those other girls back and Julio too, if we can manage it."

"I don't give a fuck about nobody but Sushi," Johnny answered me. "But we'll bring them back if we can."

We both got to our feet and made ready to head out the door. Jeanette grabbed Johnny and gave him a hug and kissed him on the forehead. "My Grandson," she said, looking into his eyes. "I am proud of you. You are much like your father. Beware when you go to these other places. You will be a part of where you are. The longer you stay, the more it will become a part of you. Always keep in your mind who you are, or you could lose yourself."

Jeanette turned to me. "Watch over my grandson." She said. "Remember, some of those you go to rescue, may not want saving."

Johnny went behind his bar. He got a sawed-off shotgun for himself and pulled out a chrome plated 9mm. He handed it to me. "I took this off a drunk that came in here to rob me about a week ago."

I looked at the gun. It was nice. Well-oiled and in good working condition. The clip was full.

"Damn, you didn't tell me about that," I said to Johnny.

"Wasn't no big deal," Johnny answered. "I got a collection of weapons in a box in the back room that I took off people in here that could arm the entire mother fuckin' Hells Angels."

We went out the door well-armed, heading toward another world.

CHAPTER 15
Into the Pit

We cruised toward Cahokia in Johnny's car. The night was cool and overcast. The sky was pitch black, not a sign of the moon or stars, the perfect night to step into a pit.

Johnny still wasn't saying too much to me. We rode along in silence for a few minutes that seemed like hours, finally I said, "What's up man? You're acting like I fucked your dog or something."

"You should of fucking called me," he said through tightened lips. I could tell he was pissed. "You should've called me the instant you saw Sushi in that club. I shouldn't be in the middle of this shit. You know that! Sushi shouldn't be in the middle of this shit. If you'd have called me, my woman and me would be on the springs doing the snake dance right now. Instead you and me are riding down the road getting ready to kill some mother fuckers tonight."

"Hold on Chuck," I said to Johnny. "You're acting like it's my fault Sushi was peeling off for those guys."

"You should have fucking called me, goddamn-it!" He shouted the last two words.

"That's why I didn't call you," I told Johnny. "You're not thinking. A man don't think too clearly when it's concerning a woman who treats his dick the way he wants it treated."

We rode in silence the rest of the way to the Masonic Temple. He pulled up outside a building that looked like an old small town courthouse.

When he shut the engine off Johnny turned to me. "Seriously Bro," he said. "Sushi does treat my dick just right."

"I know," I answered.

We both got out of the car simultaneously. He looked at me over the top of the car. "And I do get fucked a whole lot more than you do, too," he said.

I gave him the finger and said, "Fuck you."

"Won't help you that way," he answered and grinned and I knew the Johnny I knew was back. "Time to make these boys pay," he said.

"Yeah," I answered. "They got to pay with interest."

*   *   *

The front door to the Masonic Temple was open. I had the 9mm out in front of me and Johnny had his sawed-off shot gun ready, just in case some of Lanista's guys were still around and wanted to play games. If they wanted to play, we'd pitch first.

The inside of the Masonic Temple looked like a rich man's social club. Shiny polished marble floors and dark oak furniture were under softly lit chandeliers. The Masons were a rich man's exclusive club. It showed.

We weren't here to be sight-seeing. Following the directions that Paul Brady gave us, we made our way to the back of the building to an average sized office where a nice sized teak desk sat on the other side of a large rug with the Masonic symbol sewn into the center of it.

I grabbed the rug by its corner and pulled it to the side. Just like we'd been told, there was a recessed steel ring set in a trap door. I'd once seen a movie called *The Evil Dead* where a trap door like this was in the floor of a cabin in the woods. Something started beating on the door from below and just about made the woman who saw it being banged upward shit her pants. At that moment when I saw that door and the image from that movie flashed through my mind I wondered, why in the hell do I even watch those movies? That was the last damn thing I wanted to be thinking about when I grab hold of that steel ring. I was about ready to swear off horror films right then.

I reached down and grasped the ring in my left hand, keeping the 9mm pointed at the trap door.

I glanced at Johnny. "You remember about a month ago when I came into your place and got lit?" I asked.

"Yeah, and I remember the thirty times since then too," he answered.

"I told you about a nightmare I'd had where I went down a tunnel in Viet Nam and I told you about that thing that came through the doorway that I blew up with grenades," I said.

"Yeah, I remember," he answered. "And I told you, you were full of shit."

"Well, that wasn't a nightmare. It really happened. And that statue that I saw in Viet Nam and the doorway... they're the same ones that we saw in Jeanette's crystal tonight. Does that make any difference to you?"

"No," Johnny said. "You're still full of shit. Just maybe a little more than I knew."

"They might be waiting for us," I told him.

"Then let's not disappoint them," he answered.

I pulled the trap door open.

The smell of moss and decay and rotting things came flowing up around us through the opening in the floor. I didn't know where it came from but the thought came to me that this is the way it must smell in a grave. I didn't want to think that but it popped into my head and wouldn't go away.

I had expected to see a ladder leading down into the dark but what I saw instead was a set of stone stairs that went down into a dusty blackness. Goosebumps jumped up onto my arms. The resemblance to the stairway down into the Earth in Nam was too great.

I told Johnny this and also said, "You get to go first, Bro."

"What's the matter," he asked, "You afraid of the dark?"

"Yeah," I told him. "I always hate this shit. But I'm more afraid of you with that sawed-off. With the wide pattern that thing shoots, you cut loose from behind me, I'll be picking pellets out of my ass for the next six months."

He went past me and started down the stairs. "I wouldn't want you to pick your ass any more than you already do," he said. "You scare enough of my customers away already."

We headed down into the dark. Neither one of us had even thought to bring a flashlight. It was too late now to go back. We moved down the stone stairs. The light from above faded out quickly. Within minutes we were in pitch black.

I kept a hand on Johnny's back so I wouldn't run into him. The only sounds were the sounds of our shoes grating on the stone steps as we went down and our breathing.

This was not a good way to be doing this. If someone below knew we were coming they could fire into the stairway and get the both of us at one time.

After an impossibly long time of following the stairs down, we came to a level floor. A few steps after that and Johnny came to a door. The door felt cold and was slick to the touch with sweat, it felt like steel.

I went to the right side of the door and flattened myself against the wall. The wall was made of large, uneven, moist moss covered bricks. The same kind I remembered being in the walls of the stairway in Nam. I didn't like this one goddamned bit.

"Be ready," Johnny whispered.

"Just don't shoot my ass," I told him.

With a loud shriek of rusted hinges, Johnny jerked the door open and jumped to the side.

Silence.

Flickering light.

We peered around the edges of the doorway and saw the same damp musty torch-lit tunnels that we'd seen earlier in Jeanette's crystal.

I put a finger to my lips in the universal "be quiet" sign and motioned for us to move ahead.

Johnny whispered to me. "Don't be shushing me. Who the fuck you think you are anyway, Sergeant Rock or something."

He moved ahead of me down the hall, walking in a semi-crouch. For someone who had never been taught how to do this in the military he looked like he could sneak pretty damn good. He probably picked this up from all the classes he skipped back in high school.

There were no side passages. I was grateful for that. The musty tunnel curved and bent and sometimes the floor seemed to be going even deeper into the ground but at least we had no chance of making a wrong turn. We went forward. It was the only way to go. And at least there was light from the torches in the walls. Walking through complete darkness is not my favorite thing to do.

Ahead of us we started hearing a loud humming noise.

I recognized it immediately as the same hum that I'd heard issued from that portal in Viet Nam. It was a little different now, not the screaming I'd heard before. I didn't know why but this made me want to hurry.

I started trotting. Not even trying to be quiet anymore. "Move it man," I yelled at Johnny.

I didn't know why or how, I knew that the gate ahead of us was open, but it was losing power. I didn't know how long that portal would stay open.

We were getting closer to the temple that we'd seen in Jeanette's crystal. I could tell this by the loud moaning sound that we could hear coming from the oval. It was making a loud Naaaaaaaaaaaaaaaa sound.

After we rounded another turn we burst into the opening where the statue of what Paul Brady had called Asmodius stood. We could only see his head now and not his body because he stood behind the oval. Inside the oval of stone it was a shimmering blackness where stars winked at us and great distances shown. This was an opening into the void, into the forever.

In front of the stone oval the white man I'd seen dragged screaming was laying on a stone slab. His chest had been sliced open. It was an empty cavity. His eyes were open, staring at nothing. His mouth was locked forever around his last scream.

The stone oval itself had the same hieroglyphics carved into it that I'd seen in the one in Nam. The symbols were pulsating and glowing just like they'd been doing on the other one. But the lightshow here was not as bright and energetic as the other had been.

The both of us looked at the opening in the center of the oval. It shimmered like water in a lake with a growing storm above it.

"You sure you want to do this?" I asked Johnny.

"I already told you I'll walk through the fires of hell to get Sushi," he answered me.

"Then let's do it," I told him.

A voice came out of the air around us. I recognized it as Jeanette. "You must go through now!" she said. "The gateway is about to close."

Hell, she'd been watching us the whole way. "Hope you don't sneak a peak in on someone when they're taking a dump," I told her.

"Go through now," she shouted to us. "And bring my Grandson back so I can slap your jaws for saying that to me."

"You know you love me Jeanette," I told her.

Then we took a running dive into the center of the vortex.

CHAPTER 16
Out of the Frying Pan

Diving into the vortex felt something like when I was a teenager and had been visiting some relatives in northern Michigan and took a dare and dove off a dock into the ice cold waters of Lake Michigan in July. The sudden shock of ice cold water all over my body made my muscles spasm and all the air in my lungs had exploded from my mouth on that day. Now, it was the exact opposite.

I felt like I dove right into a hot lava pit. My skin burned like hell. It felt like my flesh was dissolving. I was on fire. All my nerve endings were screaming and I know I must have screamed because of the pain. But I only heard the silence of a vacuum.

I closed my eyes when I dove through and opened them now. Stars and vast yawning distances were all around us. Pitch blackness and points of light and swirling eddies of strange balls of energy floated around us. I couldn't be sure how close anything was to us. All size is relative to what it is compared to, but out here between the stars, there was nothing to compare anything to.

The only thing that I could tell was close by was Johnny. At least I thought it was him. There was this flaming writhing form of a man where he should be. It looked like the comic book drawing of The Flame from The Fantastic Four. I looked at my own arms and at my own body and it didn't surprise me that I seemed to be on fire too.

Maybe this jumping through hadn't been such a good idea. But we were moving. The only way I could tell was that ahead of us, what had been just one more pin point of light was getting larger. Not brighter, just larger. Whatever the thing in front of us was, we were flying toward it.

I wanted to slow down to at least take a look at the thing that was now the size of a dinner plate in front of us. But it was like jumping out of an airplane and deciding you wanted to take a nice slow look at the ground beneath you before smashing into it. We didn't have parachutes, so there wouldn't be any slowing down.

I tried to shout something to Johnny. To just hold on for a little while and we'd be out of this. But I knew he wouldn't hear me. Hell, I couldn't even hear myself.

Then we were at the thing that had been the size of a dinner plate. It was the size now of the oval we'd dove through. We flew out of it now, or maybe we were spit out of it the way you'd spit out a watermelon seed.

My ears popped and I went to stop my fall with my hands and missed the dirt floor and plowed up the ground with my face. I guess I wasn't cut out for acting like Superman. The dirt didn't do my forehead any good either. My face wasn't built for plowing fields.

Johnny came through next, landing on my back with his knees and falling forward over me, he ground my face into the dirt some more with his elbows. He tumbled off to the side and sat up. I pulled my face up out of the dirt.

"Thanks a lot, fuck-head," I told him. "That's just what I needed after being fried alive." My words came out sounding weird. The words tumbling from my lips weren't the same ones I was hearing in my head.

Johnny stood up and was dusting himself off and answered, "Hey Bro, anytime you want your face stomped in the dirt, let me know and I'll be on it." He stopped then. His face wore a perplexed look.

It was probably the same one I had on my face.

"This is fucking weird," I said and somehow the words I thought seemed a little bit closer to the ones I spoke.

I looked at the clothes Johnny was wearing and pointed at them.

He pointed at my clothes.

He was wearing a rough cloth tunic tied at the waist with a leather belt and sandals. A short sword was hanging from a scabbard at the belt.

I looked down at what I was wearing. I was wearing clothing very similar to what Johnny had on. A robe tied at the waist of a rough cloth, leather sandals and a sword hung from my side.

We looked around us. We were in a shallow unlit cave. The mouth looked out over green hills. The stone oval behind us was only that, a cold stone oval. The symbols were carved into it, but they weren't glowing anymore. The center was just an empty space that shone through to a bare wall behind it.

"Shit," I said. "What the fuck did we get ourselves into here," And my exterior words seemed to slowly be matching my interior words.

"Well, whatever the fuck we're in," Johnny said, "We're here now. Jeanette said we'd be a part of where we are. I guess the clothes and these weird ass words popping out of our mouths are a part of it."

"I tell you what," I said to Johnny. "I don't mind getting no free clothes, but shit man, I'd rather just do my shopping at K-Mart from now on."

There was a small leather bag tied to the belt at my hip. It was tied with a drawstring and felt like it had some coins in it. I was hoping those coins were worth quite a bit. I'd jumped into that oval doorway with around eight hundred dollars in my wallet. Now I didn't even have pockets for a wallet to fit into. I wouldn't like knowing that eight hundred dollars just vanished into nothing.

*   *   *

Outside the mouth of the cave a rough dirt road ran down the hill and into a thick forest. We went to the cave's entrance and looked around.

Where we stood looked more like a small mountain than a hill. To the west of us was water, a hell of a lot of it too. It looked like it was the ocean. Water just went on and on all the way to the horizon.

Sailing ships were out there, but not a kind that I'd ever seen before. They had big square sails and dozens of oars stuck out of both sides of the ships and, in a rhythm to a drum we could hear even from where we were, they stroked the water moving the ships forward.

To the east of us, the mountain on whose side we were on, went off into the distance farther than we could see. Next to that were rolling green hills and we could see the brown roofs of homes in a village on one of the hills. It was too far away to make out any details. Next to that was the forest that the road in front of us ran into.

Looking back and forth between the sailing ships and the village where streamers of smoke drifted into the sky. I said to Johnny, "Hey Toto, I don't think we're in Kansas anymore."

"No shit, Dorothy, you got that right," he answered. "Guess we better get our asses on down this road. This is the only way to go and we don't know how far ahead of us they are, or if they're on foot."

We started off down the road in a trot. That lasted maybe fifteen minutes. One of the things I'd carried with me from the other side of the vortex was the bruises to my ribs that Roy Wilson had put there. It wasn't long before those ribs were talking to me. And Johnny didn't do much better. It wasn't long before both of us had degenerated from running to walking at a good pace.

It was day time but angry gray clouds swirled above us and gave everything a gloomy overcast. These damn toga things we had on weren't none too warm either. In fact the going was downright breezy. I did have on some type of rough cloth underwear to keep the wind off my balls though.

The biggest surprise of the day came just before we entered the forest. I needed to take a piss something terrible. So I stepped off the road, pulled up this robe thing, pulled down these shorts and went to aim Good Charley at the tree in front of me. My hand grabbed more skin than I was used to and when I looked down it looked to me like I had a growth over the end of my dick.

I yelled, "Son of a bitch!" And sprayed piss in a circle around me in the surprise at seeing the head of my dick covered.

Johnny danced back from the flying piss. "What in the hell is wrong with you?" He shouted.

I pointed at my dick while I finished pissing.

"It's different," I told him.

"Yeah, well you're a white boy. It sure as hell is different than mine," he said. Then he looked in his shorts. "Oh shit," Johnny said and I think he went a shade paler.

He went to the other side of the road and examined his own dick closer, muttering to himself, "What the fuck is this."

It hit me then; I put my dick back into my underwear and over my shoulder asked Johnny, "were you circumcised?"

"Sir-sir-sir…what the fuck?"

"Circumcised? They do it to baby boys where they cut a little bit of the foreskin off. I think it keeps down infections or some shit like that," I told him.

"Fuck, I don't know. I don't remember shit that happened to me when I was a baby," Johnny said.

"I bet we were," I told him. "And I don't think we are now."

We came to the forest's edge and entered the woods.

"I'm really going to have to fuck this guy up that grabbed Sushi and those other broads," Johnny said. "Man, when you start messing with my dick, that's when things get personal."

"You got that right," I told Johnny. "Hell, you can skin me alive and I might not even notice it. But when you start playing around with Old Man Johnson you best have a pussy and a smile on your face or you're in some serious trouble."

Just as we stepped into the shade of the forest the clouds broke loose with some lightning and thunder putting on a nice light show for us. Then a heavy rain poured down.

The drops of water seemed to be about the size of quarters when they hit you on the head. Being under the trees, we weren't getting soaked but enough water was getting through so that we knew it was raining. Cold rain too. Where ever we'd popped out at, after coming through that portal or gate or whatever the hell it was, I was betting we were not in the tropics.

The road through the forest was overgrown so much that we could tell it wasn't used very often. If it wasn't for the relatively straight line of it and the thickness of trees on both sides, the road would have been hard to follow. Except for the width of the road, I would be calling it a trail instead.

Neither one of us knows anything about following tracks in the wilderness so I was happy this road appeared to be more or less permanent. As we went deeper into the woods one of the things that hit me was the sheer abundance of bugs and wildlife around us.

What I was used to, and not that I hung out in the woods a lot, was the overgrown spots around East St. Louis and Cahokia. As far as bugs, we had mosquitoes and that's about it. Any other bugs, except for gnats and flies, you had to look for.

Here, bugs were all over the place. Not that they were flying in my face, but they were making noises that you knew were bug noises, noises that couldn't be nothing but bug noises. These weren't just crickets either.

We heard those, but there were a thousand other bugs calling to each other that I'd never heard before. I sure as hell wasn't going to sleep on the ground in these woods.

As we were moving along I also caught the glint of animal eyes looking at us from the lush foliage on both sides of the road. Sometimes I heard the animals, startled by us, running off crashing through the weeds. More than a few times I caught sight of animals that I couldn't identify. There were birds all over too. Chirping and whistling to each other. Some of those were familiar to me. Others I'd never heard before.

The smells in this forest were luxurious. Sweet smelling flowers and strong musty smells came off the trees and weeds. And something else, I didn't smell any kind of engine exhaust. It's the kind of thing we live with and don't notice but engine exhaust makes the air smell dead or used up. The air I was breathing now smelled good. It was full of oxygen. This air made you feel good just breathing it.

Well, at least I didn't see any six-armed green men or Martian princesses or shit like that. So I figured we were at least still on Earth. Though I didn't have a clue where.

We must have moved through the forest for maybe about an hour or an hour and a half, half trotting or walking fast when the forest came to an abrupt end.

Night came suddenly and without warning. In the gloom of the forest with the rain coming down we hadn't even known that it was evening. Now, in the dark, we knew we left the trees behind because the rain came down on us unimpeded.

We left the forest and immediately realized it was going to be next to impossible to follow the road. We couldn't hardly even see the ground, much less tell the difference between the height of the grass in the road verses what was on the sides of it.

Looking ahead we could see a dim glow in the distance.

The rain rapidly soaked us to the bone.

Johnny grabbed my shoulder and pointed to the glow. I could barely make him out in the dark. "That's where they've got to be," he said.

"If they went anywhere else," I told him. "We've lost them already."

We set off toward the glow ahead that either had to be a camp or a town.

If anybody ever asks you to take a walk in the rain with them in sandals and a toga, I'd advise you to go tell them to go fuck themselves. Walking in the rain in the kind of clothes we had on was cold business.

By the time we could tell what the glow ahead was, I was even more pissed off about this situation than I'd started out being. I was cold, wet, and shivering and I wanted to kill something, hell, anything.

On the last stretch we walked that night, I pulled the sword from the scabbard and gave it a few experimental swings just to see how it felt. The thing that was strange was that the sword in my hand felt good. It felt like I'd held this sword and used it many times. I was going down the road parrying and slashing at an imaginary opponent and the blade in my hand felt familiar, like I'd been trained on how to use it and had killed with it many times before.

I knew I had never picked up a sword in my life, but when I was shadow sword-fighting, muscle memory seemed to be taking over. I was doing quick effortless movements that were ingrained inside of me. I didn't have a clue where I'd got the knowledge of how to handle a sword. But I did have the feeling I'd be grateful for this knowledge soon.

What the glow ahead was coming from was the windows in several wood buildings in a small town that reminded me of something from the old west. All the buildings were one story high. Most were made of wood. A few were made of stone. Nobody was on the street when we arrived.

We walked down the center of the muddy street. At first all we saw were what appeared to be closed down store fronts or shops of some sort. Guess they closed up around here when night fell. Signs were over the doors of the shops. The signs were written in symbols that I could have sworn I'd never seen before.

The thing was, now I knew what the symbols meant.

Some of the signs advertised clothing or shoes or weapons or dried food. Just stuff like that. One sign read, "Slaves Boarding Area." Two sturdy steel cages with steel chains bolted to the floor sat outside the doors to this storefront to advertise as an example.

Johnny stared at the cages as we walked past. "We need to get those girls and get our asses out of here," he said.

"Kind of make you appreciate the good old U.S. of A. don't it," I told him.

"Yeah," he said. "I ain't never gonna bitch about my income taxes again after this."

We went on until we came to a harbor area where a boat like we'd seen from the cave's mouth was docked along with several other small ocean vessels. That was to the west. Across an open area was a row of shops. A few of those advertising food, drink, and lodging were open.

We headed to the nearest one.

CHAPTER 17
McNuggets and the Welcome Wagon

What told us that these food, drink, and lodging places were open were the torches burning outside the doors.

As we went to the nearest of these local hotel-bar & grills I told Johnny, "It doesn't look like they got any electricity around here." I pointed at the torches.

"Yeah," he answered. "Have you noticed they haven't got any glass either?"

Now that he mentioned it, I did look for windows and where there wasn't light coming out, there were wood shutters. The windows that did have light coming from them didn't have any glass and the shutters had been left open.

After pushing open the door to the tavern we were assailed by the smell of the body odor of the customers that was so strong it made your eyes water. The rain must have diluted the aromas in the street but in here there'd been no down pour to wash away the stink. Everyone in the tavern looked to be filthy; dirty faces, dirty clothes, dirty skin, and hair that looked like it had never known a comb. Men and women, young and old alike, this was a dirty-assed bunch of about twenty people in a dirty-assed place.

Some of these people were dressed in roughly cut animal skins. Others were dressed in tied-at-the-waist rough cloth robe things like what we had on. All of the men had swords or axes with them. I was betting these people don't do their shopping at J.C. Penny or Target.

Quite a few of them, eating, drinking and farting, gave us the evil eye as we came in. Well, fuck you all, I thought. We ain't here to have a party and we're sure as hell not kissing cousins either.

The place was dimly lit by a fireplace at one end of the room and candles on each of the tables.

We went to what passed for a bar, a long wood table, and waved to get the attention of the guy who seemed to be the bar tender. He came over to us.

His smell got to us before he did. He was a big greasy fat guy with a big gut and hog jowls.

"What can I get for you gents?" He asked us.

"We need information," Johnny said. "Some men came through this town with some slaves in chains. Two of the slaves were Oriental women, one was a black woman. Where did they go?"

"The slaves don't come in here," the Barman said. "We've no place to quarter them. To the north a few paces is the only place you can keep slaves tonight. Don't think you'll find them there though. All market boats left already."

"Let's go," Johnny said to me and we turned to go back out the door.

"You don't have to hurry away," The Barman shouted after us. "I got good food and drink and I'll make the price right."

On the way to the door I glanced at what one of the guys at the tables was eating. On what looked like a flat piece of thick bread something like thick stew was steaming. He picked at it with his grubby fingers. A few bugs, cockroaches I think, ran over to the food and helped themselves to a few bites of his dinner. The guy kept on eating, not even noticing them.

"Reminds me of McDonalds," I told Johnny as we left the place.

Johnny pointed back at the guy who I'd been watching eat. The guy calmly picked up one of the roaches, popped it into his mouth, chewed and swallowed.

"There goes a McNugget," he said. We went back out in the rain.

*   *   *

Splashing through the mud puddles on the way to the next lighted building, I asked Johnny, "Just where did you get to ask about the women as though they were slaves? Last time I checked, I'd never seen a slave in my life, except maybe in *Roots* or some other damn movie."

Johnny answered, "I have no damn idea. It just popped in my head, like maybe slavery is normal here."

"It probably is," I told him. "Hell, did you notice the crowd at that last place. I was half expecting Conan to come out of the crapper scratching his balls with one hand and picking his teeth with the other."

"This place is like a fucking Barbarian Disney Land," Johnny said. "We need to get the women and figure out how to get back where we belong."

From between two buildings just in front of where we were headed six heavily armed men came out and blocked our path.

We stopped and looked behind us. At least six men were behind us too.

"The welcome wagon's here," I told Johnny.

"Yeah, all we need now is Mr. Rogers," he answered.

They formed a circle around us. All of them had their swords and axes out. We pulled our swords. The two of us stood back to back waiting for them to make a move.

I was hoping like hell I was as good with a sword as it had felt like I'd be when I'd been making my practice swings.

We stood there, none of us making a move. Then the Barman reappeared. He came to the side of us, where the two of us could turn our heads and look at him. Stepping between two of the others we saw he held a long bow and had several arrows in a quiver slung over his back.

"Good gents," he said to us in his good natured salesman's tone. "I'm afraid I lied to you before. I do know where your lady friends are and I can take you to them. Of course, you'll have to drop those swords and just trust me."

"Not likely," Johnny told the Barman. "It'll be a cold day in hell when we trust you."

"Really?" The Barman answered. "A shame, I'll have to wound you then. I didn't want to. I do hate selling damaged goods."

That was when I charged him. Slashing with the short sword and stabbing at the guys in front and around us, I ran full tilt at the Barman.

The Barman backed off and Johnny charged at the same time I did. The line of armed men closed up where the Barman was, he ducked behind them, it also moved backward away from us. We forced the line back and coming from us was all offense. We didn't even know if we knew defense. So how the hell could we plan what we were doing? We just attacked.

But the men against us didn't just let us cut them apart either. They fended off our attack pretty damn good, blocking our slashes with whatever weapon they had in their hands.

Somehow I got separated from Johnny. Then someone jumped on my back. He clamped his arms around me pinning my arms to my sides. Somebody else jumped on him and we all fell forward with me on bottom.

"Get the fuck off me!" I yelled. But a few more just piled on top.

I could hear Johnny cussing and yelling too. There was no way I was going to be able to help him. I was too damn busy with what I was into.

Some guys face was shoved in front of me and against my face. I clamped my teeth onto his nose and bit down hard. It crunched and blood squirted into my mouth. He screamed. Fuck those vampire movies, human blood mixed with snot tasted horrible. I spit a piece of nose and some blood out.

He let go and rolled off me.

I made it to my hands and knees and raised my head up to see what the hell I could do to get loose. Someone jumped forward, a rock clutched in his hand. He smashed me in the skull with it.

Everything went black.

CHAPTER 18
Rolling on Down the Road

I woke up with my head throbbing. A large tender lump was above my left ear. I moved my hands to feel the lump and chains clinked together. That's when I opened my eyes. We were in the two cages we'd seen outside the closed shop where they advertised the boarding of slaves. The cage was only about four feet by five feet by four feet. Not enough room to stand up in or really stretch out.

Johnny was sitting up in his cage. He looked at me as I tried the chains. He had a matching set on him too.

"The way that guy smacked you on the dome with that rock, I thought you might be dead," he said.

"What happened?" I asked.

"Well, after you decided to go to sleep on the job, all those guys piled on me," Johnny said. "I could have kicked all their asses and ran off, but I figured you needed me so I let them lock me up so I could take care of your ass."

"I appreciate that," I told Johnny.

"Seriously though," Johnny said. "We are in some deep shit this time. I listened to them after they threw me in here and we will end up where Sushi was taken. These guys were talking about the slave markets in Rome."

"Rome?" I said. "This sure as hell isn't Europe. At least not any Europe I can think of."

"If you'll shut the fuck up I'll tell you more," Johnny said. "Look, they were discussing how much the Emperor Caligula loves to see strange types of warriors in the Coliseum.

"I don't know when Caligula was alive, but I sure as hell know he wasn't born in the same century we were. So I'm betting we ain't even in the twentieth century.

"They're gonna try to sell me for quite a bit of money since not many blacks are in the Roman Empire. Your buddy Caesar Lanista told them we were coming. That's why they were waiting for us."

I said, "Fuck! We walked right into it."

"No way could we've known what was ahead," he said. "One thing I did find out that's good is that Sushi and Sherry St. Clair probably will be well cared for at least until they get sold in Rome."

"Why's that?" I asked.

"The current fashion in Rome is for the Senators to keep Oriental mistresses. It's like a status symbol for them to have these little chicks to service their dicks."

"You seem pretty calm about all this," I said to Johnny.

He kind of chuckled. "Only because I know Sushi," Johnny said. "She don't do a damn thing she don't want to do. Some soft rich boy takes his dick out and points it at her, she's gonna rip it off and feed it to him."

It was still dark and still raining. In these cages it was breezy but we were reasonably dry.

I tried my chains some more.

"They're not gonna come loose," Johnny told me. "I've already been through all that."

"Probably nothing else to do but try and catch some sleep," I said.

"You're probably right," he said. "These next couple days I'm guessing aren't going to be the easiest ones we'll live."

I made myself as comfortable as I could in the cramped cage. Wearing chains is not my preferred bed clothes.

I closed my eyes.

*   *   *

I woke with my cage being jostled. Two poles had been stuck through the bars and my cage was picked up and hoisted onto a large ox pulled wagon by six of the guys we'd fought the night before. The guy whose nose I'd bit a chunk out of wasn't there. He'd be nursing that hurt for a long time.

Johnny's cage was loaded next to mine. Two other slaves in cages were loaded onto the wagon. Their skin was white, though you could hardly tell it through the dirt on them. Both were men.

The Barman from last night was arguing with some other guy over what seemed like pricing. Finally he yelled, "Take him back off then." He indicated Johnny's cage. "I'll sell him to someone who knows the value of a Nubian."

When the men went to drag Johnny's cage off, the guy changed his mind and paid the Barman what he wanted.

Then with a crack of the whip we were off down the road, a long slow journey. The sun beat down on us. We moved on, not really knowing where we were going. Not sure how to get back to our own world.

The road was dusty and hot. We were part of a caravan that was hauling all kinds of things in wagons pulled behind horses, donkeys, and oxen. The ox that pulled our wagon must have been fed a steady diet of beans. He kept ripping off loud farts as he pulled us down the road. I can't think of anything that smells worse than ox farts. When he cut loose it made you see stars. We were seeing a lot of stars behind that ox.

At least with that going on I couldn't smell the other two slaves on the wagon with Johnny and me. I tried talking to them, but they weren't the talking type. All I got out of them was that the taller one, who was around six foot two and had blond hair and blue eyes, was a Norseman. When his clan raided the coast a few months earlier he'd been wounded in the fighting and left behind.

The people they raided nursed him back to health so they could sell him to this slaver. His name was Torstan.

The other guy was a red headed Scotsman who was proud of the fact that the Romans had never conquered his clan. He said that he was exiled from his clan for fucking the Chieftain's daughter. "Aye, I put the meat to her real good I did," he told us. "Put it to her so good, she pined for me night and day. No other man could ever interest her after what I put her through. Which done got her Daddy mighty upset with me. Seeing she was betrothed to the son of the Chieftain of the clan to the east of us. Daddy said I had to go. I was wandering the hills when slavers caught me."

Sounded like a story to me. His name was McRae.

*   *   *

It was sometime during the middle of the day when some guy with a basket full of vegetables walked along beside our wagon and threw each of us a few potatoes and a few carrots and some other vegetables for us to eat. Hell, I wanted about a dozen Big Macs or at least a Bucket of Chicken. But I ate the vegetables.

When the guy went to walk away back up the line of wagons I yelled at him, "Hey, how about some French dressing and maybe something to wash this down with."

He ignored me and kept on walking.

I yelled to him. "Hey fuck-head! Let me out of this fuckin' cage and I'll rip your fucking head off and shit down your throat!"

As soon as he was out of earshot Johnny said to me, "You know man, I would advise you to keep that smart-ass mouth of yours closed when you're talking to these guards. We need to try to get those women back to where they belong. You getting yourself killed over bullshit ain't gonna help anyone at all."

"Yeah, well I'm not too goddamned used to being in chains and being caged up. I ain't built for this shit."

"You think I am?" He answered. "But we got to keep our heads. These boys ain't playin'. Remember, you ain't worth as much as me. You cause some problems they'll kill your ass right off."

"Shit, you act like you know a hell of a lot more about this slave shit than I do." I said.

"If you're saying that because I'm black, then you're barking up the wrong tree, dog." Johnny said. "Look around you man. Me being black didn't get me in chains no faster than it did you. Give the Romans some credit. They ain't prejudiced. They don't give a shit. They'll slap anyone in chains. These mother fuckers are equal opportunity assholes."

"All right Bro," I told Johnny. "I'll try to keep it cool."

He leaned close to the bars and whispered to me, "Remember Bro, we're the only two people in this world that we can trust."

"Right," I told him and reached into his cage and we clasp hands.

* * *

We watched the scenery slowly roll by through the bars of our cages. The hours stretched long into days. Days stretched into weeks. The same routine, we never got out of our cages. We were fed once a day. After the third day I was eating everything they threw to me and was begging for more. Hunger will make you very agreeable.

They didn't even let us out of the cages to piss or shit. It must have been too much of a risk for them to let us take a squat in the bushes at roadside. Pissing through the bars wasn't too much of a problem, but shitting through the bars was something else entirely. You had to hang from the bars at the top of the cage and aim your ass as close to between the bars as you could get it. Then you had to really bear down to make your shit fly free of your asshole in one shot. Otherwise you'd be wearing that shit on your feet all day until it dried and you could scrape it off.

I don't know why I even bothered with trying to keep the shit off my feet. The way it always smelled with that damn ox throwing farts back on us, we smelled like shit anyway.

To the north of us, at a distance lost in mist and clouds, a mountain range stretched up to the sky. We only caught sight of it when we came to open cleared out areas. I got the impression we were traveling through farmland divided up with large stretches of forest and swamps and lakes and barren scrubland.

The agriculture itself was very primitive. None of the fields were large at all. When we did see people working fields they were plowing using oxen or horses. Mostly the farms we saw were like orchards with apple trees and fields of grapes.

We didn't meet many on the road heading in the opposite direction. When we did and tried to talk to them through the bars of our cages they'd act like they didn't hear a damn thing we'd say to them. We were at the lowest end of the social scale in the Roman Empire. Even talking to us was considered bad manners. Well, fuck them. I'd had people look down their noses at me before. That was nothing new.

The only thing that was any different was that the people outside the wagon didn't really appear to be any better off than us. For the most part the people we saw traveling on our road looked underfed, dirty, and were dressed raggedy as hell. Most of them were traveling on foot. The few pack animals we did see looked skinny and unhealthy. The Roman Empire might be the strongest empire in the world but the common people weren't living any better because of it.

Torstan laughed at my efforts to communicate with the local civilians and didn't attempt it himself.

McRae made a few attempts to talk to the locals. But after he made a suggestive remark to a farmer's wife he wasn't fed for two days. After that he didn't say too much. Hunger will make you agreeable with local customs very fast.

On the second day after McRae was not being fed when food was thrown to us, a large potato that bounced off my leg rolled toward the bars that separated McRae's cage from my own. He made a dive for it, his arm reaching into my cage, his hand snatching for the potato. I reflexively snapped out a right cross and punched his hand away and grabbed the potato. I gathered up all the vegetables and made a small pile in front of myself in the center of my cage.

McRae retreated to the boundaries of his bars and glared at me for a minute. Then a whimper escaped his lips and I heard his stomach growl.

The guard who'd thrown the food to us walked away.

I looked at Johnny. He looked back at me. I remembered what Jeanette had told us, "Always keep in your mind who you are, or you could lose yourself."

Well, just who the fuck was I anyway. I was looking one hell of a lot like a hungry son of a bitch in a goddamn cage the last time I checked.

I looked at McRae. He looked like someone who's just seen his baby die. A blank look of despair was on his face.

"Hey, Mac," I said to him. He didn't even look up.

I divided my food up in half and passed half my vegetables to him between the bars.

He ate the food down and muttered a thank you. I could tell he wasn't the kind of guy who liked thanking anyone for anything. Johnny passed me some of his food.

He said, "I know that wasn't easy."

"Fuck it. I'm getting sick of potatoes and carrots anyway." I told him. "We get out of this shit, I'm gonna spend a month in a Safeway, just going up and down the aisles, eating as I go."

"I heard that," Johnny said. "Yeah, we get out of this we might actually be able to eat some of Sushi's cooking."

I remembered how Sushi cooked.

"I don't think so Bro," I told him.

"No," he agreed. "We'd have to be a lot hungrier than this."

The next day, our little caravan pulled into Micea.

CHAPTER 19
On the Auction Block

We knew we were coming to some sort of a city at least two hours before we were able to see it. The smell of the place told us what was ahead of us. Even the smell of our farting ox didn't drown out the stench of a large number of people living close together in a time of no sewage treatment plants.

What we were approaching smelled like a huge pile of cow crap mixed with rotten eggs.

When me and Johnny started talking back and forth about this McRae asked us, "Just where do you come from anyway, that your cities do not smell like this?"

Johnny told him, "We come from the United States of America."

I chimed in, "East St. Louis to be exact."

"Never heard of them," McRae said. "So what is this place like where men don't stink?"

We tried to tell him what life in the good old U.S. of A. had been like. Most of it, he just couldn't get. The idea of a supermarket was an alien concept. Explaining cars was another thing that wasn't easy. The idea of a carriage not pulled by animals just didn't make sense to him. TV's, radios, or telephones were impossible for him to figure out and when we told him about twentieth century air travel he started laughing.

"That's enough, that's enough," he told us smiling. "I've told some mighty big lies in my day, but stories about silver birds big enough to carry over one hundred men... even I wouldn't try to put that one over on some-one."

He laughed off anything else we tried to tell him about our world. I can't say I blamed him none either. If I'd have grown up and lived in the world he did, I wouldn't believe what we were telling him.

*   *   *

When the sun was still high in the sky the gates of the city appeared before us. Micea had a stone wall around it that stood roughly fifty feet tall. The gates that we passed through were made of thick rusted iron bars.

The caravan moved into a courtyard and the different owners of the different wagons parted ways and went off to where they needed to go. The guy who had been arguing over Johnny's price had four wagons holding a total of sixteen slaves. He had the wagons arranged in a half circle so that all of us could be looked at and bargained over at the same time.

McRae leaned close to the bars so he could whisper to Johnny and me. "I'm pretty sure that most of us are going to be tested here to find out what they are going to use us for. At least we'll get a good meal before they do it."

I wasn't quite sure what he was talking about but I was betting they weren't going to keep us waiting for long. I leaned close to Johnny. "No matter what happens," I told him, "We got to be cool about it until we get them to believing there's no fight left in us at all. Then we escape. Won't be no trying either, we make it or die."

A stocky guy with a short sword in his hand was walking back and forth in front of the cages. He was slapping the flat of his sword against his palm like a lion tamer cracking a whip. When he noticed me talking he came over and slapped the flat of his sword against the bars of my cage. "Silence slave!" He barked at me.

I didn't say anything else. I even had to look the other way. Otherwise he would have seen the murder in my eyes.

He walked away.

I looked at Johnny.

Johnny just nodded back at me. There was no doubt about the message we passed to each other. Just take the shit they throw at us in silence, until we can make them pay.

Looking into the other cages that had been brought with us I saw only one female among the sixteen prisoners. She was a skinny, scared, and grimy looking little teenaged girl.

There were a few skinny teenage boys and a few old looking guys. The rest looked like us, mean prisoners of war.

After a few minutes, five guys dressed like they thought they were royalty showed up with their guards. They began inspecting us, making comments on every aspect of our appearance from our teeth to our toes. They went over every one of us in the cages, one at a time.

When they got to me, I smiled at them and gave them the finger. They didn't know what it meant anyway.

One of the bidders called the guy who'd brought us here Chilo. So I figured that was his name.

Most of the others had been purchased at between fifty to eighty sesterces. The little teenaged girl had to practically be given away. She was weeping the whole time that the bidding was going on for her. Chilo kept poking her with a stick to make her reveal a breast or a bit of leg for the bidders. She just shrank back to the far corner of her cage hiding her face.

When McRae was up for bid he proudly told the group, "If any of you have a house of pleasure, I'm the man for you. I can please any woman on the Earth. If you have a nagging wife just give me a shot at her and her nagging will be over. She'll walk around your home with a grin as big as the sky and stars in her eyes and bowl legged as well."

The bidders discussed McRae's powerful looking thigh muscles then he was bought for ninety sesterces. When Chilo asked the winning bidder, a mean looking dark skinned guy, why he'd went so high the Bidder said, "I just want to see the look on his face as he's being gelded."

Torstan went for seventy sesterces. He was sold to a short, fierce looking, black haired man named Flaccus, who said he'd make a great arena fighter.

I was bought by the same guy for fifty sesterces.

The bidding got really hot when Johnny's turn came. A black man in Rome was very rare. A few of the bidders had never even seen a Negro before. The bidding reached one hundred and fifty sesterces before the guy who'd bought me and Torstan added Johnny to his collection.

I was grateful as hell that guy bought Johnny too. If we'd been bought by two different bidders I'd have had to have found him and the girls. Finding the girls is going to be hard enough.

After the bidding was done we were taken out of our cages at sword point. I'd been bent over so long in that damn cage that it hurt just to try to stand up. Outside my cage, off of the wagon, the first step I tried to take my knees gave way and I pitched on my face on the dirt.

A guard kicked me in the ass. I stood up and told myself, *the first chance I get you're a dead mother fucker.* I didn't voice a word of it. Yeah, be cool, until it counts. Laugh now mother fucker, I will laugh last.

* * *

We were prodded at sword point down the street and into a building that looked like a horse barn except for the chains screwed into the floor. They slapped the chains on us in there and we were brought some bowls of a type of stew and large chunks of coarse bread. After all the days of raw potatoes and carrots, this meal tasted better than anything I'd ever eaten.

Flaccas bought five of us from our caravan, Torstan, Johnny and me, the crying girl and another skinny teenage boy.

While we were still eating Johnny turned to me and said, "Did you see the way they were bidding on me. Shit, they like brothers around here don't they? If I'd of shown them my dick, they'd still be arguing over me."

Torstan scowled at Johnny and with an evil smile said, "Yes, they would still be arguing over who would get the pleasure of cutting your dick and balls off."

"Man, that shit ain't funny," Johnny said. "Don't you people have any sense of humor at all?"

"You are a slave now," Torstan told him. "Speak when you are spoken to. Do what you are told. You will live longer."

"Well, you ain't my master, mother fucker," Johnny said. "I'll speak to you any goddamned way I feel like it!"

"Take it easy," I told Johnny. "He didn't mean anything by it."

"I know," Johnny said. "I don't wear these damn chains too well my-self."

We ate the rest of our meal in silence.

The idea that we might spend the rest of our lives in chains wasn't a good thing to be thinking about.

* * *

A few minutes after we were done eating six guards came marching into the barn. One of them was carrying an armful of thick chains and manacles. Starting with Johnny first, they put a thick metal ring around his left ankle and using a type of pliers, an anvil and a hammer, they beat on it and riveted it shut.

They moved from him to me, then on to everyone who was already chained to the floor in the room, fastening a manacle around each of our left ankles. For the full grown men, the guards kept their swords pointed at us, ready to run us through if we gave them any trouble.

After that, again starting with Johnny at the beginning of the chain, they used the pliers to squeeze a ring closed and fastened our leg manacle to the long chain. When they were clamping the final ring onto the end of the chain and fastening the last of us, the weeping girl to the rest of us, Johnny whispered to me, "Hell, I 'd rather be in the back of a bus in the 1950's in Alabama than being the leader of this train."

"I heard that," I answered. "After this, if anybody in the U.S. complains to me about being treated bad, I'm gonna bust him upside his head."

One of the guards yelled at us to shut up, which we did. We were then prodded at sword point out the barn doors and down the street.

Walking with a chain attached to one leg ain't easy. Every time one of us stumbled a guard would smack that person with the flat of his sword and kick the stumbler until he got in step with everyone else. Not my preferred method for learning how to march, but it was effective. Before we'd walked fifty paces, all of us were in step and moving along pretty good.

I don't know how far we marched. It must have been at least a mile when we came to a compound that looked to me like the outside of the prison in *Papillion*.

High walls, iron bars on all the windows and doors, spikes at the top of the walls.

A large door was opened for us and we were prodded inside. Across an open courtyard we heard the clash of steel. Men were slashing and stabbing at each other with strange weapons of all kinds.

This was to be our new home.

CHAPTER 20
Gladiator School

The smell of dust and sweat was in the air. Mixed with it, almost over-powering, was the smell of spilt blood. I knew this smell well, a pungent, unpleasant, repellant aroma. I'd never smelled it this strong before.

Here, many people had died, and their deaths had not been pleasant ones. The smell of a person's death when it comes violently is strong. The air will reek of the fecal matter the body throws off in its final fight to live. That stench was heavy.

Off in a far corner of the courtyard two men were nailed to crosses. Cru-cifixion has to be a terribly painful way to die. Their final agonies were etched on their faces.

In the open courtyard, separated from us by a fence of steel bars, men were training with swords, spears, and three pronged tridents and nets. Some were sparring, their hands wrapped in cushioned bandages. Others were training with apparatus that swung wooden poles at their heads that they ducked under then swung a pole at their ankles that they jumped over in succession. Those poles looked like they would knock hell out of you if you miss timed a duck or a jump.

A few seconds after I started watching a guy using one of these training machines the guy didn't jump fast enough. The swinging pole cracked him loudly across the ankles. He went down. As he was getting up the top pole swung and knocked a handful of his teeth flying through the air. That boy looked like he wouldn't want to be kissing anyone for a while.

In another part of the courtyard, sandbags hung from platforms. Some guys with blunt iron swords were slapping these around. More bags, hung the same way, were being punched at by more guys with wrapped hands. The guards let us watch this for a few minutes then the door we'd entered through swung open and Flaccus, the man who'd bought us, walked in.

He walked back and forth in front of us, looking us over. He didn't seem overly impressed. He stopped his pacing and addressed us as a group, like an army drill Sergeant would.

"Before these chains are taken off of you, I will tell you this," he said to us. "I am a business man, and you are my property. I supply fighters for The Circus Maximus in Rome. The Emperor himself watches the shows that I supply to. Some of you will be granted the honor to fight and die in front of our great Caesar Caligula. All of you will in some way contribute to the shows put on in Circus Maximus.

"Disobedience will not be tolerated and will be punished. Attempts to escape will be punished," he pointed at the two crucified men, "In this manner."

"Obedience and bravery and giving an entertaining show will be rewarded, sometimes by letting you have a woman. Do as you are told and you may be happy here. Some are. Disobey and die."

He walked toward the back of the line again looking us over. Flaccus stopped in front of the scared teenaged girl and reached out to touch her cheek. She shrank back from him. He backhanded her hard, knocking her from her feet.

Flaccus looked at one of the guards and motioned to the girl, "Take this one to the females."

He walked toward the door and said over his shoulder, "Have the others bathed. They stink of their barbarian homes."

Flaccus left.

*　　*　　*

The girl was unfettered from our chain and led away.

The chains were taken off us and the image of the two men nailed to crosses in the courtyard did stop any idea I had of springing at the throat of the nearest guard. I can think of quite a few better ways of dying than being crucified. So I did as I was told and acted like a good boy.

We were taken into a large room where several wooden washtubs were filled with water. Each of us climbed out of our clothes and into the wash tubs.

A female slave was at each tub to help us in and scrub us down with an abrasive sponge. The water was cold, but after weeks without a bath the cold water felt great. The slave that was helping me wash was probably in her thirties. She was attractive, but never looked up and never met my eyes, even though I tried to get her to. I tried to talk to her but she just looked away and wore a stony expression on her face.

I asked her name but she didn't answer. Hell, here I was sitting in a bath tub in the raw in front of a nice looking woman and I couldn't even get a peep out of her.

"Come on, you can tell me your name." I said to her, "There's no harm in that."

But she just stayed stone silent and kept working at my dirt like a well-trained mechanic working on an engine. After a few minutes, I gave up and just enjoyed the scrubbing.

She also gave me a shave with a very sharp knife. I was hoping she knew what she was doing when she had that knife at my throat. I kept my mouth shut during the shave. At that moment I didn't want to be pissing that woman off.

At length, a guard came in and clapped his hands together. "Finish up now," he barked. Man I could have stayed in that tub all day.

My attendant had me stand up and she dried me off using a coarse cloth. Someone brought some clean clothes for me and took my soiled ones.

Outside the tub she handed those to me and went to step away. As she did, I touched her arm. She stopped and for once met my eyes. "Please," I said to her. "Let me know your name. What can be wrong with that?"

She smiled a sad closed mouth smile and shook her head no. She stepped away from me then glanced around for the guard. He was looking in another direction. Her eyes looked sad when she looked back into my eyes. She opened her mouth and pointed to it with her right hand.

I could see that she had no tongue. Someone had cut her tongue out.

*   *   *

We were marched to individual cells by four guards who had swords out but didn't seem overly worried to be walking us around. In here, it would be crazy to attempt an escape. There were so many armed guards that you'd be cut down in just a few minutes. So our guards weren't too concerned about us trying anything. Just before we were put in the cells the leader of the guards told us, "Get as much rest as you can. Tomorrow, we will decide who of you are worth training."

Then I was shoved into a small dark chilly room and the thick wood and iron door was slammed shut behind me. It's a bad feeling when you're locked up. I'd been locked up before, but never like this.

After a minute my eyes adjusted to the dim light. There was one piece of furniture, a wooden cot for sleeping. A few blankets were thrown on it. Well, it was better than I was used to in that damn wagon.

A basket of fruits and vegetables was sitting on the bed. Guess they wanted us well fed for whatever was going to happen tomorrow.

In one corner was a bucket. It was empty. I was guessing that's where I'd be doing my pissing and crapping.

In the other corner was a bucket full of water. I wanted to make sure I didn't get these buckets mixed up in the dark and take a piss in my drinking water or go to wash my face with a handful of shit.

The walls, like practically everything else here, was made of a grey stone. There was an opening in the ceiling that had bars across it. People walked past overhead. They didn't even glance down at me.

In the wall opposite the door and over the cot was a barred window. I could see out into the courtyard where fighters still worked out on the bags or sparred with each other with swords, spears, tridents, or fists.

The sun was setting and it was getting cooler. In another place and in another life I'd be planning to head out and run the streets all night. I know I wouldn't be able to sleep without my trusted friend, Jack Daniels, with that clashing of sounds going on outside.

Here, I sure wasn't going to be running any streets tonight. I took the basket off the cot and sat it on the floor and lay down.

At least I could stretch out. I got an apple from the basket and slowly ate it. This was a weird twisted world that I found myself in. But aren't all worlds twisted. In some ways, I could understand this place better than my own world.

Here, the strong survive and dominate use the weak to get anything that they want. There's one law to survive here. Be hard.

Just about everything here seems to be made of stone. People's hearts must be made of stone too. If I'm going to have any chance of getting out of this alive, I'm going to have to be harder than the stone that surrounds me.

I ate the apple and watched the fighters in the courtyard. Some of them were damn good. I'd better keep it in my head to try things that they had never seen or I was in for a serious bruising and worse.

The breeze blew in. It actually seemed like fresh air. It surprised me how quickly I'd gotten used to the awful smell of this place.

A large crow landed on the head of one of the men on the crosses and started pecking at his right eye. The guy on the cross looked like he was past caring. They'd probably leave him and his buddy up there till they rotted off.

They were a damn good reminder of what a failed escape attempt can mean. Until I was certain we weren't going to fail, I wasn't going to attempt anything.

After a time, after I ate another piece of fruit, I did drift off to sleep.

CHAPTER 21
Testing Day

Morning came quickly, too quickly.

Light streaming in through the barred window followed quickly by yells and shouts from training fighters was what brought me around. You'd think that sometimes I'd wake up not knowing where I was and think I was back in East St. Louis, but that never happened. Not even once.

Things were so different here I always knew instantly where I was. The smells were stronger and harsher. The sounds were always either deafening loud or total silence. Even the sun seemed more raw and hard on the eyes.

I took a raw potato and carrot from the bucket and ate them, then took a piss and a shit in the correct bucket.

There wasn't any toilet paper for me to use. Man, I tell you what, I was seriously beginning to miss toilet paper. Try not wiping your ass for months on end and you'll know what I mean. You start getting this crusty feeling right in the crack of your ass from clumps of shit stuck to your ass hairs. And if I ever did get some Roman woman to do the wild thing with me and she goes to give me some head, she'd better be holding her breath. The smell coming from this unwiped ass has got to be deadly.

I threw some water on my face from the other bucket and cupped water in my hands and drank some too.

The door to my cell was thrown open and I was motioned out by a guard with a short sword. Twelve other slaves were already in the hallway. I saw Johnny and we passed a look. That was all we could do. We were too far apart to pass any words.

The guard herded us down the row of cells and through a door out into the courtyard.

In the dusty yard they lined us up against a blood stained wall. A new guard came to take a look at us. He paced back and forth looking us over.

This guy hadn't said anything, but from the way the other guards reacted to him and the way he moved around us, I knew he was either the commander here or the head trainer. I later found out his name was Miletus.

He was around six feet tall and muscular and knew how to use his size to intimidate. He had a face that would have looked at home on a bulldog's body. His attitude matched his face.

After looking us over for a minute he stopped in front of the skinny teen-aged boy who was now trembling.

"You!" He barked and pointed a finger at the kid. "Step forward!"

I thought the boy was going to faint, but he did manage a step, even with his knees shaking so badly he could barely stand.

Miletus turned his back on the youth and let his gaze wander over the courtyard in front of him. He sighted on a pair going at it hot and heavy with two of the blunted iron swords. Pointing at the shorter of the two, Miletus shouted, "You, Paulino! Over here! Bring the ferrum. You are to test the boy."

Paulino strode to where we were, carrying the two heavy blunted swords. Up close I could see he had a wide scar on his left cheek that gave him a demented look, like he had a big constant smile on his face.

The practicing gladiators stopped and watched as Paulino stood in front of the kid. I'd seen this before in boxing gymnasiums. Every time a new guy comes in to spar, everybody always wanted a first look at somebody they might be fighting someday. Maybe they could spot a weakness that no one else would notice.

Miletus ordered the boy to step forward. Paulino tossed the blunted sword into the dirt in front of him.

The youth stared at the blade with a mixture of horror and fascination. He looked to be frozen with fear.

"Pick it up!" Miletus barked at him so loudly it made all of us jump.

Laughter and derisive comments floated over to us from the watching gladiators.

"Pick it up, now!" Miletus yelled at the boy.

The kid bent over and lifted the sword from the dirt, glancing fearfully toward all of us. If he was looking to us for help, there wasn't a damn thing we could do for him.

Paulino smiled a sneer. He looked at Miletus then lunged at the boy in a feint. The boy stumbled backward, his nervousness on display for everyone. Following the off balance kid, Paulino feinted a stab at his stomach. The boy dropped the heavy blade too far to bring it back up fast. Paulino slapped the flat of the blade against the kid's shoulder with a resounding thwack.

"There goes your arm," Paulino shouted and laughed. "It's lying in the dirt at your feet." He stepped back like he was watching the boy do something. The kid hadn't moved, other than to rub his right shoulder.

Tears were starting to form in the boy's eyes.

"Good," Paulino told the boy. "I see you've picked up your arm and put it back on." He smiled. "We can begin again."

Paulino came in at the kid. This time the boy whined loudly and just re- treated. Tears burst forth from his eyes and ran down his face. He sank to his knees and cried, "Please don't hurt me. Please, oh, please." He let his sword drop to the ground.

The other gladiators were laughing loudly. Paulino stopped and looked at Miletus who was shaking his head in disgust.

Miletus shouted to a guard, "Get him out of my sight. Take him to the house of entertainments. He will be taught to pleasure the gladiators who prefer a boy's ass to women."

The boy glanced back at Paulino as he was lead sobbing away. Paulino sneered at the kid and blew him a kiss.

"I'll be seeing you later," he shouted.

Miletus pointed at me. He barked, "You! Step forward."

I came out to where the discarded sword lay in the dirt. I kneeled in front of it and took some dirt in my hands and worked it into my palms.

Why was I doing this?

I don't have a fucking clue. I think I saw it in a movie once and it looked good. There wasn't any director there to yell cut when the going gets tough. So I guessed I had better not hold up the show.

Picking up the sword, I faced Paulino. I smiled. "Please, don't hurt me," I told him.

"It will hurt," he said. "When I bend you over and drive it deep."

You'll regret saying that, I thought.

Paulino came in at me. It was that same feint he'd tried on the boy.

I flicked his blade to the side and stood my ground. He almost fell into me. Stepping to my own right, I was inside his guard. I brought my left elbow around as a short left hook into his teeth with bone rattling force.

He staggered back a step. I knew he was seeing stars. Faking a kick to his nuts, I recharged the kick and sent it to his lowered right wrist instead.

Paulino's sword flew from his grasp.

I wanted to get a little payback for the kid right now.

"Hey, fuck-head don't hurt me," I said and swung the blunt blade at Paulino's head. It was really just a feint.

He ducked down and charged me. Not a good move. Guess he hadn't paid attention to that last kick. Ready for his rush, I planted a kick right in the middle of his in charging face.

I'll give Paulino some credit. He takes one hell-of-a shot.

He came straight up out of that crouch with blood pouring from his nose and busted lips.

I fired off a left hook that would have put the lights out in a moose, if it would have landed. I wish it would have landed, because as soon as my fist sailed past, within a half inch of Paulino's face Melitus shouted, "Stop now!"

I did stop. I had to remember where I was. I couldn't let myself go having too much fun.

The other gladiators cheered me and sent some derisive remarks Paulino's way. It felt good being cheered too.

One of the other gladiators came over and took me to where some of those bags were hung. They had all been through this initiation ritual so many times they all knew the parts they were supposed to play. He started preliminary instructions on how to work out on the bags using the heavy blunt swords.

Every now and then a gladiator would wander by to congratulate me for kicking Paulino's ass. I was definitely in, but I wasn't letting down my guard no matter how these guys were acting. I had to always remember, I was a slave. Any one of these guys would be ready to cut my throat without a moment's hesitation.

Paulino went off to lick his wounds and get bandaged up. He gave me a long lingering look of death as he left the courtyard. I knew I'd better never turn my back on that one.

I watched the other guys get tested. As it turned out I hadn't needed to beat Paulino to qualify for training. All I'd needed to do was not show fear and fight back.

Johnny passed his tryout with no problem at all. I didn't expect him to have a problem.

Torstan didn't have any problem either.

Most of the guys tested that morning passed their tests to become gladiators.

The few that didn't were sent off to be trained to perform duties nobody would ever want to do.

Now, we were professional murderers. On a moment's notice, we could be ordered to kill and we better do it too, otherwise we'd be the one dying.

Killing was nothing new to me.

Doing it for somebody else's profit was.

CHAPTER 22
Oaths & Roman Hospitality

All of us new gladiators spent the next few hours training with our individual instructors. Somewhere around noon, and all time telling now has to be an estimate as my Timex is long gone, we were rounded up and lined up in front of the same wall in the courtyard where we'd started out. Eight of us were against that wall.

Melitus was back in front of us again doing his pacing back and forth.

He shouted for us to be silent. This guy had a thing about shouting. Melitus just had to do it, day and night.

"You are slaves," he shouted. "There are no choices you can make in your own life. All of them are made for you. Except for one choice, the one you can now make. You can choose to be gladiators and fight and die like men or you can choose to be a cowardly piece of shit who will serve those who fight."

"A gladiator is well fed. He sleeps in open barracks among his brothers and is given a woman or boy as he earns them. The other slaves get nothing and are treated like the worms that they are."

"You will now take the oath of a gladiator. All who choose to be men step forward one pace and repeat what I say."

All eight of us stepped forward. You'd have to be an idiot not to.

Melitus began, "I now swear to become a gladiator and obey all orders without question given to me."

As a group, we repeated what he said.

"If I should disobey, I agree to suffer myself to be whipped with rods, burned with fire or killed with steel."

Well, I said the words, but he could kiss my ass about me letting him do any of that shit to me.

* * *

We spent the rest of the afternoon with our instructors swinging those heavy swords. When evening came the instructors took us all to a large room where everyone was walking around freely and sitting where ever they felt like at several large tables.

Slaves were bringing plates of food out to the seated gladiators. Most of the ones serving the food were women. The few men among them were old and decrepit.

I found Johnny and we sat as far from everyone else as we could to talk.

"How'd you like that oath we took?" I asked him.

"Shit," Johnny answered. "That mother fucker better think twice before he thinks anyone's gonna be burning me. This is one nigger that will fuck him up. When I come down on him, he'll think the entire Zulu nation is pulling a train on his ass."

Food was brought to us.

I wasn't exactly sure what the meat was. It could have been rabbit, chicken or squirrel. Hell, it might be big rats for all I knew, but it tasted damn good. We were also given a salad of some kind of barley stuff. It wasn't as good as the meat, but I was hungry so I ate it all.

We whispered about the possibility of escape and quickly came to the agreement that escape right now was too dangerous and didn't make sense anyway. We knew the girls would probably end up on the auction block in Rome, but on our own we didn't have a clue as to how to get there. It wasn't like we could just pop into a Seven-Eleven and buy a road map either.

So, if we just rode this out and took our training we'd probably end up in Rome too. At least we'd be closer to the girls that way. We'd figure out what we'd do after we got to Rome. Besides, learning how to use these weapons the right way might come in handy.

*   *   *

We had to quit our talking when another gladiator came and sat beside us. He didn't want to talk much and we were thankful for that. There's not a lot we had in common with the majority of these guys. Conversation wasn't going to be easy with very many of them.

Like what were we supposed to ask, "Hey there dude. How's your spear thrust coming along?" As if I'd give a shit. Glad we didn't have to go into it.

After dinner we were lead to the open barracks that Miletus talked about. Open barracks hell, looked like the county jail to me. It was a hallway with five cells on both sides.

Six of us were to a cell. Each of us had his own wooden cot with hay and blankets spread on top. Each of us had his own piss/shit bucket and there was again a basket of fruits and vegetables lain on each bed.

The accommodations wouldn't be making me forget the Hilton, I tell you that.

These cells were open so we could see into the other cells through the bars. That's probably what Miletus meant by open. They were really just big cages. I don't think I could ever completely get used to living in a cage. If I ever get out of this shit, I know I'll never look at the animals in the zoo the same way.

We were given the choice of which cells we went to before we were locked in. Me and Johnny stuck together.

Four other gladiators shared our cage. Two of them were older guys with worn out looking bodies and faces. The determination on their faces told me they'd probably make it through training. I wasn't betting that they'd make it through too many bouts of hand to hand combat. The spirit might be willing, but if the flesh is weak, pity wouldn't be found here.

Of the other two, one was a young guy, looked to be in his late teens. He would be fast on his feet. He could be dangerous, if he could keep his head.

The other guy named Pugnax, had a sadistic attitude and the size and strength to make it work for him. He was somewhere around six foot two and weighed around two-twenty. He was the local equivalent of a boxer. This guy had scars all over him from previous battle wounds. Too bad one of those wounds hadn't been fatal.

He started out by ordering the younger guy off his cot so he could claim it for his own. I think he did that just to let us know what he was about. This guy had the potential to be a problem.

After eating a little fruit, taking a dump in the correct bucket and talking for a few minutes we were all getting ready to settle down to some heavy sleep when the guards came for me.

*   *   *

Two guards came with the one who unlocked our cell. He stepped in and pointed at me with his sword. "You," he said. "Come with us."

They lead me through breezy torch lit hallways and when I asked where I was being taken I was told, "Silence!"

When we came to a row of cells similar to the one I'd been in the night before, we stopped in front of one of the doors and it was unlocked.

The door was swung open. I looked inside but could see nothing inside except blackness. A torch beside the door blinded me from seeing anything.

The guard who'd silenced me earlier now said, "You are given a gift for your showing against Paulino. You showed more than expected." Then I was shoved into the room and the door was slammed shut and locked behind me.

All was darkness within. I could see nothing at all, not even my hand in front of my face. Where my cell the night before had at least a window and an opening overhead, this one had nothing.

I stepped forward slowly into the darkness, feeling my way. I didn't want to walk into something in the pitch blackness.

I found the bed and sat down on it.

I'm being given a gift, I thought? Being thrown in a pitch black hole, these Romans are some fucked up people if this is their idea of a good time.

My eyes were adjusting gradually to what little light came in from under the door. I could make out vague shapes in the room I was in, the cot I was sitting on, the basket of fruit, the two buckets. And something in the far corner that was hunched over and making sniffling noises.

As my eyes adjusted further I could tell it was a small person. I went to the corner and saw that the person's back was turned to me. It was a woman. She was trying her best to hide, in a place where there was nowhere to hide.

I went over to her and as softly as I could I said, "Don't worry, I won't hurt you." I reached out and touched her back. She screamed in terror.

I went back to the bed and sat down as my ears throbbed from the echoes of her fright. From there I told her, "Look, I'll just leave you alone. Nobody's going to hurt you in here tonight."

She stayed crouched down in the corner covering her head with her arms and sobbing. From the sound of her voice I could tell this was that skinny teenage girl that Flaccus bought with the rest of us.

I guess I was supposed to be a part of her training. I was supposed to rape her, to get her used to doing what she's told, whether she likes it or not. I listened to her cry for a while. Little moans escaped her. She sounded like an injured puppy.

Well, I'm not one for rape. Never could understand how a guy could get off on hurting a woman. And besides, she was still a kid. These Romans are some fucked up people to be doing this kind of thing. I might be so horny that I could fuck a knot hole in a tree, but I could not rape a kid. Wrong is wrong. No matter where you are.

There were two blankets on the cot, so I took one to her. When I laid it over her shoulders, she screamed again.

"No one's going to hurt you tonight," I told her again and meant it.

I didn't even want to think about what this kid had probably been through all day. And that boy that Paulino had eliminated from the ranks of the gladiators, for all I know he might have had it worse. I doubt they use Vaseline in the Roman Empire. That boy better learn how to suck a mean dick, otherwise he's in for some rough rides.

I knew I'd better get some sleep so I stretched out on the cot. Even though I was tired as hell, sleep was not easy in coming. The extreme cruelty of what I was seeing was bothering even me.

I'd killed a lot of people, but I didn't torture and rape and nail people to crosses. And I was getting the feeling that I was only touching the tip of the iceberg. I knew there was going to be a whole lot more ugliness to see before we left the good-ole Romans behind.

Just before I drifted off to sleep, there was movement on the cot beside me. There wasn't much room but I slid over as far as I could and the kid cuddled up to me like the lost child that she was.

I wished there was something I could do to help her, but I knew there wasn't.

CHAPTER 23
Who Makes the Glands Dance?

By the time I woke up the kid was gone. I must have been so tired that when the guards came in to take her, I just slept through it. It's probably better that I was a sleep. One bad move from one of those guards and I might have started acting like a hero and try to protect the kid.

That would have only gotten me killed.

Fists, feet, knees and teeth against swords is not an even contest. Who was I to be thinking about protecting anyone? With the situation we were in, Johnny and me would be lucky to get out of this alive with all our limbs attached. We would have to be extremely lucky to get Sushi, Sherry, Terry and some of those others back to our own time and place. Trying to help anyone else was pure insanity.

So what? I'd been called fucking crazy before. This wouldn't be the first time I'd done something really stupid.

*　　*　　*

We spent the better part of the next week just getting used to the training we were going through. After the first day, I had aches in places I'd forgotten existed. Over the next two days the soreness went away. Muscles I hadn't used for a long time hardened. My wind got better. My reflexes became quicker.

They were feeding us three good meals a day of small game animals and fruits and vegetables. I was very surprised at how quickly my body was reacting to the good food, exercise and rest.

Even when I was a professional boxer I never took the training seriously, it was always just a way to make a buck. Here, I didn't have a choice. There was no cutting this training camp and going chasing pussy all night. Here, you did what you were told when you were told to do it. There wasn't no playing around with these trainers. These guys were serious.

When you didn't do what you were told a whip was cracked across your back. One lick with that whip and you were ready to do anything they said.

Near the end of the first week the martial arts training that Johnny and me had received started to show. We were clearly better at defending ourselves than most of the guys who'd been brought in with us.

This really wasn't all that surprising considering that most of these gladiator trainees were just farmers or thieves. They were starting from square one.

Torstan was the exception.

He was big and strong and mean as hell. He liked the heavy weapons. Anything that had some weight to it Torstan liked swinging at someone's head.

There were some contradictions in our training.

Before we began our training, the day after we passed our tests, Miletus stood us against the wall and shouted at us, "While you are here you are never to strike with your weapons to cause injury. This is a place of learning. Not the place of combat."

When we were sparring with the blunted swords or other weapons and a fight did break out, Miletus usually just stood back and let the two go at it until it got too serious for his liking. If he really didn't want us injuring each other, he should have stopped those fights immediately.

In Johnny and me, he was dealing with two guys who could end a fight and a man's life in a split second. Him, waiting for a signal for us to look like we were going to hurt someone just wouldn't work.

Near the end of that first week of training while having the midday meal, Johnny and me came to an agreement.

When no one was close to our table I told Johnny, "You know I don't think it would be a good idea if we let Miletus and these other guys know just how much hurt we can put on them if we want to."

"I've been thinking the same thing," he answered. "They might slap guards all over us and keep us in chains right up until they throw us in the Coliseum."

"Let's not show them all our tricks. OK?" I said.

"Fuck," Johnny said. "I got tricks I don't even know I knew. I just won't let them see I can kick their ass any time I feel like it."

"Until it makes a difference," I said.

We shook hands.

"Yeah," he said, "Until it makes a difference."

* * *

Training became routine.

Get up, eat, stretch then work out with different weapons until Miletus chose you to specialize in one. Whatever you looked best at doing, whatever would make you worth more money, Miletus had you specialize in.

Miletus chose Johnny to be a retiarus, a fighter with a trident and a net. A retiarus didn't wear much armor since his mobility was a key to his success. I think Miletus chose this type of combat for Johnny just to be able to show off his black skin. The word was given to the rest of us. If we sparred with Johnny, make sure you don't hurt him. If you do, you'll be nailed to a cross.

A black man in Rome cost too much to be wasted before a profit was made from his hide.

I was chosen to be a caestus fighter. Those are the guys who have their hands wrapped in bandages and punch the bags around and spar for their training. Here we would always wear padded gloves while sparring. In actual combat in the arena, leather straps studded with nails would be stretched over our knuckles.

After taking a few licks with those babies you get a serious case of the uglies for the rest of your life. Miletus probably chose this type of training for me because I'd been boxing for so long that throwing straight punches and short compact hooks was instinctive. Throwing a straight punch was something I could not force myself not to do.

I would rather have had my main training be with a sword but I didn't have any choice in the matter. Sword training would be more valuable to me but not make me more profitable for Flaccus, and that's what it was all about.

* * *

Days came and went with a swiftness that was hard to believe. The routine of training occupied most of our waking hours. We trained hard and every three days we were sent to the bath house where we were scrubbed down like the prized livestock that we were.

I lost all track of how many days went by while we were at Micea. One week, two weeks, a month, I'm not sure.

I only know that I continued to get stronger and quicker under the training we were going through. The thing was, at my age, I know I should have reached a certain level of fitness and not been able to surpass that. There should have been a wall I'd reach where my body would say, "That's it, I can't do any better than this."

The other older guys reached their plateau after a few weeks. You could see it in their worried expressions when they watched the younger guys smoothly go through movements that they had to struggle with. It's got to be a bad feeling to know you're going into a fight to the death with less physical tools than your opponent.

I'm glad I didn't have to have that on my mind.

It seemed like every day that I worked out on the bags or sparred or dodged the swinging poles from the training devices that more years were peeling away from my body. I was feeling younger every day. Never had I been this fit in my life.

I was feeling like if they threw me into a pit with a big black bear, I could rip his nuts off and shove them down his throat before he could do any damn thing about it.

When I mentioned this to Johnny he said, "I've been noticing the same thing, as far as feeling younger. I'm not sure what the hell caused it, but I know we went through some physical changes when we came through that portal."

I told Johnny, "The life expectancy in these times is a lot shorter than our time. Maybe, whatever happened to us is compensating for that difference in life span."

"I tell you something," Johnny said and pointed at my left temple. "Back in our time, you were starting to turn gray. You don't have a gray hair on your head now."

"Your gray is gone too," I told Johnny. "But you're still as ugly as an old prune anyway."

"Sushi calls that my rugged good looks," Johnny said and smiled.

"You miss her very much?" I asked.

"Yeah," he answered. "It's like a part of me is gone. No offense Bro, but I could tell her things that I couldn't tell anybody else, personal things." His eyes had a faraway look, like he was seeing something that I couldn't. It looked like any moment now he'd start crying.

I said, "You could tell her things like, get down there and suck my dick girl. Tube steak's served for dinner tonight."

Johnny looked at me hard for a second then burst out laughing.

"I'm gonna kick your ass for that someday," he said.

"I didn't need to have you going all misty on me," I told him. "These Romans won't give a shit about you nursing a heart ache. They'd use it to torture you."

"I will tell you one thing though," Johnny said. "I do miss Sushi for more than just the sex."

"I know Bro," I said.

"But that knob job that she could throw at you," Johnny said. "Damn man, she could sure make my glands dance."

CHAPTER 24
Party Time

After a hard day of training, at the evening meal, Miletus strode into the room and announced to all the hungry gladiators, "In honor of Venus, whose festival begins tomorrow, tomorrow will be a day of rest. Tonight we will celebrate." Then he marched out.

Johnny and me looked at each other.

"What the hell do you think that means?" I asked.

"I don't know," he answered. "Knowing these assholes, they might want to torture each other and call that a good time."

After we finished eating, we were marched to the bathing room where we got a good scrubbing a day ahead of schedule. Then they marched us across the courtyard and up a stairway to the third floor.

The other gladiators seemed to be happy about what was to come so I was kind of relaxing myself when we were directed through a large wooden door and into what looked like a Roman tavern.

There were probably a few hundred gladiators in this huge torch lit room where heavy wooden benches and tables were the main furnishings. Gladiators were sitting at the wooden benches drinking from large wooden mugs. Wooden kegs of different kinds of drink were scattered throughout the room.

In the center of the room was a huge long table where all kinds of foods were laid out. There were fruits, vegetables, cheeses, breads and different kinds of meats that I couldn't identify. I took a closer look and some of the meat looked like big snails. On another plate they had something laid out that looked like stuffed mice. I might try some of the bird or rabbit looking stuff later but I was staying the hell away from those snails and mice.

Slave girls and boys were continually running between the kegs and the seated gladiators refilling mugs as they were emptied.

Guards were wandering among the gladiators. Some were sitting with the groups of gladiators on the benches, others just roaming around. They weren't drinking. Although you could see some of them laughing with the gladiators, they knew what their jobs were. I even caught a glimpse of Miletus wandering around.

Near the center of the room there were two tables pushed together. Two men and a woman were standing on the tables playing musical instruments and singing. Well, not really singing. It was more a loud harmonized moaning. The musical instruments, and these words popped in my head when I saw them because I'd never seen these things before, were a harp, a lute and a lyre.

The music they were making was slow and almost trance inducing.

I motioned toward them and told Johnny, "Check them out. I think I'll stick to my Rolling Stones and Led Zeppelin."

"Yeah," Johnny answered. "Motown ain't missing a goddamn thing by not signing them."

We took a seat at a bench near the eastern wall of the room. As soon as we sat down two girls brought us some mugs full of a dark purplish liquid. They smiled at us and seemed to take an extra-long look at us.

I smiled back.

Johnny asked them, "What is this stuff?" He pointed at his mug.

I'd already taken a drink and the liquid had a bitter-sweet flavor that I couldn't quite name. It burned the back of your throat while making your mouth water for more.

"Spiced wine with ground sea slugs added," one of the serving girls told us, a doe eyed beauty with flowing black hair. "It is said to give the manhood of Hercules to all who drink it." She blushed a bright red as she looked at Johnny then she glanced at the wall behind us where there was a long row of doorways that had cloth curtains over the openings.

We now saw that gladiators were going through the doorways towing serving girls by the hand behind them. It was obvious that this was a type of whore house and we were to do our fucking on the other side of those curtains.

"If you want anything at all," The serving girl said blushing, "just let me know. I have always been curious about Nubians."

Johnny smiled back. "Thanks for the offer," he said. "I'll consider it."

Then those girls were off to serve someone else.

"Damn," I told Johnny. "You should have jumped on her. Man, she practically laid that pussy on the table and yelled, Come and get it!"

Johnny just shook his head. "I made some promises that I'm not going to break," he said.

"Hey man, let me clue you in on something," I told him and took another drink of the spiced wine. It tasted better with every drink. "Sushi will never know if you fuck one or ten of these broads in here tonight. I sure as hell ain't gonna tell her."

"That ain't the thing," Johnny said. "I'd know and that's what matters. When I make a promise, I don't break it."

"Good for you," I told Johnny and we clacked our mugs together. "I tell you what though, I'm gonna be tearing me some pussy up tonight."

I glanced around the room looking to spot a woman to my liking when my eyes fell on a welcome sight. That woman who'd had the job of scrubbing and shaving me when we first got here was moving among the tables carrying two wooden mugs in her hands. I liked the way the weight of the mugs made her breasts stick out in front of her.

She moved lightly on her feet like a ballet dancer as she dodged guys making grabs at her ass. She didn't seem to want to just be grabbed and dragged away to be fucked. She placed the mugs on a table then turned away before the invitation to sit was even given.

I walked up behind this nameless silent woman and like I was patting for a dance touched her on the shoulder. She spun around and if she could have made a sound I think she would have shrieked.

When she saw me she recognized me instantly. She smiled and if she could have sold that smile for what it was worth she would have been the wealthiest woman in the Roman Empire.

I motioned for her to follow me. She grabbed my hand and we went back and sat across the table from Johnny. If I haven't said what this woman looked like before, I'll tell you now. She was around five-five and had all the right curves in all the right places. She made that slave toga thing she was wearing look good. I could see the points of her nipples thrusting forward under the fabric. Small but obviously firm breasts, just the kind I like. It was making my tongue tingle just thinking about taking them in my mouth.

She had chestnut brown hair and large brown eyes, a dainty small nose and lips just the right size for some serious kissing. It also gave me a dick twitch thinking about those lips wrapped around old Ben Johnson.

As soon as we sat down she reached over and laid her head on my shoulder. She reached over and rubbed my stomach with her hand. I was glad this working out had my stomach back to being as hard as a rock. Other parts of me were getting as hard as a rock too.

"Looks like you've found a recruit," Johnny told me.

"Un hunh," I told him and reached around and felt of her waist then moved her head and kissed her on the neck.

She moaned. Guess she could still do that even without a tongue.

"Man, go get a room," Johnny told me. "I know you need me to tell you how to fuck, but I don't want you to be bumping uglies on this table. I'm gonna be eating here in a while."

"Just for that, you don't get to watch," I said. We stood up and walked toward one of the curtained doors.

From behind me Johnny said, "Just remember what I warned you about back at my bar." But Julia was the last thing on my mind.

*   *   *

Through the curtain there was a short hallway that ended at a brick wall. The hallway had four doors. The doors opened inward and all four doors were open. From all four, dim candle light shown.

At least these doors were made of wood so we could close them for a little privacy.

We went into one of the rooms and shut the door behind us. There was no latch to lock the door. That shouldn't have surprised me. We were slaves, we didn't even own ourselves, we were lucky they even gave us a door to shut. Make no mistake about it; I knew that this little get together was only to make the gladiators perform better. This was to make more money for our master, it wasn't for us. It was only for Flaccus our owner. A gladiator with a stiff dick sticking out in front of him couldn't be expected to fight very well. How well we performed determined how much Flaccus made off of us.

I turned to this nameless silent woman and realized she had never known any gentleness in her life. Everything she did was forced on her, especially the sex. Suddenly, I wanted to make her feel very good. To show her what kind of pleasure a man can give rather than just take.

The thought ran through my mind, that's probably why she liked me so much. When I met her, I asked her for her name. I didn't demand that she give it to me. I asked her. She probably wasn't used to anyone asking her for anything. In her world, everything was always just taken.

A small straw covered bed on a raised stone platform was against the wall.

She started to undress. I stopped her and looked into her eyes in the candle light. I kissed her on the forehead, then on the cheeks and worked my way around her face and kissed her long and slow on the mouth probing her mouth with my tongue.

I untied the rope at her waist and pushed her garment off of her shoulders and let it slide down to the floor at her feet. She looked up into my eyes and I smiled at her.

"You're beautiful," I told her and kissed her again.

I laid her down upon the straw covered stone slab and gently ran my hands over the contours of her skin feeling her softness and warmth. I took my clothes off and kissed down the front of her body, nibbling at her skin.

Her breath came in short gasps when I sucked on one of her nipples that sprang out into a hard little bud. When I switched to the other one and sucked on it and slid my hand between her smooth thighs she made mewing sounds from deep within her throat and her lips formed words that her tongue-less mouth could no longer speak.

I kissed all the way down the front of her. Over her small smooth stomach and down to her pubic hair. When I went to part her thighs to lick her pussy she looked down and gasped in wide eyed surprise. Her legs were suddenly tight almost clamping shut on my head.

"It's all right," I told her. "I won't hurt you."

A look of doubt crossed her face. No one had ever wanted to do this to her before.

"Trust me," I whispered.

After a moment she relaxed and I began by lightly kissing the insides of her thighs. First one, then the other all the way up to the moist warm center of her. I teased her with my tongue until I found the little nub of hot flesh that made her moan from deep down in her throat.

I worked at her clitoris until she was twitching all over and her legs were shaking. She was panting and drooling like a Saint Bernard that just won the Kentucky Derby in one hundred and twenty degree heat. And when she came, damn did she cum.

She grabbed me by the hair of the head and pulled my face into her pussy so hard I could barely breathe. Death by pussy suffocation, that'd be a new one.

She was grinding her teeth and slinging her head back and forth and going "Uhh Uhh." It looked for about a minute like she was having an epileptic fit. I could tell this woman had never had an orgasm before. She probably didn't even know they existed.

After she came, she laid back with an expression on her face that had written all over it, "Jesus, what the fuck was that?"

We rested for a moment then I raised myself over her and slid into her moist warmth. She raised herself and came up and engulfed me as I came down. This nameless woman whimpered softly as I pounded myself into her.

At the same time we both came to a shuddering orgasm.

We laid back then and I held her in my arms. I spoke soft words to her in the dimness of the single candlelight. I did not make her promises of a better future for us. There was no future for us. Both of us knew it.

CHAPTER 25
The Party's End

When we came back out into the main room Johnny was having a face-off with that idiot from our cell, Pugnax. The skinny teenaged girl who I'd been sent to fuck my second night here was hiding behind Johnny.

"You will give her to me!" Pugnax stated through tight lips and tried to reach around Johnny for the girl.

Johnny slapped the big guys hand away with a loud pop. "Don't be so grabby," Johnny said. "Remember what your momma got for grabbin'."

"I never knew my mother," Pugnax said with a snarl. "I don't know what she got."

"She got you, you stupid son-of-a-bitch," Johnny told him.

I started to step forward to go to where Johnny was and the nameless woman grabbed my arm to hold me back. Her eyes were pleading with me to not leave her side.

"I gotta go help my friend," I told her.

Her grip was still tight on my arm.

I looked deeply into her eyes. "There are some things I've just got to do." I told her and she let go of me.

I gave her a quick kiss and as I turned away to help my friend, her eyes still begged me to stay with her. I would never forget that look, because I would never see her again.

At Johnny's side I asked, "What's up Bro?"

Pugnax was rapidly turning redder with every second. He was breathing hard and clenching his teeth. This boy was in bad need of some anger management classes. I doubt he'd be getting that training here.

Johnny said. "I was talking to the girl cause she seems to be scared to death of everybody else here when this gargoyle-lookin'-mother fucker up and grabs her by the arm and tries to jerk her off the bench from beside me. So, I did a little trip and shove on him, and put him on his ass, and he still thinks he's getting the girl."

"I will take her!" Pugnax roared at Johnny.

Johnny waved his hand in front of his face. "Oooooo," he said. "Man do you gargle with shit? Your breath is fucked up." Then he got serious. "You ain't taking a motha-fucking thing," he told Pugnax. "Except for my dick up your ass if I ever feel like fucking something as ugly as you are."

I thought that that would be it and Pugnax would charge Johnny and we'd both have to do a stomp job on his head. The veins in his forehead almost popped out. You could see them pulsing with the pounding of his heart.

To the surprise of the both of us he got hold of himself and actually smiled. His voice was so tight and constricted from his denied rage that he sounded like an angry alligator when he spoke. "Miletus ordered me to take her and show her what will be expected of her from now on."

Johnny glanced at me and I glanced at him. We nodded simultaneously. *I was thinking, well I just got one of my best fucking's of the last few years it might be a good day to die.*

Miletus didn't appear to be around anywhere. Otherwise he'd probably be in our faces ordering us to give the girl over. He's probably enjoying one of the slave girls. It wouldn't have made a difference anyway. That wasn't going to happen. Neither one of us would hand over a kid to be raped.

Slave or no slave, no kid deserves that.

"Why didn't you say that right off?" Johnny asked Pugnax. "Shit man, what Miletus says goes." He stepped to the side. "Ain't that right Bro?" He said.

"You got that right brother," I said and stepped to the other side of Pugnax leaving a clear path between us to the girl.

Pugnax, not the smartest boy in the world, stepped forward between us.

I hit him with a hard overhand right just behind his left ear, a split second later Johnny smashed him with one hell of a left hook to the right side of his jaw. He went so limp it looked like all the bones vanished from his body at once. He went down and out in a heap.

One of Miletus' guards yelled, "Stop now!"

He stepped forward, hand on his sword, about to draw it but he hadn't drawn it yet. He expected us to just freeze at his order. We weren't freezing for shit.

I stepped to him and grabbed his wrist and locked his arm to his side jerking him to me with my other hand and smashed my forehead down onto his nose. Blood flew and he staggered backward blinded. Then I snapped a kick up under that Roman soldier skirt thing they all wear. The way my toes sank into his gonads I knew he wasn't wearing anything at all under that skirt. The guard changed color and hit the floor.

Other guards were coming now. Johnny grabbed the girl's hand and we hauled ass across the room. The other gladiators just got out of our way as we ran to the door we'd entered through. None of them showed any interest in wanting to help us and we didn't have the time to take a poll to see who was unhappy enough with his life to want to help us get the hell out of there.

We reached the door with about eight guards just a few steps behind us. The door was barred from the other side. It was made from thick planks of wood. We weren't just going to ram this door down.

We turned to face the guards.

They had their swords drawn.

We saw now that the swords they held were ferrum, the blunt training swords. The ferrum were more like billy-clubs than anything else. Believe me an entire crowd of guys swinging billy-clubs at you can raise some serious knots on your head. It's better than having your arms hacked off, but not by much.

The girl cringed behind us against the door.

There wasn't anything else to do.

I charged that entire crowd of mother fucking guards. It was a better idea than I'd even planned on. I was on them so quick they didn't have time or room to swing the ferrum. As a stabbing instrument, ferrum are useless.

Diving right into the middle of four of them I took one of the guards down with a ridge hand to the throat, kneed one in the crotch, elbowed another to the stomach, tried to jab my fingers in another's eyes then I was slammed up-side the head with one of the ferrum.

The entire world spun and spots danced in front of my eyes. My knees sagged and I realized I was on my knees and two of the guards were on both sides of me using my head for batting practice.

I grabbed one of them between the legs by the ball sack and dug my nails in and jerked like I didn't have a pair of my own and wanted to keep his. He screeched like a cat thrown into a fireplace.

Another guard bludgeoned me on top of the head. The thought ran through my mind that I'm not putting my fucking hat on for a long fucking time. I blacked out.

Nails were tearing into the flesh at my wrists. I was hanging by the nails, legs dangling, pain, unbelievable pain, in my arms, looking down at the ground, a long way down.

Nailed to a cross, throat dry, sick to my stomach. A big crow sits on my shoulder pecking at my eyes. He tears my eyelid loose. Bright white light burns into my brain.

"Get the fuck off of me!" I yelled at him.

I came awake again kicking out with my feet from my back. I connected with a guard's knee. He grunted. I kicked him again. He fell sideways.

I saw Johnny. Four guards had him pinned to the wall, two on each arm. He yelled, "Fight me one on one, I'll fuck you all up!"

They were not going to take him up on his offer.

I scissor kicked a guard off of his feet and spun away from another's grasping hands and made it to my feet.

Ferrum were being swung at me from all sides. I tried to block them with my forearms. The blows made my arms go numb. Charging the guards in front of me again, this time I was met by a ferrum swung over hand. Stars danced in front of my eyes.

Someone climbed on my back, locked an arm around my throat. My arms were wrenched out to the sides then behind me. I was tripped and met the floor with the side of my face.

The crowd was on my back. They tied my arms behind me and bound my legs together. Someone pulled a bag down over my head. It was tied at my neck.

I heard Miletus yell, "Take them to the cages! I'll decide what to do with them by the morning."

Several arms picked me up and carried me. I was thrown onto a hard cold floor. A rusty hinge screeched as the door was slammed shut.

CHAPTER 26
The Alter of Slaughter

I slid around on the floor of what I was in to try to get my bearings as to what the size of this new cell was. With a bag over your head you can't see too much of anything. A breeze was blowing on my arms and I was able to figure out that the cage I was in was about the same size of what Johnny and me were transported to the gladiator school in.

There was muffled talking. The words I couldn't quite make out and the floor beneath me shook and there was a banging noise. The banging noise and the shifting of the floor beneath me came two more times.

I heard animal sounds and the shuffling of bodies not far away and just generally had the feeling that I was outside.

What I was figuring was happening was that they'd loaded me up onto another wagon and was going to take me to somewhere else.

There were more scraping noises and I moved toward it until my head made contact with an iron bar. I winced back from the bar. The top of my head was sore as hell from being clubbed with that ferrum.

"Hey," I said through the bag. "Why don't you give me a hand and take this sack off my head." I leaned as close as I could to let whoever was on the other side of those bars reach over and untie the drawstring at my neck.

No one answered. No one reached over a hand to help me.

"Come on, goddamn-it! We're all in the same boat here. Shit! Help me out."

But there was no help coming to me.

I could hear them breathing on the other side of the bars.

I asked a few more times than lay down on my side. I tried to get comfortable on the cold bottom of the cage but getting comfortable with your arms tied behind you and your legs bound together isn't the easiest thing in the world to do.

After a while, there were some more talking voices. The floor rocked again, a crack of the whip and we were rolling down the road.

With my head covered, blind as a bat, not knowing where I was being taken and totally at the mercy of these sadistic bastards, this was not feeling like a pleasure cruise.

*   *   *

It's a lonely feeling when a bag's over your head and nobody will say anything to you. Every now and then I'd hear somebody talking, but no one was answering anything I'd say at all.

I think the other slaves were afraid to talk to me. I was obviously in the shit. I must have fallen asleep because the next thing I knew I was being poked in the back with something sharp and someone was shouting at me to wake up. Light was filtering in through the bag so I knew it was morning.

The way the floor was rocking I could tell the other cages were being off loaded.

When I showed signs of life the guy yelling at me said. "I am going to have that sack taken off your head. You give us any trouble and you will be fighting today missing an arm or a leg. You decide how you will have it."

"I'll do what you tell me," I told him through the bag and leaned close to the bars with my head.

The drawstring was untied and the sack was pulled off.

The inrush of cool air felt good going down my throat. I had to squint against the brighter light that scratched at my eyes.

After a few seconds I could see again. A big ugly guy in need of a bath and a visit to the dentist was unlocking the door to my cage. Outside, four guards were waiting for me with swords drawn. These were not those training swords either. Nothing blunt about any of these blades.

There was a long line of slaves lined up in front of the cages they'd just come out of. All kinds of slaves were in that line: young, old, male, female. Most of the females were old. I saw that the skinny teenage girl Johnny and me tried to protect was in the line. She had a busted lip and her left eye was purple and swollen shut.

Pugnax was in the line too. We locked eyes and he gave me a stare of pure death.

I looked for Johnny but didn't see him anywhere. Might be he was considered too valuable to be wasted in these kind of fights. It didn't matter. I knew Johnny could take care of himself. I was going to need to concentrate on keeping my ass alive today.

I went to the end of the slave line, and with two of the four guards watching me very closely. We were marched through some huge doors into a foul smelling room where the walls were lined with cages.

One wall of the room was a steel gate made of crisscrossed metal bars. Beyond that gate was a large killing field. Covered in ugly reddish dirt it was a round central open area enclosed by stone walls.

Over the stone walls the spectators sat on ascending rows of stone steps. This arena was structured like a bowl, so everyone could get a clear view of the carnage below them.

Miletus was in the room we entered. He pointed at me. "This one," he barked. "Put him there." He indicated a cage next to the gates where I'd have a clear view through the bars to the arena floor.

I was put in the cage he said and the door was locked behind me. At least these cages were large enough to stand and stretch.

After all the slaves were placed in cages, Miletus walked over to where I stood with my hands on the bars.

"I knew you would be a problem the first moment I saw you," he said. "I could see it in your eyes. You and that Nubian would always be a problem."

"Where's Johnny?" I asked.

He ignored the question.

"You will not be a problem after today," Miletus said as he was walking away. He stopped and looked back at me. "Flaccus paid for you to die in front of them." He pointed toward the spectators. "Do yourself proud," he said, "Show them a death they'll remember."

Ain't this a bitch, I thought. This mother fucker's giving me a pep-talk so I won't just lay down easy and let myself be massacred. The harder I fight, the more money Flaccus makes on the next group of sacrificial lambs brought here, the better it makes Miletus look to Flaccus. This was fucked up.

Well, I wasn't going to lay down for anyone, for any reason.

"Fuck you Miletus," I yelled at him. "Why don't you just step your ass out there in the dirt and have a go at me? Don't have the balls, do you?"

That made him smile. He laughed and walked away.

*   *   *

It was still early in the morning and there weren't many spectators in the stands yet. Some slaves came through with sacks of vegetables and fruits and handed them out to the slaves in the cages. Some of the cages were still empty.

On the arena floor to start off the day's festivities, they began by having a beast hunt just a few minutes before another group of slaves were brought in. A beast hunt is a sad thing. All kinds of animals are turned loose on the arena floor and trained bestiaries hunt them down and kill them. The bestiaries might use swords or knives or spears or they might even be bare handed. No matter how they did it, it was a sad thing to watch. Hell, the animals, whether they were deer, antelope or even lions and tigers were in an enclosed area. Eventually they were going to die.

After a little while, I was rooting for the lions and tigers to eat a few of the bestiaries. The struggle was so unequal I wanted to see the underdogs get in a few good licks before they went down.

When the new group of slaves came in I was surprised as hell to see a short attractive black girl among them.

That was Terry, the sweet looking black woman who was just starting to play a symphony on my skin flute when Sherry so rudely interrupted us. She was placed in a cage two away from mine.

As soon as the guards had all the slaves locked up, they left to perform other duties. I shouted, "Hey Terry, over here," And waved at her through the two sets of bars that separated us.

For a moment she looked at me like I was crazy. She didn't recognize me at all.

"It's John Dark," I shouted to her.

At my voice, recognition flashed in her eyes. "Mr. Dark," Terry gasped and involuntarily reached toward me. "What are you doing here?"

"Just out for a stroll, figured I'd drop in. Now what the hell do you think I'm doing here? Me and Sushi's boyfriend came after you, Sushi, and Sherry, "I told her. "We kind of got sidetracked."

She smiled. "I can see that," Terry said. "I know Johnny, if you guys came to rescue us, who's coming to rescue you?"

"That's the part of the plan I'm still working on."

"Where's Johnny?" Terry asked.

I told her about the gladiator school and us trying to stop the girl's rape and pointed her out across the room.

"You best learn something about where we are," Terry told me. "Here, you better help yourself and that's it. You try to help anybody else, you gonna get fucked up."

I had to smile at that. "We came here to help you," I reminded her.

She smiled at me and those big African lips contrasting nicely with her white teeth made my balls twitch. I had a mini flashback to her wrapping her lips around my dick in her dressing room. It must have shown on my face because Terry said, "You know we have unfinished business."

"You got that right," I told her. "Can't never leave a man unfinished."

"Might cause you some long term problems," she said and giggled.

"Yeah, like a stiff dick that never goes away."

We just smiled at each other for a minute.

After a moment of silence I asked her, "How'd you end up here?"

"That's a long story," Terry said.

"I ain't going anywhere," I told her and listened to what she had to say over the screams and cries of wild animals being butchered.

CHAPTER 27
Terry's Tale

Terry told me that her, Sushi and Sherry were taken directly to Rome and put on the auction block in front of a bunch of wealthy Romans.

"With my dark skin I was bought for some damn good money," Terry said. "I don't know who Sushi and Sherry went to. I was sold first so before their bidding even started I was taken away."

The guy that bought Terry was a short plump effeminate man that turned her stomach at first sight. "I just knew, he put a hand on me, I was going to have to kick the shit right out of him," she told me.

Turned out, he hadn't bought her for himself. The man named Apronius Marcelus, bought her for his fifteen year old son. The boy named Seneca was so withdrawn and shy that he couldn't even look at a female without turning a bright shade of red. Talking to girls for him was totally out of the question.

When Terry was introduced to Seneca and told her duties would include instructing the boy in sexual techniques her first thought was, this wasn't going to be such a bad job. "The boy was cute," Terry said. "And when I got him loosened up and speaking a little he had a way with words that got me all hot and bothered just talking to him."

The boy reminded Terry of the guy that starred in the beach movies shot in the 50's, Frankie Avalon. "Except, he was smaller," Terry said. "But I liked him."

It took Terry a few weeks to get Seneca at ease enough to get him into bed, "The trick was," she told me. "I had to make it seem like it was his idea so I wouldn't bruise his ego. I needed to make him feel like a man and I was his conquest, or some shit like that."

Seneca had a separate house in back of his father's mansion. He was given this house so he could have privacy for his studies. Since she was Seneca's personal body servant, Terry was given a room in the same house.

After she'd spent quite a bit of time doing little things to get the boy interested in her, like rubbing up against him by accident or revealing a bit of naked thigh, also by accident, Terry figured it was time to take a more direct approach.

In the middle of a night lit by a bright full moon Terry awakened Seneca by sitting beside him on the bed and pretending to weep.

Sitting up, he asked her, "What is wrong Terry? What brings these tears from your lovely dark eyes?"

"I had a dream," she told him. "It was horrible. I'm afraid to go back to sleep. Master," she asked, "Could you just hold me in your arms and make the nightmares go away?"

With that she shrugged out of her clothes and slid in beside the boy. It didn't take much urging from Terry for Seneca to begin doing naturally what his body had already been bidding him do. They made love all the rest of that night.

"I couldn't believe how much energy that boy had," Terry told me. "Once I got Seneca that first night, he wanted to be fucking me, morning, noon, night and day. He found out what that thing between his legs was for and was going to make sure he got the most out of it."

"I'd be lying if I said that I didn't like it too," Terry went on. "Every different position I showed him, man he got to it. I was his new toy and he loved playing with me. After a few weeks I was trying to figure out new things to teach the boy. He was a very willing pupil. My favorite student, if you know what I mean.

"Seneca was a very gentle lover too. One peep from me that anything we did hurt and he'd stop. He was always asking me how things felt. And he got to be like a magician at pulling orgasms out of me. Once he found out that my moaning and groaning was because I was feeling good, he'd do his very best to make me squeal."

"I wanted to make sure Seneca knew as much as I could teach him. For one thing, he was practicing on me and I was getting the benefit of cumming like no woman on Earth had ever cum before, and Seneca was also whispering words of love to me when we were in the middle of our hot and heavy lessons."

"There was a library in the big house. I checked it out for books on sex. You know they had nothing in there about a guy giving a woman head. They had all kinds of stuff about girls blowing guys but nothing the other way around. Guess these Roman's ain't too concerned about a woman feeling good. When I taught Seneca about that, man he about had me climbing the walls. He liked to lick my pussy hard just to hear me scream."

"I'm not sure if I love Seneca or not, but he loved me," Terry said. "He treated me good and never talked to me like I was a slave. He asked me if I would marry him. I said I would. I know I could do a whole lot worse in this world than being married to the son of a rich man."

"When Seneca went to tell his father of his plans to marry me that was the last time I saw him. He went to the house, about fifteen minutes later some guards came out with a chain. They threw me in a cage and here I am."

Terry's face had a sad look on it. Like she was seeing in her mind what might have been. "Guess Apronius didn't want his son marrying no slave," Terry told me.

"I'm sorry," I said and meant it.

"Ain't nothing but a thang," Terry said. "Something good'll come along again. It's bound to."

*   *   *

The beast hunt was winding down. Out of what seemed like at least a hundred animals let loose into the arena, only a few of them were still alive. Of the bestiaries, just a couple of them received minor injuries. It was a rigged fight that we'd just witnessed, rigged but real. There was only one possible ending.

The spectators were divided into different areas for the different classes of people that watched the show, one area for the lower classes, another for the rich and one other for the elite class.

The elite sat in marble throne-like seats that were covered with an umbrella type of sunshade.

After the beast hunt ended a different type of slave came out and started working in the arena among the dead animals. These were guys who had meat cleavers and bundles of cloth bags thrown over their shoulders. They were chopping up the bodies of the animals where they lay and putting the pieces into the bags. Then they'd toss the bags to the spectators in the seats for the poor, where they would fight over the scraps.

We watched this for a little while until I realized Terry probably didn't really have a grasp of the seriousness of what was happening today. Something about her attitude didn't seem right. She seemed to have an, *I don't give a shit attitude* about her.

"Terry, you do know where we're at don't you?" I asked her.

"Course I do," she answered me. "I seen this kind of shit on channel 11 on the *Saturday Afternoon Cinema*. Saw this stuff in that movie *Barabas*."

"Good, cause you better start waking up," I told her. "These people do some ugly shit to slaves."

"They won't do shit to me," Terry said, "Wouldn't make no sense."

I told Terry, "They'll do anything just for a good show. When we fight today, it'll probably be to the death."

She laughed at that. "I doubt I'll be fighting anything, except maybe some Roman's big dick. It just wouldn't make no sense," she said." "They can only kill me once. But they fuck me a thousand times. So why would they kill me. It just don't make no sense."

"Don't bet on anything these damn people doing making any sense at all," I told her.

That was when the guards came in and opened up Terry's cage and dragged her kicking and screaming out into the arena.

CHAPTER 28
Slaughter

Other slaves were dragged out of their cages. Not many of them kicked and screamed like Terry did. In the open killing field, five pairs of slaves were spaced out evenly. While they were held at sword point by guards who each held an extra short sword in his left hand, an announcer of sorts walked to the center of the arena and read from a scroll.

The announcer shouted directly to the spectators in the elite seats. "For your entertainment, an exhibition of the faultlessness of Roman Justice, these criminals have been collected from throughout the empire."

Terry and her opponent-to-be were no more than fifty feet from where I was standing on the other side of the bars of my cage and the gate. I could see Terry's mouth drop open and her eyes were wide in surprise. She mouthed the word, "Criminal?"

"These committers of the vile acts of murder, arson, thievery and deception will be given the chance to atone for their actions. They will fight for you today and noble combat will cleanse the evil from their hearts. Those who survive will be given the chance to show the courage of a true citizen of Rome. When they show this courage, their crimes will be washed away and they will once again be accepted by all of Rome as one of her children."

With that he strode to an exit door, paused before leaving and shouted, "Let it begin!"

The guards that were with Terry and her opponent, tossed the short swords from their left hands into the dirt at each of the girl's feet. Then they backed off so that they were behind each of the women. It was obvious that they were there to force the girls to fight and to keep the fight going at a fast and furious pace.

For a moment Terry stared dumbly at the sword at her feet not comprehending what was really happening.

Her opponent, a wiry, strong looking woman with dirty brown hair and skin like tanned leather did not hesitate, she snatched up her blade and came at Terry at a run.

"Get your fucking sword!" I screamed at Terry.

That seemed to jar her out of her funk. She grabbed up her blade and brought it up just barely in time to stop a slash across her head.

The force of the blow knocked Terry to her back. She rolled away and her opponent missed another slash at her head purely by accident.

The other fights were going on too but I was only watching the one unfolding directly in front of me.

Terry didn't have a clue as to what to do with her sword. Thank god the other woman didn't either. The other woman waded after Terry, ripping the air with viscous strokes of her blade. She had no skill at all, just meanness and a ruthless desire to kill.

Terry just kept backing off, putting her blade in front of the swinging sword that was coming at her. She was making little whimpering noises. This was not something that she had even remotely been prepared for.

The crowd roared when in another part of the killing field a man was stabbed and went to the ground. The spectators sounded like hungry animals that were somehow devouring the feeling of the kill. Whenever a blow or slice or stab struck home, the crowd ate it up. That's what they were there for.

I was watching Terry's fight so intently that I didn't even notice when Miletus walked up. He stood beside the bars to my cage.

"Your friend," he said to me and laughed. "She has no courage. She has no skill. She has nothing of any value. She will die."

"Call it off," I told Miletus. "Look at her, she's not a fighter. You know that. She sure as hell didn't do what that guy said the rest of them did. Call it off!" I yelled at him.

"You are in no position to order anyone," Miletus said. "Anyway, it doesn't matter. We were paid to show them death today. We do what we are paid to do. We will show them death."

Terry backed up into one of the guards, who shoved her forward. Stumbling, she almost ran full onto the woman's sword in front of her. Somehow, she twisted just as the thrust came and jumped sideways.

"Miletus," I shouted at him. "You said she's useless. Hell, take a look at her. Wouldn't you rather be fucking her than just seeing her die? Take a good look. I can tell you from experience, she can suck your dick like you ain't ever had it sucked before. Call it off! This makes no fucking sense."

This made him laugh again. "I can have a thousand slave girls tonight if I want them. What would one mean to me?"

Terry's opponent was slowing down. She'd been doing all the fighting. She missed one of her big swings and threw herself off balance. She stumbled, turned her ankle and fell to her knees in front of Terry. Terry drew back her sword to swing the killing blow down upon the unprotected head. Then she stopped.

"Get rid of her," I yelled at Terry. "Fucking kill her! Do it! Do it!"

Terry kicked the woman instead, knocking her to her side in the red sand.

Miletus scowled. "Your people are weak," he said. "Yes, I know where you come from. Many of you have come through my school. I spit upon your country and your empire. That you should come after we are gone is an affront to the gods." With that he walked away.

Terry was breathing hard but wasn't as tired as the other woman. She circled around behind her, keeping her sword in front of her in both hands. She spoke to the other woman.

"Listen girl," Terry said between her gasping breaths. "We can call this even right now. We don't have to kill each other. How about it? We both get out of this alive. I don't want to kill you and I sure as fuck don't want to die."

The woman slid around to face Terry while still on her hands and knees. She looked up into Terry's eyes. She smiled and nodded her head yes.

The woman reached out her left hand to be helped to her feet and Terry reached for her hand. It was at that moment when I saw that the woman's blade was to her left side. Her right arm was tensed.

I shouted "No!" as she ripped the blade upward in a backhand swing that caught Terry's left hand just above the wrist and sliced clean through it.

Terry's scream was like the metallic screech of grinding steel.

Blood flew through the air in a spray. Terry's hand swung at the end of her arm like something made of rubber attached to her wrist only by a few layers of skin below her thumb. Everything else, bone, muscle, veins and ligaments had been sliced clean through.

Terry screamed, "No! No! Oh god no, please no!"

There's something particularly gut wrenching about hearing a woman screaming in pain. This was worse. I knew this woman personally and I couldn't do a damn thing to stop what was happening.

I grabbed the bars in front of me and shook them straining against the steel that held me back. Crying out in frustration, I beat at the bars and tried to rip them loose from their moorings like my desperation would transform me into some type of all-powerful superhero.

But today was not a day for superheroes. The bars did not give. I could only watch.

Terry's opponent came at her like before but this time Terry buckled beneath the blows. She went down from a chop to her thigh and as she lay on her back begging for mercy. Her opponent stood over her grinning.

She seemed to be enjoying Terry's cries and after kicking Terry's sword away did not make her end fast.

When Terry kicked at her, she chopped chunks out of her feet. When Terry tried to put her hands up to ward off the blows, her other hand was sliced off.

Terry tried to crawl away on her knees and the two stumps of her arms. She couldn't move fast enough. Her opponent followed her, hacking at her legs, her buttocks, her back and shoulders. Every sword stroke bit deep.

Each time the blade came down Terry screamed in pain. Each scream was weaker than the one that preceded it.

I turned away and couldn't watch. After what seemed impossibly long, Terry was silent.

She was dead.

At least her pain was over.

I looked back out at Terry lying in her own blood. Her face was turned toward me. Blood ran from her lips and her nose. Her dark eyes seemed to look at me, accusing me, asking, "Why didn't you save me?"

CHAPTER 29
Rape of the Innocent

I watched as three slaves pulling an ox cart gathered up the bodies. A few of the fights still went on. They were more evenly matched contests than the ones that ended quickly.

The slaves with the cart handled the bodies like city laborers collecting road kill carcasses from the shoulders of rural highways. They just picked them up and unceremoniously tossed them in the back of the wagon like trash. What a few minutes before were people were now just useless meat.

As far as I knew the Romans didn't practice cannibalism, but it wouldn't have surprised me if they did.

On this long day, my surprises concerning what the Romans considered entertainment were far from over.

*   *   *

When the last fight ended, the victorious slaves were lead away to be bandaged up and gotten ready for their next fight. There was no announcement of the names of the winners.

No congratulations.

The blood thirsty crowd in the stands could care less who won or lost, they only wanted to see the blood spilled. The faces of the people in the stands looked like demons to me, creatures from hell who fed upon pain.

I wasn't going to let them feed on me. They could get their thrills off of someone else's blood. I was about to see them do just that.

Miletus came back into the slave holding area as the slaves on the killing field were finishing cleaning up the mess left on the sand. There were still the odd body parts lying around waiting to be taken away.

Miletus walked to the Iron Gate and leaned on it watching me.

I asked him, "What are you doing back here? Come to give me some more of your sermon on the wonderful Roman way of life."

Miletus smiled. "I came to watch your face," he said. "One of the things I really love about your people is how I can give you pain without even touching you."

I had a bad feeling about what I was going to see next but no matter what it was I wasn't going to beg this guy for mercy. Miletus didn't even know what the word meant.

The Announcer strode to the center of the killing field again and shouted, "Continuing our theme of Roman justice. This woman, this vile harlot who will next be revealed to you used the charms of her young body to seduce a noble Roman Senator and then poisoned him to rob his home. Let her meet the beast and the fate she deserves." He strode away again.

The sun was high in the sky. It gave off a stifling suffocating heat. The smell of blood and human excrement was in the air. Anyone who dies violently evacuates their bowels at the moment of death. It's not a pleasant smell. Quite a few people had died violently here already. More were to follow.

Two guards came through the doors and went directly to the teenage girl's cage who Johnny and I had tried to protect. They went in and one grabbed her by the hair and slapped her hard across the face.

The other grabbed the stunned kid's arms and wrenched them behind her. They started dragging the screaming, begging child out of her cage then out onto the killing field.

On the killing field a man leading a leopard on a leash went to the center of the arena. He was accompanied by another man who had a bucket in one hand, a large paint brush in the other and animal skins slung over his shoulder.

They stopped and waited with the leopard as the two guards dragged the struggling girl to them.

Miletus was smiling as he watched the proceedings. "Go ahead," he said to me. "Beg for the little one's life. You are the one who put her where she is. If she had done her job like the rest of us do and proven she was useful, she would not have been used like this."

The guards threw the girl on the ground and when she tried to get up to run, one of them punched her and knocked her back down. The two guards ripped the clothes off the cringing girl.

Two more guards came out and grabbed the girl's arms and held them to the ground. The original two guards each grabbed one of the girl's legs and forced them apart, exposing her nakedness to everyone in the arena.

The girl screamed out in shame, begging them not to do this to her. She might as well have been screaming at the sun to not shine down so hotly upon her, for all the good it did.

Her cries were heartrending, but I kept a stone face. I wasn't going to give Miletus the satisfaction of letting him know it affected me at all.

The spectators seemed to really be getting off on what was going on. There was hooting and cheering in the stands. Miletus had a weird expression on his face as he watched what was happening to the girl. Something about this excited him in a sexual way. He even reached down and rubbed himself at his crotch.

"You are some sick fucking freaks," I told him.

Miletus laughed. "Freaks, we are not the freaks," he said. "We are the purest people. Our empire lasted longer than any in history because we did not lie to ourselves. We know we are animals. We are the strongest animal."

The man carrying the bucket dipped the paintbrush into it and stirred around. The large cat's head instantly snapped up as though he smelled something. Whatever scent caught the cat's attention, it was so strong he couldn't ignore it.

The man with the paintbrush and bucket took the brush out. It was dripping red and he slapped a large red swash of the reddish liquid onto the girl's privates, leaving a large red splotch there.

The girl screamed again and one of the guards at her arms punched her and she was quiet. The punch must have knocked her out. With what was coming, it would have been better for her if the punch had killed her.

The man who had painted the girl slung the animal skins off from over his shoulder and laid them on the semi-conscious teenager. The guy who had the leopard on the leash led his pet to her. The leopard was obviously a male.

He was erect. Whatever the guy had painted the girl with it must have had the scent of a female leopard in heat in it.

The leopard didn't need any prompting. It did what its instincts told it to do when presented with a female in heat. He mounted the girl and started fucking her in a frenzy.

Miletus actually reached down into his tunic and was fondling himself as he watched this.

What in the hell is wrong with you fucking people I thought as the girl suddenly and violently came fully awake.

She shrieked and screamed at the creature that was on top of her and fought with a desperation brought on by madness to get loose from the four strong men who held her.

The leopard, excited to the point of frenzy by the yelling crowd and his sexual instincts, snapped his teeth down onto the neck of the girl beneath him. One jerk to the side was all it took for him to end her life.

The crowd applauded and cheered. Miletus looked at me and laughed. He pulled his hand out of his underwear and wiped it in the dirt at his feet. "That was a good one," he said. "Yes, it's not easy to train the big cats to perform in front of crowds but Crixus really has a way with them."

He started to walk back out of the slave holding area but paused at the door and told me, "You are next!"

CHAPTER 30
Pulling a Train

As the cleanup crew was taking the girl away four guards came to my cage. Three of them had their swords out. Guess they figured I could be more trouble than a skinny teenage girl.

The other guard held leather straps that had sharp steel spurs worked into them. The straps were tied around the fighter's fists and worn like brass knuckles.

"Put your hands through the bars," The guard who held the studded straps ordered me.

"Fuck you!" I told him.

"Have it your way," he answered. "The other fighters will wear the caestus whether you use them or not."

I put my hands through the bars.

"I thought you would see it that way," he said as he tightened the straps around my fingers and wrists.

They lead me out to the center of the killing field. The red sand crunched under my feet as I walked.

No announcer came out to broadcast the reasons for my fight. I was probably considered so unimportant that no announcement was thought necessary.

The people in the stands were milling about. They weren't interested in the least in me having to battle for my life.

That was fine by me.

I wasn't here to give them a show.

The sun suddenly seemed much hotter than it had been just a few minutes before. The smell drifting up from the red sand was that of rotten meat.

I took a good look around, up into the stands before my opponent was brought out. For the most part, it was a motley bunch that showed up to see today's blood sacrifice. The mob reminded me of a crowd at a wrestling match, except that these people knew the blood shed here was real.

There were the middle and lower class sections of the seating, dirty, ugly, rude, crude in-breeds; the cream of Roman society.

When my eyes wandered to the upper-class seating I was in for a surprise. Among others of the ruling class was a good looking, tall, slim built woman seated on the central marble throne. Next to her was the reason why I was here, Caesar Lanista.

I walked toward where the aristocracy sat and the guards did not stop me. Lanista had a smug smile on his face. From the body language that passed between him and the woman he sat beside, it was obvious that she was in a position of dominance over him and that there was also something sexual going on there.

I shifted my gaze to the lady on the marble throne. We made eye contact. I showed her with a look I was interested. She blushed red. Not an embarrassed blush but a blush of excitement.

Lanista turned red from the open threat I'd made to his position in this powerful woman's bed.

I raised my right sharp spurred fist to the lady on the throne and saluted her. She smiled.

"For you my lady," I shouted to her, "I give my blood today."

Then I scratched myself on my right cheek with one of the studs and drew blood. As the crowd "Ahhhhhhed," I wet my fingers with my own blood then blew a kiss to the lady on the throne.

My opponent strode out to the center of the killing field. I moved toward him and prepared to shed blood.

*   *   *

The guy sent against me was a tall, lean, long limbed, blond, snarling twenty year old. He came at me slowly at first, then with a burst of speed charged me and dove at my legs.

I was ready for it. We were taught at the school in Micea that there were no rules in these fights. You had to expect anything. I circled around to his back and he spun in the sand trying to keep me in front of him.

From where I was at I could have tried a kick to his head but I knew just barely enough about ground fighting to know I didn't want to be down on the ground with this guy. My thing was slipping punches and kicks and firing back precise counters to mess the opponent up. I didn't want to be in a wrestling match.

I was going to force him to play my game whether he wanted to or not. The stakes were too high to even consider letting him deal the cards.

We played for life and death.

I motioned for him to get up.

He stayed down, crab walking toward me. He threw a kick at my legs. I avoided it.

In a mixed martial arts match that would happen in about two thousand years, an oriental wrestler named Antonio Inoki used these tactics against Muhammad Ali. Their match ended in a boring fifteen round draw.

I doubt these Romans would put up with a fighter boring them for very long. They'd shoot us full of arrows just to see us jerk.

The only way I could attack was to go to the ground with him.

Fuck that! I wasn't going to do it.

I moved around and motioned some more for him to get up. There was a scattering of boos in the stands.

"Come on," I shouted to him. "They want to see some knuckles flying." I motioned to the crowd.

A few shouts came from them. "Come on! Come on!"

I stopped moving and put my hands on my hips and looked around at the crowd with an exaggerated expression of confusion.

More boos came. More joined in to the chorus of cat calls until it was so loud the sand beneath my feet felt like it was vibrating.

The mass of blood thirsty idiots in the stands were not booing me.

My opponent took the bait.

He climbed to his feet. He came toward me.

Some things never change. Insult a man's manhood by making him look like a coward and you just might make his emotions over rule his head. This guy's balls were going to override any brains he might have.

Not a good idea.

Moving around, I feinted him out of position, made him miss with a sweeping right and dropped him with a left uppercut.

Miletus told me I was going to die today. So I asked myself, why I was being matched against this guy. Miletus would know I could take him easy. Something wasn't right.

Give the kid some credit though, he was stubborn. He started climbing to his feet. The kid had a lot of guts. No brains, but a lot of guts.

The kid got to his hands and knees and was taking his time trying to stand up. He was so dizzy you could almost hear all the little birds chirping as they flew around in his skull.

I took two jumping, skipping, running, steps toward him and just as his hands came up out of the sand I planted a rising kick in the kids face.

Something crunched when the kick landed.

The kid went over to his back. His feet flew in the air then slowly settled back down to the sand. From his back he coughed and spit blood into the air.

The kid was done.

He was out.

I wiggled the toes of my right foot to make sure I hadn't broken one of them. They were OK.

I raised my arms to the blood thirsty mob in the stands to a smattering of applause.

Well, at least I'd got the attention of a few of these sick sons-of-bitches.

The body brigade came out and loaded up the kid and as they carted him away I found out why I'd been given such an easy opponent.

My next opponent made his appearance.

So that was how it was going to be, I realized now. They were going to keep having me fight until either one of these guys got lucky or I fell apart from fatigue.

The new guy was one of the older men from the school in Micea. I recognized him.

He was a little smaller than me; a little shorter and thinner. His black hair had streaks of gray in it. His face was weatherworn like just about everybody here except for the very young. For a guy his age, he was in damn good shape.

I'd sparred with this guy and knew offensively he was no threat. He couldn't punch too hard and his hands were not terribly quick. He also never attempted to throw any kicks.

The problem with him was, he could slip punches damn good and he instinctively seemed to know to not move straight backwards. He moved from side to side really well.

In a straight up match I'd just track him down and force him into exchanges that he couldn't win and knock him out. It might take a while, but I knew I could do that. The thing is with the way things were set up, I couldn't fight him straight up. I didn't have the option of waiting and using up the energy it would take to chase him down.

Not with another opponent coming right after him I didn't.

I waited for my opponent to come out to where I was then moved toward him. He moved backward, away and to his left. Coming after him, I moved forward but I didn't just go straight at him. I stepped to my own right. That way, for him to move in a circle out here he'd have to take three steps for every one step I took. He'd have to be moving very fast too, otherwise I'd run him into the wall eventually.

I was just giving him a lesson from Boxing 301: Cutting the Ring Off. In a twenty foot ring I'd have this boy in a corner in less than a minute. Out here in this football field sized arena, it would take longer.

He wasn't seeing what I was trying to do until we were close enough to the wall for me to look past him and into the area where he'd come out of. Past the gate of crisscrossed metal bars I saw a long line of fighters standing there with the caestus tied to their fists. From that quick glance I figured there were at least ten guys waiting in line to come out and try to knock my brains out.

Suddenly the opponent I was fighting at this moment didn't seem very important. How fast I tracked him down or not didn't matter, I wasn't getting out of this arena alive unless I did something about this setup.

Caesar Lanista and the tall slim built woman were seated directly above where the fighters were. I stopped there, totally ignoring my opponent and pointed at Caesar Lanista.

"This is between you and me," I shouted to him. "Guess you don't have the balls to fight your own battles."

He stood up. "You are nothing!" He shouted. "I would not dirty my hands with the likes of you."

I hadn't totally forgotten my opponent. While I was having this little talk with Lanista, he was creeping up behind me.

"I call Caesar Lanista a coward," I shouted at the top of my lungs.

The woman beside Lanista gave him a look of pure venom. "You call yourself Caesar?" She hissed at him.

I knew I'd gotten this boy in some shit now.

"In my home country, where he steals women, he called himself Caesar," I shouted to the lady. "I don't know what he calls himself here."

My opponent chose that moment to charge me from behind. I wasn't as oblivious to him as he would have liked.

I threw a spinning back fist that caught his onrushing face square. The studs from the caestus crunched the cartilage of his nose. Blood and snot flew through the air.

He went to his hands and knees. His ruined nose looked like a stomped on tomato.

Lanista shouted to the guards, "Seize him and kill him!"

CHAPTER 31
Close Cut

The guards were coming at me fast so I figured it was time for me to make my exit. The Iron Gate and wall in front of me were a combined nine feet high. That's all that separated the fighters from the spectators.

I scaled the gate and the wall easy. I was just reaching the top of the wall and was pulling my head up when a guard on the other side of the wall above me took a swipe at my head with his sword. I hadn't seen that boy from the arena floor. I ducked and he missed so close I didn't figure I'd be in need of a haircut for six months.

He stood above me and with an evil grin took aim at my hand with that sword of his. I didn't feel like wearing the nick name of nubbins for the rest of my life so I let go and went flying backward.

I landed in the sand on my back and all the wind was knocked out of me.

Guards were starting to come out of doors. That was when I heard a woman's voice shout, "Do not harm him!" It was the woman beside Lanista.

The guards froze. Evidently when she spoke it carried more weight than when Lanista spoke.

I was climbing to my feet when Lanista started to say something and a look from the woman silenced him.

The guards were looking back and forth between me and the woman. She was the obvious authority figure here. She was the one who would be giving the orders on this day. I was kind of hoping she'd say, "Game's over, everybody go home." But that wasn't what happened.

She smiled at me, a warm inviting smile. I smiled back and blew her a kiss. She spoke directly to me. "I want to see how far you can go," she said. To the guards she said, "Let his fights continue as before."

Ain't this a bitch, I thought. I was figuring I'd just impress her with the Dark dick and everything would be all right. Evidently, seeing blood spilled got her off better than a good orgasm.

My next opponent came out of the slave holding area. It was that big Viking Torstan. This was not going to be easy.

CHAPTER 32
Fighting George Foreman

The sun beat down on our heads. It felt like gravel being ground into my skull. There wasn't a breeze in the air, but it felt like I had all the maniacs in the stands breathing down my neck. To make it short, it was hotter than a mother fucker out there.

Torstan walked across the red sand toward me. He wasn't hurrying, he wasn't creeping along either. He moved like a guy out on an afternoon stroll. He had a smile on his face.

"I wish I were not a part of this," Torstan said when we were close enough to talk and indicated where the line of slaves with caestus wrapped hands stood. "I would enjoy a good clean fight against you. But this has no honor."

"You take what you can get," I told him.

"Yes," he said. "We'll make it a good one, but not for them, for us!"

Then he came at me.

If I had to describe Torstan's style by comparing it to a boxer most people in America are familiar with I'd have to say he moved like a young George Foreman. He came in with a pawing jab trying to set up huge right hands and roundhouse left hooks.

He wasn't as fast as the younger guy I'd fought, but he wasn't as stupid either. And Torstan was one strong, tough, son of a bitch.

After a few minutes of feeling out sparring I started circling around him stabbing him with quick left jabs when Torstan let fly with a crusher of an over-hand right over one of my jabs. Since I'd been expecting it I ducked the right and turned to slide away to the left and found out the first punch was just a lure.

I ran straight into a left hook that caught me square in the pit of the stomach. In my old days of hard drinking every night, that body blast would have made me shit down both legs and vomit into the air at the same time. As it was, the punch knocked the wind clean out of me.

I crossed over a neat right hand that caught Torstan above the left eye and opened a mean looking cut. I backed off and moved out of range to catch my breath.

The people in the stands applauded our exchange. I looked down and saw that Torstan's caestus had torn the skin at my stomach. Blood ran down the front of me. This was the first time any of these guys marked me.

Torstan reached up and dabbed at the blood from his cut eyebrow. He looked at it then wiped it on his chest in a big X painting himself. He turned and looked at the Romans in the royal box.

"May all of your mothers be fucked by dogs," he shouted at them.

Hell, I was beginning to like this guy more every moment. Too bad I was going to have to fuck him up.

He came at me again.

That first exchange told me there was no way I wanted to be standing still and slugging it out with Torstan. He had the kind of raw power where I could land twenty punches and all he'd have to do is land one or two to erase whatever I'd done by putting a serious hurt on me.

I moved and circled.

Torstan came at me with his big slow thudding punches.

After a few more shots with the caestus, Torstan had cuts over both eyes and his nose was bleeding. He did land some glancing blows on me so that my lips were busted and my right cheek was gashed open.

Even though he kept a warrior's grim half smile on his face, I could tell Torstan didn't like the pattern I was forcing him into. He would come at me and if he threw only the controlled punches like a jab or a short hook or a straight right, I would just step away from him. When he tried one of the killer punches that threw him off balance and left him open, I'd step in with a counter and rattle his teeth.

It was a hot day and Torstan was starting to breath hard. I wasn't feeling very fresh myself and the heat was getting to me too when Torstan gave it a do or die charge.

He went from calmly stalking me to running at me like a madman so suddenly that he caught me off guard and got me with a good left hook that split my right eyebrow wide open.

Stars danced in front of my eyes but I still knew what was going on so when he tried to finish me I did something I hadn't ever tried before and threw a foot sweep.

His foot being kicked out from under him surprised the hell out of Torstan, who found himself on his hands and knees before he knew what happened. From there, he dove at my legs and got hold of one of my feet.

As I fell backwards I drove a hard right fist down into the side of Torstan's head nearly tearing his ear loose. That blow had to have stunned Torstan good, but he kept that hold on my ankle until I rained three more crushing shots to the same spot.

The instant Torstan's grip loosened I slid away from him and got to my feet.

Maybe Torstan didn't have enough practical experience in arranged fights to know to stay down when you're hurt bad, or to at least stay in a posture where you couldn't easily be attacked. Or maybe Torstan was just too stunned to be able to think about anything at that moment.

Whatever it was, he lurched to his feet staggering around like a drunk. I came in, showed him a right hand and ripped a double left hook to the body then head and followed with an overhand right.

Torstan's eyes rolled up into his head but it took another hellacious left hook to put his ass in the sand.

At this point I know any boxing match in the twentieth century would have been stopped. But we weren't in the twentieth century and the bastards in the stands were thirsty for blood.

Torstan rolled over and spit a mouthful of blood into the sand along with a few teeth. He laughed and looked up at me from all fours with a crazy gape-toothed grin.

"Stay down!" I told him.

He just laughed some more. "You'll have to do better than that," Torstan said and reeled to his feet once again, his legs as unsteady as a sailor on the deck of a ship in the middle of a hurricane.

My breath was coming in harsh barks too. Even though Torstan was still barely ticking he was taking one hell of a licking. I was wearing myself out beating on his thick Viking skull.

Torstan came at me with his lips shredded, one eye closed and his nose broken. Blood flowed from a dozen cuts all over his face. Through the pain he kept that crazy ass grin plastered across his face.

He swung a wide overhand right at me.

"You stupid son-of-a-bitch," I yelled at him and countered with a right hand of my own that snapped his head back.

Taking Joe Louis's advice, I didn't wait for Torstan to fall. I kept nailing him with quick punches in a rat-a-tat-tat series of combinations until he collapsed onto his face in the sand.

When Torstan went down face first I knew this fight was over. I stood there with limp tired arms hanging from my shoulders like slabs of lifeless meat.

I looked around the arena into the faces of the cheering maniacs in the stands. I wasn't sure what they were cheering for. They didn't know who I was. They only liked the show I was putting on.

I looked up into the royal seating and Lanista was gone. Only the tall nice looking woman surrounded by guards and slaves was there now. I looked into that woman's eyes and gave her my best smile. With all the blood pouring from the cuts on my face I doubt I looked very appealing but I tried anyway.

She smiled back and raised a bright red handkerchief in front of herself. What the fuck this was about I wasn't sure, until a guard ran out and tossed a dagger at my feet that I picked up.

So, this was the old thumbs up or thumbs down thing.

The woman raised her other hand beckoning an opinion from the spectators. A chorus of, "Kill him! Kill him!" answered her.

With that sweet smile on her face she let the red cloth fall.

CHAPTER 33
Midday Snack

A deafening cry went up throughout the arena. The mob wanted death.

I looked down at Torstan. He was on his back now. He looked up into my eyes. That same grim, half smile, played across his bloodied, crushed features.

"Do it," he mouthed.

The woman in the royal box and the mob all wanted the same thing, for me to kill for them.

Standing over Torstan, I held the knife above my head and looked into the eyes of the lady in the royal box. She had that same look of anticipation that a woman who likes to fuck gets on her face just before you drive the meat home.

She'd have to use someone else to get her rocks off today.

"When I kill," I shouted to her and everyone else in the arena. "I kill for me! No one orders me to kill!"

I threw the knife into the stands.

She didn't seem very surprised by me doing this. Her smile never left her face.

I was exhausted and my next opponent came running out to meet me.

* * *

That ugly, scarred-up, sadistic bastard Pugnax was the guy who came out. Pugnax had matching knots on both sides of his head from where I'd tagged him with the right hand and Johnny had cracked him with his left hook. On him, the lumps looked good. Anything new on his head had to make him look better. There's no way he could look worse.

The crowd was still booing me for not killing Torstan when Pugnax raised his arms over his head and shouted to them, "I will crush this one's skull for the glory of Rome."

That got him a loud cheer.

What a fucking idiot, I thought. You're doing this for the glory of Rome and then you'll go back to your cage like everybody else who's just fighting to survive.

The adrenaline rush from the last fight had worn off. I felt dead on my feet. When a second wind is mentioned on a boxing match what they are talking about is when the first rush of energy has burned off fatigue sets in, then the body draws off of inner resources to keep going. The inner resources being used up are the second wind.

I was past my second wind.

After two quick fights and one blood and guts slugging match, this engine was running on fumes. There weren't any fuel reserves in my body to draw off of anymore. I was dogged out tired and knew the only thing that would help me would be a good meal and some sleep. I doubt that these guys would give me that kind of a break.

Pugnax knew I was tired too. There wasn't any way to hide it. He came at me in a half crouched, hands out in front of him type of a wrestler's stance.

I snapped a jab off and slid to the side. My feet were heavy. My movements were slow.

Pugnax stepped with me. He knew how to cut off a ring. I realized this at the same instant that he dove at me.

We went down in a tangle of legs and elbows. Before we even hit the ground, Pugnax ripped two hooks into me, one to the body and one to the head.

It was my worst nightmare. I was on my back and this sadistic son of a bitch was raining blows down on my head.

I took five, six, seven … ten or fifteen shots before he actually knocked me to a position where he couldn't keep pounding me.

Stars were swimming around my head. The world tilted crazily. There was no up or down, just everything crooked. Black spots danced in front of my eyes. Blood washed into my vision.

Everything cleared for a moment. He was trying to grip my face with his left hand to slam me with the right and accidentally wiped the blood from my eyes.

I turned and twisted my head just as the right came down. He missed, overextending the punch, he hit the sand.

Pugnax fell forward on top me.

His face was at my face. His nose was at my mouth. I snapped my teeth shut onto his nose.

Pugnax screamed. He jerked away, couldn't get away.

The crowd shouted for blood.

I ripped away at his nose, my teeth bit deeper. I wrapped my arms around his head and held on like a star high school quarterback riding his favorite cheerleader.

Pugnax climbed to his feet and lifted me in the air. I bit down harder and felt the cartilage part and tore backward with my head.

Then I was thrown loose and Pugnax was on his knees with his hands to his ruined face. Blood poured through his fingers.

I kicked him once in the face and he went to his back. Spitting the ragged piece of meat and skin that had once been Pugnax's nose into my hand I held it up to the woman in the royal box.

"Your prize," I shouted to her and hurled the chunk of nose at the woman.

The blood thirsty maniacs cheered me. A few minutes before, they hated me.

The sun felt cool. Like cold ice water was poured over my head. Everything was very bright. Everything was white.

The sand beneath my feet pitched and rolled.

I fell to my knees. I laughed like a madman and everything went black.

PART III

O' Death! The poor man's dearest friend.
                    -Burns, Man was Made to Mourn

When life is woe,
And hope is dumb,
The world says, "Go!"
The grave says, "Come!"
                    -Arthur Guiterman, Betel-Nuts

Like the dew on the mountain,
Like the foam on the river,
Like the bubble on the fountain,
Thou art gone, and forever!
                    -Walter Scott, The Lady of the Lake

Love is everything, and
Love is nothing.
                    -The Walker in Darkness

CHAPTER 34
With the Dead and After

I heard the loud sound of squeaks and creaking like a giant in a rocking chair. On top of that were the shrieks of birds and a loud buzzing filled my ears.

My eyes felt like they were glued shut. I tried to open them and couldn't do it. With the sound of creaking I felt side to side rocking. Everything was coming to me through a wall of fog. A layer of gauze was between me and the real world. It felt like I was inside a cocoon that I didn't really want to break out of.

Every bone and muscle in my body hurt.

The smell around me was awful; rotten meat mixed with piss and shit.

The rocking stopped, jerked to a stop.

"Here, this one," a harsh voice yelled. "Get them off quick."

I tried again to open my eyes. This time I succeeded. Bright sunlight scorched down into me. I opened my mouth to speak and only a dry rattle came out.

Someone leaned over me. His shadow shielded me from the sun for a moment. I heard a gasp of surprise. The shadow moved back. The sun fried my eyes again.

"What do we have here?" The harsh voice barked. "Get out of the way!"

From the corner of my sight the first figure was shoved aside and the second figure moved in front of me. Both of them were just black outlines against a flaming sky.

"You were supposed to check them, make sure they were dead." The harsh voice barked.

"I did, I thought they were," The second voice said.

"I'll finish him," The harsh voice spoke. There was the sound of sliding metal, a sword being drawn.

"Wait!" the second said. "I know this man."

"Just another slave," the harsh voice growled, "I'll make it quick."

He stood over me blotting out the sun. He raised his sword above his head. "Pray to whatever gods you have," he said. "Your time has come."

I tried to raise my arm to ward off the blow and can only raise it for a moment before it falls.

Something crashed into the head of the one who was going to hack me to pieces. He pitched forward, falling across me.

With a grunt he raised up to his knees.

I see that I am in the back of a wagon filled with corpses, the rotting bodies of those who were killed in the arena. They were out here dumping them in ditches on the sides of this road.

Rising above my butcher is the man who wanted him to wait. I recognize him now. It's McRae, the Scotsman. He had a large rock in his hand. He slammed it down onto the head of the Roman guard again. The guard pitched forward on top of me once more.

McRae then got on top of the guard and pounded his head with the rock until his skull was caved in and the blows with the rock made wet smacking sounds.

McRae dragged the soldier off of me.

"I have got to get you out of here," he told me and gave me a drink of water from a rawhide flask he had untied from his hip.

I tried to smile and thank him but my face muscles weren't up to it. I probably looked like a gargoyle. The way I must have looked I have no idea how he ever recognized me.

I tried to sit up and passed back out.

*   *   *

The next time I woke up was to the sound of a crackling fire, the smell of roasting game animals and the cool feeling of my face being washed with a wet cloth.

I opened my eyes and it was a teenage girl who was washing the caked on blood from my face. The girl squealed and slid away from me in the dirt. I sat up and it seemed like everyone in the camp turned and looked at me at the same time.

It wasn't a big camp, maybe ten or fifteen people. They were a ragged bunch, a few women in their twenties and thirties, a few teenage girls, and McRae. The rest were old men and women. They had a few wagons with six horses tied among the trees.

McRae saw me wake and came over. I remembered him as being the laughing joking guy from the cages who was so proud of his skill at giving women orgasms. The smile was gone from his face.

I stood up and my head throbbed. I was figuring it wouldn't stop throbbing for about a month. It wasn't like I could get hold of any Tylenol either.

We shook hands. "I want to thank you for helping me out," I told him. "If it wasn't for you, I'd be with the rest of them in that ditch."

A half smile curled his lips. He said, "I was going to kill 'em anyway the first chance I got. He's the one who put the knife to me."

For a moment I didn't know what he meant then I remembered what the buyer of McRae at the slave auction said right after he'd bought him. He said he'd paid as much as he did only to see the look on McRae's face as he was having him gelded.

I didn't ask McRae if he had had his manhood cut away. I didn't have to. His face expression and his attitude told me. There was nothing I could say to him. That's the kind of thing that you can't just tell a guy that in time they'll get over it. What they had done to McRae, there wouldn't be any getting over.

He showed me around the camp and introduced me to everyone. All of them were run-away slaves. They were reasonably certain that they wouldn't be bothered this deep in the woods at night. Slave hunting parties didn't like coming out here because it was nearly impossible to avoid ambushes. But just in case, there were sentries posted outside the camp.

After my little tour we went back and sat on the bed of grass that they'd had me sleeping on. McRae asked me if I had any plans now that I was a free man again.

I told him about Caesar Lanista's kidnappings and how Johnny and me followed him. Then I told him about what happened that got me put in the arena. I finished with, "The first thing I got to do is get Johnny loose. Then we find the women and get our asses back to where we came from."

"Getting your friend out of that gladiator school in Micea looks to be suicide," McRae told me.

"I don't have any choice," I answered. "I don't turn my back on friends."

"Then I'm in," McRae said.

I looked at him and the surprise showed on my face.

McRae grinned and the way his face looked was frightening. "What we're going into at that school in Micea is a fight to the death. The way I am now, do you think I want to live long? I just want to make sure I take quite a few Roman bastards with me when I die."

"Good," I told him. "Just don't die too quickly. There's a lot of Romans there to be killed."

We started planning the days ahead.

CHAPTER 35
Camping Out

McRae and the other people in the camp knew the countryside we were in fairly well. As it turned out I was the only one who spent his entire stay in Rome in a cage or in chains or in captivity of some sort.

Most slaves in Rome had jobs to do. So except for being owned property that could be disposed of and done with as the owner wished, slaves usually did have a sort of freedom. All of the slaves in the camp except for McRae just walked away from their owners. Now they were all wanted criminals because they didn't like what their lives were and left them behind.

I spent the next few days eating game animals and practicing with a sword McRae gave me. It always surprised the hell out of me just how natural handling a sword felt. When I fenced with McRae it felt like I was born with a sword in my hand. I had knowledge inside of me about this weapon that I could not account for.

The lumps on my face went down and the purple bruises gradually faded away until I looked human again. Maybe I still didn't look very pretty, but at least I did look like I was a member of our species.

After a week of recovering and honing our sword skills we were ready to set off toward Micea.

Micea was only about forty miles away. So, two nights of horse riding should bring us to its walls.

*   *   *

The escaped slaves were going to head north the morning after McRae and me were leaving. They were hoping to cross the mountains, then leave the Roman Empire and find a peaceful secluded spot away from the rest of the world to live out the rest of their lives as free people.

Unless they joined some larger community they would always be at risk from roaming bands of robbers and cut throats. This was not a good world they were in. Their chances of finding a safe haven were slim.

The week I spent among those people was peaceful and calming. They didn't have much but what they had, they shared with me. Those people, without any questions, accepted me as one of them. For a short while it was like I had a family.

These people were just ordinary folk. In America, we'd call them lower-middle class. In another time and place, just about everyone in America could be wearing chains. The night McRae and me rode out of the camp, if I would have been a religious man I would have prayed for their safety. As it was, I wished them good luck.

So, outfitted with swords, daggers, ropes tied in bags slung across our horse's backs and clothes that made us look like ordinary travelers, we set out.

*　　*　　*

We rode down the wagon trail toward Micea mostly in silence. There wasn't a lot for us to discuss anyway. We knew what lay ahead.

We were also quiet so we could hear what was in front of us. Night time outside of a city in ancient Rome was, except for moonlight, pitch black.

We were both wanted criminals. McRae was more wanted than me. He'd killed his overseer. I was only supposed to be dead.

Every time we heard the sounds of approaching horses and wagons we got off the road and into the woods and hid until they passed. This didn't happen very often. Three times the first night. Four times the second night when we were close to Micea. No one would be out after dark unless the party they traveled with was well armed and large enough to scare off any bandits that might be around.

Just out of sight of Micea we turned east so we could travel parallel to the city walls and approach one of the smaller gates that would be guarded by a single sentry.

For a half mile we skirted the city walls then the small eastern gate was in front of us.

From the tree line with the crickets singing their eternal song around us we planned our next move.

McRae wanted to bribe the sentry to get through the gate. I didn't have any money so I didn't know how we could make that work.

"You start it off," he said. "I've got something that will get his attention."

We came out of the tree line on foot leading our horses.

We approached the sentry showing our palms to him so he saw we held no weapons. "We're just travelers looking for lodging." I said to him.

"Your roof will be the trees of the forest tonight." The sentry answered.

"Look, no one will know if you let us in," I said to him coming close enough to talk. "We'll pay you to let us through. We want to get a meal and there aren't any cafés out here."

I fiddled with the money sack at my belt knowing it was empty.

McRae put a hand on my shoulder, "Keep your money my friend. You've paid the last few days. I'll pay tonight."

"It'll be expensive to get through my gate," the sentry said.

"No problem," McRae answered. "I've enough for all," and stepped forward toward the man. He reached behind his back like he was going for a hidden money sack.

With a movement too fast to be caught by the eye in the gate's dim torchlight, McRae stabbed the sentry in the ribs with his dagger.

I clamped a hand over the sentry's mouth and tripped him and we all three went to the ground. In silence McRae stabbed the sentry three more times then slit his throat.

We quickly went through the Sentry's pouches and took the gate key and what money he had. We propped him up in a sitting position like he was taking a nap. Then we entered Micea and locked the gate behind us.

CHAPTER 36
Savagery

Micea was still awake. The streets were lit by torches that served as streetlights. In a dark alley between two buildings we divided up what money we took off the sentry. It wasn't much. The sentry must not have been much better off than most slaves.

Well, at least he could have looked for something better if he wanted to.

We moved down the streets fast to put some distance between us and the gate in case the sentry was found dead before we wanted him to be. We didn't run. We didn't want to attract any attention.

At a café we bought a duck leg each and a glass of water that was a long way from clear. When I get back home I'm going to make it a point to send the guy who runs the water treatment plant a Christmas card every year. After drinking this shit, you don't know what could be swimming around in your stomach.

We also got directions to the gladiator school. I'd only been inside the school the entire time I was here so I didn't know my way around town.

We took our time eating to let the night get even later, and then set out in the direction of the gladiator school.

*　　*　　*

Back out on the street at about what I was estimating was 1 AM things were starting to get quiet. It was almost a mile walk to the school.

On the way to the school the only people we saw on the streets were prostitutes, their customers and some thugs looking to kick the shit out of someone and take their money. The way the prostitutes looked, their customers must be desperate to fuck anything. The faces on those women looked like they'd worn out three bodies each. But there were guys willing to rent them.

The thugs were a mean looking breed. With the cuts and bruises still healing on me, and McRae's general attitude, we looked meaner. They gave us the once over and searched for easier prey.

The school itself was separated from all the rest of the buildings around it by a wide walkway so we couldn't just hop from a building to the school's roof.

One thing that surprised me was that there was no sentry walking around the entire school. There was a guy at the front gate but that was it. No one else appeared to be stopping anyone from getting in.

We made a complete circle around the building making sure there was no one else on guard but the guy at the front gate. There was no one.

Then it hit me that it made sense. You would never expect anyone to be trying to break into this place. Hell, inside is only a lot of pissed off guys training to kill you.

There's nothing in there you could make money off of, so there's nothing you'd want to steal. All the security they had was for keeping the guys in, not for keeping someone out.

My plan, what I'd told McRae back at the forest was to climb up on the roof and come down into the open courtyard where we practiced. From there, get to the small cells where the girl had been sent to me. I was figuring if Johnny was still here, that's where they'd have him.

There being only one guard, we changed our plans right then.

McRae stayed hidden around the corner to the right side of where the guard lounged against the front gate. I came around the corner to his left walking with an exaggerated stagger.

The guard came to the alert as I approached him. I didn't recognize him at all and I knew he didn't recognize me.

I staggered up to him. "Open your mother fuckin' door," I slurred at him loud enough to cover McRae's movements behind him. "You mother fuckin' gladiators think you're all so fuckin' tough. I'll beat the shit out of you all."

He grinned at me. An evil grin and put his hand on his sword. "Move along," he said, "Before I have to hurt you."

"Hurt meeeeee," I said and that was when McRae clamped his left hand over the guard's mouth and shoved his dagger between his ribs from behind. The guard's knees buckled and McRae withdrew his blade and stabbed him four more times, then threw him to the ground.

I could tell McRae was really enjoying himself tonight. That wouldn't be a problem as long as he remembered why we were here and didn't just go kill crazy on me.

We took this guard's money, got the key from him, and unlocked the gate. I took the guard's sword as an extra and sheathed it, keeping mine in my hand.

Inside all was quiet. It was dark except for a few torches that were still burning out in the courtyard. The courtyard where the training took place was separated from the entrance by a fence made of steel bars.

Through the steel fence by the dim light of two dying torches, I saw in the far corner of the courtyard a man was hanging from a single cross. The man was black.

It was Johnny.

"Oh shit," I said and McRae looked at me. I pointed to where Johnny hung from the cross. "He's over there," I told him.

"You should have expected that," McRae answered and he was right.

I told McRae to guard the door that lead into the main part of the complex and kill anyone who came out. He would have done the killing part without a word from me.

A crude ladder was leaning against a wall near where Johnny was. The gate to the steel fence that lead out to the courtyard was unlocked. I went out into the courtyard and got the ladder and leaned it against the cross Johnny was on.

As I was climbing up to get him down I told Johnny, "Hell Bro, least I can do for you now is give you a decent burial."

A voice as dry and raspy as fall leaves rustling in the wind answered, "You ain't buryin' shit!"

Johnny's head moved slowly up to look me in the eyes. His eyes were swollen and his lips were busted from a beating, but he was alive. I saw now what I couldn't see in the torchlight from the ground. Johnny wasn't nailed to the cross. He was tied to it.

"You're alive!" I said in a shouted whisper.

"No! I'm a fuckin' spook," he rasped. "Get me down."

I cut his right arm loose and he slung his arm around my neck so I could cut his left arm loose.

"If you kiss me, I'll drop you on you fuckin' head," I told him.

"If you drop me," he answered, "I'll kiss you with my size ten hambone upside your head."

That's just what friends are for, to appreciate being rescued.

I got Johnny to the ground and was trying to massage some life back into his arms and legs when we started hearing shouts and the ringing of steel against steel.

I gave Johnny the extra sword and we were heading back to where McRae was when the door he was guarding burst open.

Two Roman guards came flying out of the open door. Before they knew anyone was in front of them McRae cleaved one's skull in half and with a neat backstroke disemboweled the other.

A crowd was behind them coming fast.

The guards from the complex were being pursued.

Johnny was up and on his feet even if he wasn't very steady. We went to help McRae but when a flood of maybe ten of the guards came through the door he backpedaled out to where we were.

Screaming maniacs with weapons were on their heels slashing and stabbing at them. We retreated to the corner of the courtyard where I'd just got Johnny down from the cross.

The guards from the gladiator school, numbering somewhere around fifty, flooded out of the door and were prevented from exiting by the front door by a few of what I now knew were escaped gladiators that somehow got around and came in the front door. The guards were boxed in.

They went to the only place they could, the courtyard.

This escape must have been in the planning for a long time because all the gladiators that I saw, somewhere around thirty, were well armed.

We would have been all right in our little corner except the escaped gladiators didn't just want to escape. They wanted blood. They were going to make every one of the guards pay for every beating they received.

The gladiators drove the guards backward across the courtyard right at us in our corner.

Desperate men fight with desperation, and the guards were attacked from the front and the rear. They were finding out what the word "desperation" meant.

As the guards were forced at us in our corner by the screaming horde on their heels, a strange ancient form of bloodlust seemed to take hold of me. A handgun and bare fists will always be my weapons of choice but in that corner I began to love that sword. I began to love the way it felt when I drove the blade home and heard my foe cry out in agony.

Time after time, one of the guards would rush me slashing away. Using skills that I had no idea I had ever had before, I would parry the attacks then rip their guts out or run them through the heart. There was something about taking an opponent down with a long blade that was addicting. Feeling his heart shudder and stop when you run him through and seeing his blood spill at your feet was a primal savage feeling. And I liked it.

When the guards had thinned down to around five I spotted the guy who appeared to be the leader of this force of freedom fighters.

He was stocky, had dark brown hair and the most scarred up vicious looking face that I'd ever seen. When the last of the guards were lying in the dirt with his blood coloring the soil I went to shake this leader's hand.

"John Dark," I said and extended my hand in greeting.

"Spartacus," he answered and shook my hand and gave a smile that would make children cry and run away.

"Well hell," Johnny said and shook his hand too. "You sure as shit don't look like Kirk Douglas."

CHAPTER 37
Micea in Flames

Spartacus ordered the other gladiators around like he believed he was some kind of army commander or something. It was effective because they did do what he told them to do.

He posted guards dressed like the former guards of the school at every entrance so no one would know that there was anything unusual going on. Then he sent groups of five to search the school to kill any remaining guards and release all the rest of the slaves from their cells.

Without a second thought, McRae joined up with Spartacus newly formed army and followed his orders without hesitation. One look at Johnny and Spartacus told me to take him to the mess hall and get him some food and water.

I wasn't much for taking orders but since he told me what I intended to do anyway, I played along with him. On the way to the mess hall Johnny told me that after he'd been told his black skin was worth too much alive to just kill him, Miletus ordered that he be beaten then hung on the cross. So that's what they did with him every day.

"They kicked my ass and hung me out to dry, daily," Johnny said. "I sure know what an overused sweatshirt feels like, because I've been put through the wringer around here."

We ate some food that was in the kitchen beside the mess hall and Johnny must have drunk two gallons of water. I guess hanging out on a cross all night was thirsty work.

Then I wanted to go check on the slave girl that I'd fucked the last night I was here. I could do with having a repeat of that horizontal tango we danced.

We got to the women's quarters about the same time that the search parties were setting them free. There was a celebration going on but my celebration was short.

Verona, as I found out her name was, had been sold the day after I was hauled away to a wealthy merchant heading back home to Carthage. She would probably be on a ship by now out on the Mediterranean Sea.

*   *   *

After the school was searched and secured Spartacus started proving himself to be about as blood thirsty as the Romans he'd just freed himself from.

He sent out what he was calling, "His Soldiers," to break into the nearest houses. There, they were to kill all the Roman citizens and free all the slaves, arm the slaves and send them out to do the same thing.

An hour and a half after Spartacus sent out his soldiers, screams of terror and pain could be heard on every street in Micea. Fires were everywhere. The gladiators and freed slaves raped women and children and killed the men.

Sometimes they killed the women and children too. It just depended on what mood the party that invaded that particularly house was in.

Johnny and me stayed out of it as much as we could. Neither one of us wanted to be a part of butchering innocent people. Keeping slaves was not right but what we were seeing was savage and heartless murder on a large scale.

When the sun came up Micea looked like a wasteland. Corpses were everywhere.

The gladiators and the freed slaves claimed the spoils of war and stripped the city clean of anything of value that they could carry.

Spartacus made clear his intentions of going from town to town, killing all Romans and freeing all the slaves to raise his army. Standing on the top of an empty slave cage, on top of an ox drawn wagon in the same open courtyard where we'd been auctioned as slaves, Spartacus shouted his intentions to his troops at noon. His army now probably numbered just under a thousand.

They cheered his every word. A look came over Spartacus' face that I'd seen before. It was a steely resolve, a power, a need to take everything and own it and bend the world to the shape that he wanted it to be. I didn't like that look. I'd seen it in black and white newsreel footage. The man who I'd seen wearing that look when I'd seen it before was Adolph Hitler.

CHAPTER 38
On the Road

Johnny and me slipped away from the orgy of death that was going on downtown and stole some money, clothes, and supplies from a devastated house. Then we caught some horses that were running free in the street, grabbed a map from a burnt out shop, and rode away from Micea.

*   *   *

We were heading to Rome.

Sushi and Sherry St. Clair were exotic looking women. On the auction block in Rome they would fetch a high price. We were betting they were still in the city of Rome, sold to some local rich guy.

If they weren't....well, we'd cross that bridge when we came to it.

The road to Rome was hot. The map we had didn't give us very much detail, just enough to let us know what towns we'd pass as we passed them and landmarks so we knew what road we were on.

Getting food wasn't very hard. There was a lot of traffic on the roads heading to Rome, mostly farmers taking crops to the city to sell. We sometimes bought fruits and vegetables from them. Other times we'd spot an apple tree off the road and go raid it.

We weren't having the kind of meals we were used to back in the good old U.S. of A. where meat was always available at a cheap price but it didn't seem to be doing my body any harm to be doing without it either.

During the night we got as far off the road as we could without taking a chance at losing where the road was. We'd taken some blankets when we'd stolen the clothes and money and in the forest camped out with a small fire burning.

McRae had taught me what stones to knock together to make sparks to start a fire with. I was grateful as hell for that now.

When there were no forests, we slept under the stars in the open fields. Looking up into the untouched heavens it was easy to see how someone born to this world in this time could be awed by its size. In our time almost all the Earth had been explored. There was an accurate map that covered nearly every square inch of the Earth by the end of the twentieth century.

During this time, maps were only guesses, sometimes not even very good guesses.

To the north was an unknown frozen land where it was rumored Frost Giants ruled. To the west was a vast ocean that it is said flowed off the face of the Earth into never ending nothingness. To the south across the Tyrrhenian Sea was a land of steaming jungles where great beasts roamed. To the east were ancient kingdoms, where it is said the ghosts of the Elder Gods feast on the souls of unwary travelers.

Looking into these skies, no airliners with their blinking lights and fifty plus passengers sailed overhead. The only satellite that looked down on us on this night was the face of the moon.

*   *   *

About half a day's ride from Rome we came around a bend in the road and ran right into what looked like an ambush. Actually, the ambush had already happened.

Four guys, who looked a lot like cutthroat thieves were beating the hell out of a chubby old man dressed in dark robes beside his covered wagon. They were backhanding the older guy and demanding that he tell them where he had gold hidden.

The old man wasn't telling them anything. So they were going to kick his ass some more. He was bleeding from the lips and nose.

The four didn't see us until we were right on top of them. With a glance between us to communicate what we were both thinking we went after the assholes.

I can't tell you why I went after those guys so fast. I'm not a hero or anything like that. Maybe it's just knowing that someday I'm going to be old and I'd like it if somebody helps me out when I get there.

Johnny got to them a fraction of a second before I did. A big ugly looking guy, with a dull expression on his face like he'd been kicked once too often by a horse, yelled, "You'd best mind your own…"

That's when Johnny's foot landed upside his head and knocked him to his back in the dirt. If that boy hadn't been kicked once too many times in the head, Johnny was out to correct that.

We both dismounted and two of the three guys still on their feet drew knives and one drew a short sword. They charged us.

Three common thugs who don't know shit and don't have long swords charging two guys who just broke out of a gladiator school is not a good idea.

Johnny was in some kind of a Bruce Lee mood. He whipped out his sword like a Samurai, held it over his head, and met the charge of the three all by himself.

I would have hopped right into the middle of it but the way Johnny was swinging that blade of his around I had to give him some room. If I wouldn't have backed off he probably would have taken a chunk out of me by accident.

The two with the knives darted at Johnny with their knives held out in front of them. Just like Samurai Delicatessen chopping bologna for sandwiches, Johnny sliced both their hands off cleanly at the wrists.

Johnny had a look on his face like I probably had back in that courtyard when I practically fell in love with my sword. It was a combination of blood lust and concentration. There was nothing he wanted more in the world than to see all three of these guys dead in the road.

The two fell away screaming about their lost hands.

Johnny moved on to the third guy who didn't look too excited about a fight where the odds were even up. Beating up on an old man with two friends to help was more his speed. He wasn't given a choice in the matter.

Leaping into him and howling like a banshee Johnny ripped the others sword loose from his grasp with a savage backstroke then nearly ripped him in half with a swing of his sword that any major league home run king would be proud of.

The two that were still alive vanished into the bushes at the side of the road. The other guy's blood spewed out into the dirt in the road. He shuddered out his last breath.

The guy Johnny booted in the head was getting to his feet now.

I drew my sword, kissed the blade and smiled at him. He chased his buddies into the bushes.

We turned to the man who we had just rescued.

CHAPTER 39
Welcome to Rome

Johnny helped the old guy sit down and lean back against the wheel of his wagon. I got him some water.

He had the look of some kind of a cleric with his non-callused hands and round soft face, but he sure wouldn't have passed for a Catholic Priest with his shaved head and purple robe.

In his own way the old dude was kind of tough. Although he was chubby, physically weak and the robbers had kicked his ass, he was still trying to not show his pain as much as he could.

After he'd taken a long drink from my water flask, through swollen and bleeding lips he said, "I offered them food, but they refused it. I only carried enough money to get the supplies for the Brothers." He indicated the wagon which we later saw was filled with a good supply of fruits and vegetables.

"They would have killed me if it wasn't for the two of you. Thank you. For as long as you need, the Brothers of Isis will shelter and feed you. We are eternally grateful."

Johnny and me glanced at each other. We both knew what the other was thinking. The last time we'd heard the name Isis was from that guy in Johnny's bar who had the portal below the Masonic Lodge in Cahokia. If they got another one of those portals, when we get the girls, this might be our plane ride home.

"Seeing as we don't have your local discount Diners Club card with us," Johnny told the old guy. "We'll be happy to accept the Brother's hospitality."

We helped the old guy get himself together and when we stood him up he shook our hands. "My name is Marius," he told us and the strength of his grip surprised me.

Maybe the Brothers of Isis take a vow of chastity and develop a good grip because of that, I thought.

"And what might your names be?" He asked and we told him our real names because in this world we were totally unknown anyway. Hell, I could have told him I was Mr. Magoo and Johnny was Corky the Clown and it wouldn't have made a difference.

We traveled that day sitting in the wagon with Marius. Marius insisted on handling the reins and our horses were tied to the back of the wagon.

I was happy to be out of the saddle. The inside of my legs were chafing from so much riding. I was beginning to wonder how cowboys got such a reputation for being studs anyway. All that bouncing up and down on your nuts all day can't be doing them very much good. Maybe the cows talk and give them that reputation.

Nights out on the range can get lonely and a big mooing cow looking at a guy with those big old cow eyes, well things could happen.

*   *   *

Marius wasn't a bad conversationalist. Once he got over his lips being sore as hell, he became the most talkative monk-looking guy I'd ever been around.

When he asked us what we were doing going to Rome I told him that we were farmers whose bad crops had forced us off of our lands. The look he gave us told us that he knew it was a lie.

"All right, I'll come clean with you. We were the personal guards of the King of Siam," Johnny said. "John fucked the King's favorite concubine and that was OK till she wanted to fuck me too but I told her she was too damn ugly for my black dick, so she told the King we raped her and we had to leave real quick before they chopped our heads off."

Marius laughed at that. "I don't believe that either but it's a better story than the first one."

"You're an asshole," I told Johnny.

"For what?" He asked.

"For lying to Marius like that," I told him. To Marius I said, "He's the one that fucked that ugly bitch. I didn't. If he knew how to sling his meat right, we'd still be living high on the hog."

For the next hour after that, Marius told us what an incredible city Rome was.

Rome, the eternal city, has the highest buildings, the most people, the best restaurants, and the best entertainment. The list went on and on. By the time we got there, I really expected to see something fantastic.

Maybe for this time Rome was something incredible. For two average Midwestern city boys from East St. Louis, Rome wasn't shit.

The same kind of stink that met us outside Micea before we saw that city assailed us outside Rome. The thing is, the smell this time was stronger and hit us farther out. The aroma of raw sewage and the body odors of millions of people packed close together who didn't take regular baths was eye watering.

We passed into the city down an avenue where all kinds of vendors sold things of all sorts. Everything was on sale, from bladed weapons to furniture, to fruits and vegetables, and even prostitutes were out there selling themselves.

One thing about the shopkeepers at these open air stores were that they weren't the same kind of sales people we see back home in K-Mart or Safeway. All these shopkeepers were heavily armed, tough looking, sons of bitches.

I found out why when we passed one of the food stands and a guy tried a grab and dash on a hanging chicken. The shopkeeper cut him down in mid-stride before he got three steps away with a chop to the leg with a short sword.

The shopkeeper dusted off the chicken and hung it back up. The would-be thief crawled off down the road, his thigh spurting blood.

I never thought I'd hear myself say it, but I was beginning to appreciate the police force back in my neck of the woods. There, at least most people didn't have to fight for survival on a daily basis. Here, the strong take what they want and anything you have, you have to fight to keep.

We passed a few of the tourist spots and Marius gushed over them before we got to the Temple of Isis. The only tourist spot that impressed me was the Coliseum.

Now that was a big stadium.

I'd gone to Busch Stadium back in St. Louis a few times and drove past it more times than I even know. Busch Stadium was big but the Coliseum made it look like a midget. And it was made completely of stone, too, by slave labor. I don't want to even think about how many people they beat to death to get that thing built.

As we rode past the Coliseum a huge roar erupted from inside that made goose bumps jump up on my arms. Probably some poor bastard just got his head cut off or something.

Yeah, the noble Romans do love their sports.

We rode on.

About a half hour later, we arrived at the Temple of Isis.

CHAPTER 40
Beneath the Temple

The Temple of Isis was a modest place. It looked like a medium sized stone elementary school house to me. Inside the wood double doors was first a large room that had wooden pews all in rows. Strangely this first room reminded me of an old fashioned Southern Baptist Church.

There was a guy standing behind a pulpit who was speaking to ten of the robed Brothers spread throughout the room. The Brothers of Isis were listening intently but it didn't sound like he was preaching to them. It sounded more like a business meeting than anything else.

"That is Brother Clovis," Marius told us, motioning toward the speaker. "I'll introduce you in a moment."

Clovis wrapped up his little speech by giving out work assignments, things like, who was going to sweep the floors, fix the meals and empty the piss and shit buckets. Glad he didn't know we were back there. If he'd have told me to empty anyone's crap, I'd have had to tell him where to shove that bucket.

The Brothers dispersed and Marius waved to Clovis and he came down to greet us wearing a warm smile.

"Brother Marius," Clovis said. "I am relieved to see you back. With so many bandits out in the countryside, I had some concerns about letting you go outside the city to get cheaper prices for our supplies. You don't look like your journey was uneventful." He indicated the bruises on Marius's face.

"That is why these two gentlemen are with me," Marius said introducing the two of us. "If it wasn't for them, I would be laying dead on the side of the road." He told Clovis what happened outside the city.

"We are in your debt," Clovis told us. "Anything the Brothers of Isis have, we will share with you."

"Well, we could use some grub," I told Clovis.

"I'm getting hungry as hell," Johnny agreed.

Clovis led us to a place that was like a cafeteria and got us a bowl of something that was like beef stew. It didn't taste bad either. While we were eating he asked us about who we were.

We gave him a condensed version of the story that we told Marius, about being guards for the King of Siam.

He smiled at that.

"It is interesting that you should be coming from that part of the world," Clovis said. "There won't be any trade between the European nations and the South Eastern Asian countries for, oh, I'd figure at least seven hundred years yet."

Johnny and me looked at each other.

Clovis' smile broke into an even wider grin. "Michael Clovis from Dallas, Texas," He said and extended his hand. "From the way you talk I'm guessing you two are from the twentieth century as well. What really brings you to our enlightened city?"

We shook his hand and since it didn't seem to make any difference, this time told him the truth that we were hunting for two kidnapped women from our own time.

*   *   *

After we described the women we were looking for, Clovis sent one of the Brothers, a guy named Anthony, out to ask around at the different slave markets to see if any Oriental type females had been bought in the last few months. Orientals were rare in the heart of the Roman Empire, so if they had been sold here we should find out.

Then he told us a little about himself.

Michael Clovis was studying to become a Catholic priest back in Dallas. He aimed at becoming a priest because he wanted to help people. He wanted to do the things that conscientious Christians want to do like feed and house the poor and help the abused learn how to live better lives.

What he was learning how to do at the seminary was to become a politician who wore a white collar; he found out quickly that being a good Catholic priest and being a good man were too very different things.

Part of Michael Clovis' training involved an internship at a ghetto church under another priest. While there, he was invited to observe a secret ceremony of the Cult of Isis in a factories' basement. It was then that he met the Goddess Isis in the flesh and found his calling in life to be a social worker in the Roman Empire of Caligula's era.

At this place in history, a lot of people were in need of a helping hand. Clovis was going to do what he could.

* * *

After we finished eating, Clovis and Marius showed us the room where their portals were. I think they had the feeling that soon we were going to be in need of a speedy exit. I had that feeling myself.

Beneath the Temple of Isis there was a stairway that led down into the Earth. After about fifty stone steps we came to a steel door. By the light of the torch that Marius held all of this looked extremely similar to the entrance to the portal room back in Cahokia.

All the places where these portals were, this room, the one on Cahokia and the one in Viet Nam gave you a feeling of being disconnected from everything else. When you head down the steps and step through the steel door it's as though the rest of the world doesn't exist. You are suddenly separated from everything else. It's as though you are in another dimension where time and space does not exist. I know you're hearing the theme song from *The Twilight Zone* in your head now, I don't give a fuck. That's just how it is.

Inside the portal chamber beneath the Temple of Isis were four stone ovals. There were eight of the Brothers sitting on the floor, two in front of each portal, meditating and chanting.

All four of the doorways were active. The high pitched screeching I'd heard from the other portals was absent this time. We could see the yawning distant winking of the stars inside the center of the stone ovals.

Johnny asked Clovis, "Where do they go to?"

"We don't know," Clovis answered. "We don't use them. The Goddess just tells us to keep them open. It is not for us to understand why."

"So when we go through one," I asked, "We're just taking our chances, right?"

"All of life is a chance," Clovis answered. "Would you have it any other way?"

"This time I would," I told him.

CHAPTER 41
Lost Forever

At the top of the stairs we were met by Anthony, that guy Clovis sent to gather information about Sherry St. Clair and Sushi. He seemed to be nervous. He consciously avoided eye contact with Johnny and me.

"I need to speak to you in private," Anthony told Clovis.

"If it's something about what happened to those women, one of them is mine! You tell us now!" Johnny said. He didn't look like he was in the mood to be playing checkers.

After a moment of awkward silence, when I was certain that Johnny was going to begin Jap-slapping Anthony upside the head, Clovis told Anthony. "Tell us all what you have found out."

"Those two women are lost to you forever," Anthony told us. "I'm sorry to tell you that they were bought about six weeks ago." He took a deep breath and placed a hand on Johnny's shoulder. "They were bought by the Emperor Caligula himself."

*　　*　　*

It surprised the hell out of me how well Johnny kept control of himself. He acted as though everything was OK. He thanked Anthony, Clovis and Marius for everything and asked where the Emperor was.

We were given directions to the palace where the Emperor stays when in Rome. Then Johnny said we would just go over there and attempt to buy the women back tomorrow. I was tempted to say, "Buy them back with what?" We didn't have that kind of money, but I kept my mouth shut.

After that, we asked for a place to sleep.

The Brothers directed us to a small spare room and while resting on two cots by the dying evening sun we talked.

"So, where's all this money you got hid?" I asked Johnny.

"Ain't got no fuckin' money. You know that." He answered.

"Didn't think so," I told him. "So, we're just going to take a short little nap and pay the Big Boss a visit tonight."

"You learn quick," he said.

"Only because I taught you," I told Johnny.

CHAPTER 42
To the Palace

It must have been around midnight when Johnny was shaking me by the shoulder to wake me up. I was in a deep dream where Julia was wrapping her thick African lips around my Irish sausage and reached out my hands to guide to her head farther into my crotch.

"Mother fucker!" Johnny said and that woke me up completely. "I will bust you upside your goddamn gourd head."

I sat up, and then stood up. "Didn't know who the hell you were there." I told him.

"No shit." He answered.

We got dressed, buckled on our swords and crept out of the Temple of Isis and into the street.

After retrieving our horses from the Brothers' stables we rode down the street toward where Caligula's palace in Rome was. The streets were torch lit just like in Micea. There wasn't much difference in the nightlife on the streets of Micea and the streets of Rome.

The prostitutes were out and so were the drunks and the gangs of tough guys who would slit your throat for what was in your money pouch. We rode our horses down the street with our swords out and resting across the horses' backs ready to be used at any moment.

We passed into a better neighborhood a half mile before we got to Caligula's palace. On the border of this neighborhood was a horse boarding stable. We woke the guy who ran the stables up by banging on his door. He was pissed off until we agreed to pay him twice the rate for boarding our horses for one night.

From there, we went on foot.

Passing into this Patrician or "upper class" area the first thing I noticed was the difference in streetlights and that there actually did appear to be some sort of a police force.

In the other parts of the city, the torches burning to light the streets were pretty much randomly distributed. There would be a torch placed in front of a tavern or a whore house by the people who owned the businesses so customers could find the way to what was being sold inside. But there was no plan to the city's night lighting at all. Some streets were pitch black except for what moonlight was shining down.

In the Patrician area, where the Senators and the Emperor of Rome were staying, burning torches were evenly spaced and all of them were lit. The torches were roughly about one hundred feet apart and the illumination they provided wasn't half bad.

It wasn't as good as the streetlights back in the good old U.S, of A, but it was enough so that the guards marching around on these streets had a good view of what was going on.

The police force I mentioned were groups of threes of Roman soldiers who were patrolling the streets in the Patrician neighborhood. I was guessing that it was the same here as everywhere else, even back in our time in the USA. The rich get the best protection, the best that money can buy. Everybody else gets what's left over. In Rome, that didn't amount to shit.

As soon as we entered this neighborhood we ducked behind some bushes to keep from being seen by these guards. The way we were dressed, they would know immediately that we didn't belong here. Any questioning by them and we couldn't give good answers.

So, we played it like what we were, thieves in the night. Only these two thieves were out to steal two women and take them back to where they belong.

Johnny hadn't been saying very much since he woke me up. He was all business tonight. No playing around. I figured one good session of tongue-fu and fuck-fu with Sushi would put Johnny back to being himself.

But, who the fuck was going to cure my bad mood?

Well, maybe I'll talk to Sherry St. Clair about that. I get Sherry out of this mess and she'd owe me big time, and I'm the kind of guy who likes to collect, especially when it means laying the meat to a sweet thing like Sherry.

We were sneaking through yards, jumping small stone walls and avoiding the foot soldiers patrolling the streets for maybe about an hour before we got to Caligula's estate.

You might wonder how we knew it was Caligula's palace so easily. Well, what was engraved on a huge stone tablet that was over the front steps to the massive house gave us a good clue.

Caligula: Emperor of Rome.

We snuck around back of the place. The building was about the size of a medium sized city courthouse. Come to think of it, it looked like one too, with its stone columns and wide steps in front of the building and arched roof.

I don't think I'd ever want to live in anything with a roof as high as that one. It would feel like I was sleeping in church.

Since there really was no easier way to do it, we decided to just find an open window or door, try to stay out of eyesight of any of the guards and just start looking in bedrooms.

Maybe it wasn't the most efficient way to go, but there really didn't seem to be any other way to search for the girls. This wasn't no damn hotel, where they had a sign-in desk and we could just ask what room they were in.

Finding an open door was no problem at all. The first door we came to in the back of the building was unlocked. It was kind of unnerving.

Johnny whispered to me in the darkness behind the building exactly what I was thinking. "This is too fucking easy," he said.

"Yeah, I know," I told him. "I'd expect the Emperor to have guards up the ass."

"Maybe he does that too," Johnny said. "I just expected him to be protected a lot more than this."

We bypassed the first door without even looking in.

We checked the next door.

It was unlocked also.

"I don't know what the fuck is going on here," Johnny said. "But I'm not staying out here all night. I'm going in to look for Sushi."

"And Sherry too," I reminded him.

"Yeah, right," he answered. I knew he didn't give a fuck about her. He was only here to take his woman home.

We entered in through that second unlocked back door and with swords out crept down a dimly lit shiny marble corridor.

We searched the first floor moving like shadows in the night. No one was on the first floor. Not even a guard, asleep or awake. The first floor looked like it was reserved for meetings and banquets. There were only a lot of couches and chairs, some tables and decorations like statues and paintings.

The idea of there being no guards inside was strange as hell to us.

We came to a central staircase and after passing a look between us, started up.

The stairway was wide and open. If there were any guards at the top they couldn't help but see us. That was the weird thing though. We weren't running into any guards at all.

The place had a strange unearthly silence about it, a kind of hush almost as though the walls themselves felt a need to be quiet.

Large windows opened on the front of the building. When we reached the top of the stairs the moon came from behind the clouds and illuminated the entire inside of the building.

The entire place looked deserted. In the bright moonlight if any guards had been posted we would have seen them from the top of the stairs and they would have seen us.

But, there was no one there.

We moved along the marble walkway to the right of the stairs and came to the first door. Turning the latch I carefully pushed the door open.

It was a bedroom.

There was a candle burning beside a large well cushioned bed. A naked female ass peeked out from under the covers. It was a nice looking ass too. The long blond hair on the pillow told us she wasn't one of the women we were looking for.

Too bad I was busy tonight, I thought. If I wasn't, I'd slip right in that bed and play hide the salami.

CHAPTER 43
Hello Darlin'

Everyone was sleeping soundly.

It was after the fourth door we opened that we found what we came for. Stretched out on silk sheets, naked as the day she was born, her breath coming in the rhythm of a deep snooze, was Sushi.

That may have been my best friend's woman on that bed laying with her mouth partially opened and the rest of her exposed but at that moment she looked like a machine that was built for fucking.

Johnny went to the bed. I turned my back to them and made like I was guarding the door.

From the bed came a startled little cry, then Johnny was saying, "Shhhhhh…, shhhhhh. It's me. I came to get you out of here," And he was hugging her and kissed Sushi.

"Where's Sherry?" I asked Sushi from over my shoulder.

"She was sent to the Coliseum," Sushi tossed back at us without hesitation. "She'll probably be fighting tomorrow."

There was something about the way she said it that just didn't sit right with me. I can't explain it, it was only a feeling. Her statement was too matter of fact, like it just didn't matter at all to her.

I turned away from the door to see Johnny trying to hand Sushi her clothes and having her push him away.

"Come on," he said. "We got to get the fuck out of here before some guards come." He pushed the clothes at her again.

"There are no guards," Sushi told Johnny. "Caligula is out of town on business, he's the most powerful man on earth. No one would even dream of stealing anything from him or hurting anyone in his household."

I looked at Johnny and he was looking at Sushi. A strange look was coming over his face, almost a hurt desperation.

"Sushi, come on Babe. I'm taking you home," he said.

"Oh Johnny," she answered. Sushi breathed heavily. "I can't go with you. I live like a queen here. I have my own slaves. This is my home now. You couldn't do this for me. This is the kind of life I need."

Shock came into Johnny's face.

"You're my woman," Johnny said. "I came to take you home." His voice had a pleading sound to it.

"I'm not your woman anymore," Sushi told him.

"So this is my goddamn Dear John speech after everything I went through to get to you? I was hung up on a mother fuckin' cross," he spit out. "I fucking did that for you!"

"This is my home now," Sushi said.

"I was in a mother fuckin' cage, like an animal," Johnny hissed at her.

"I'm sorry," Sushi said and reached out to wipe a tear off of his cheek.

Johnny slapped her hand out of the air in front of him. "Get the fuck out of my face," he said and Sushi did back away from him. She climbed back onto her bed, and pulled the blankets around her.

Then Johnny did something I never thought I'd ever see him do. He dropped down on his knees beside the bed and with tears pouring out of his eyes he cried, "I love you! Don't do this. Oh god, please don't do this. I don't know if I can live without you." Johnny buried his face in his hands and started weeping.

From the bed came a giggle. Sushi said, "You are really pathetic. You know that."

Johnny's head snapped up. The look he gave Sushi had pure murder in it.

That was my cue. I grabbed Johnny from behind and hauled him toward the door saying to him, "We got to get the fuck out of here!"

At the door he regained control of himself. Johnny marched out of the room. He was shaking so bad I knew he wanted to start screaming but somehow he held it back.

CHAPTER 44
On the White Horse

Johnny was silent as we moved through the massive house and exited through the back door we came in. In the darkness behind the huge structure he turned toward me.

"You know that wasn't really me in there acting like that," he said.

"You don't have to worry about it Bro," I told him. "Women will make you do some fucked up things."

"That just wasn't like me," he said.

"I know," I told him.

"I want to thank you for dragging me out when you did," he said. "I don't know what I would of done if you hadn't been there. Probably broke the bitch's neck."

We moved out of that section of town a hell of a lot faster than we came in. Johnny was leading the way and he was just about a hair away from being reckless. He was acting pretty much like he didn't give a shit. Which, I guess, he really didn't.

He was leaping stone walls and hedges like he was in a hurdles race. The only thing he didn't do was stand in the middle of the street and yell at the Roman patrols, "Hey mother fuckers, I'm over here! Come and get me if you got the balls." He was sure acting like he wanted to though.

I figured it was by pure luck that we made it past the border of the Patrician neighborhood without having to fight our way out.

As it was when we went to pick up our horses and woke the stable keeper up again, and when the guy complained Johnny told him flat out, "If you don't shut the fuck up, I'll cut your fuckin' head off!"

And the guy did shut up, so I couldn't argue with the results.

Riding back toward the Temple of Isis in the waning hours of the night Johnny asked me, "Have you ever really thought about how really fucked up this situation is?"

"Well, I know Sushi did you wrong," I told him.

"No, I'm talking about... like everything. The whole entire fucking deal between men and women, the whole thing is fucked up. A guy finds a woman he gives a shit about, a woman he loves and he'll bleed for her. He'll go through the tortures of hell for that woman.

"And what the fuck does he get back. He gets fucked a little bit and on a really good day when the woman is in a really charitable mood, she might just suck his dick some. Another thing, the thing that gets guys off the most is knowing they get the woman off. The thing that makes me feel the best is hearing the woman moan. Ain't that a bitch?"

"Most guys will work their entire fuckin' lives, giving their woman a good life, so she can sit on her ass and enjoy it and what does he get at the end? A fucking box in the ground, if he's lucky!

"I'm tired of the whole fucking deal. This riding in on a white horse to save the day shit is over for me. I ain't never doing this shit again."

I had to admit, I didn't want to go through this shit again either.

*   *   *

We rode the rest of the way back to the Temple of the Brothers of Isis in silence. When we got there we boarded our horses in their stables and headed to our room. It was just getting light outside.

I figured we'd go to the room and come up with a plan to go and get Sherry St. Claire.

When we got to the room I sat down on my cot and turned to Johnny, "All right," I asked, "You got any ideas as to how we can get down to the slave holding area at the Coliseum without getting killed so we can get Sherry?"

"I'm not going," Johnny snapped at me. "Like I said, I'm done with this hero shit. These bitches are going to have to get along without my help. I done learned my goddamned lesson. I'm going to get some sleep, then go down and hop some of these portals till I hit the right one."

I looked at Johnny. He'd lain back on his cot. I thought about whether or not I should just jerk him off that fucking cot and punch some fucking sense into his head.

To tell you the truth, I didn't blame him one bit.

"Fuck it," I told him and stood up and buckled my sword back on. "I'm heading down to the Coliseum. I'll think of something on the way. I don't need your fucking help anyway."

CHAPTER 45
At the Coliseum

By the time I got my horse from the Brother's stables the sun had just come up. The day time vendors were coming out and setting up their wares. The night time vendors were packing up and leaving.

Most of the night time vendors had been skanky looking prostitutes. That was one thing that hadn't changed from this time to the twentieth century. The street prostitutes mainly came out after dark. I didn't know why that was. Even if the laws in force in Rome made it illegal for street walkers to be screwing in broad daylight there didn't seem to be enough of a police force to enforce the laws. Maybe these Romans were too shy to make balling in daylight profitable.

As for myself, I didn't give a shit. I'd take a blowjob at high noon on the county courthouse steps and grin at the Chief of Police as I shot a wad of spunk in a chick's eye. You gotta be bold or you get old. Come to think of it, you do get old anyway. So why not be bold?

I rode toward the Coliseum.

People were dragging out the stuff they were going to sell that day. Shoemakers had those Roman sandals most Romans wore hanging from ropes. They also had some crude types of leather boots. If I was planning on staying in Rome forever, I'd get me a pair of those.

There were people selling plates and bowls of either wood or pottery. Other guys were selling knives and swords.

I stopped at a place, bought a joint of beef, and ate it as I rode down the street. In the early morning sunshine, these were some sweaty stinky people going about their everyday business of living from day to day. Most of these people couldn't even dream of a world like the one that would be here in about two thousand years.

I had to keep reminding myself to never forget what my world had been like.

*   *   *

The large circular avenue was blocked off from all traffic except for foot travel. So I again paid to have my horse boarded at a stable just off the main street leading to the Coliseum.

The money I'd taken in Micea was dwindling fast. Most of it was going to sticking my horse in horse hotels. I walked on foot to the playing field, where the game was death.

The Roman Coliseum: the most famous sports arena the world has ever known. The contests played on this field were played for the most basic reward. The winner lives. The loser dies.

Somewhere in there was Sherry St. Claire. I wasn't going to leave without her.

If I have to guess as to the Coliseum's height, I'd have to put it at around forty stories high. Not as tall as some buildings in our time, but this thing was big around too. Was it a mile around, two miles? I don't know. I only know that it is one hell of a big fucking building when you're standing next to it.

Throngs of people were milling about on the wide avenue outside the arena. Most of the vendors out there were selling food and refreshments of all kinds to enjoy while watching the fighters hack each other to pieces.

There were a lot of entrances into the seating in the arena. This kind of surprised me until I was told all seating was free. You were just given a ticket and a seat number on the way in to keep people from fighting over the best seats. The shows were all free.

This was the one area, at least on the street outside the Coliseum, where it looked like all the classes of Rome mingled together. You'd see the dirt poor peasant lining up right next to the Roman Senators to get their seats for that day's bloodshed. Kind of heartwarming isn't it, seeing what will bring people together, witnessing the blood and guts and pain of your fellow man. Pain and death are a great equalizer. No matter who you are, no matter how rich and famous you are, you're going to get pain and death at some point in your life.

I walked around among the people in the street. I didn't want to just go in and get me a seat. I wasn't here to watch the show. I was here to try to stop someone from being a part of it.

Different barkers were yelling about what they were offering from boxes and holding up samples of wine, legs of lamb or turkey legs for people to see.

People were bustling about.

Then I heard this guy yelling about how he was taking bets on the fights and another guy close by him was handing out printed programs of what order the fights were going to take place in and who was fighting who.

The guy handing out the programs were giving them out for free, so I grabbed one.

The program was very crudely printed. In fact, I think it was just stamped on the stuff they used for paper. They had the beast hunt listed first, after that some executions, then some caestus bouts, after that were some women's weapons fights.

I wasn't really interested in what was after that because listed in the women's bouts was the name Sherra, slant-eyed barbarian who spurned the Emperor's offer of sacred love. That sounded like Sherry to me.

Sushi obviously didn't turn down Caligula, probably jumped on his pole like a crazed tongue-fu master. That's why she's living so well and Sherry is being fed to the slaughter.

Another name caught my eye in the caestus matches before Sherry's fight. Phonetically, it came out as, Pabow Paaz, barbarian fist fighter. I was guessing that was my friend Julio "Padre" Paez. Well, I was here to get Sherry. Besides, Pablo is a man. I wish him luck, but I got to do what I came here for.

It was early enough so even the morning beast hunt had not begun.

The guy who was taking bets started having an argument with a guy over the odds he was giving.

"How can I know if what you are saying about these fighters is true?" The guy questioning the odds shouted. "I haven't seen any of these fighters."

"Then go see them," the odds maker yelled back. "They are down there on display in the holding area. Pay the guards. They will let you take a good look. Go see if I don't give good odds."

That was all I needed to hear.

I headed in the direction of the entrance with the intention of getting as close to Sherry as I could.

CHAPTER 46
Beneath the Coliseum

I waited through the line and got my ticket for my seat. The line wasn't very long, so it didn't take but about a half hour. It felt like I was waiting for weeks.

Inside the stadium the seating was divided up like it had been in the arena where I fought. The different social and economic classes had their own sections. I looked so ragged that morning that I was given a ticket to the section of society that was barely above being a slave.

I stopped a guy hurrying by and asked him where I had to go to get a look at the fighters. He pointed to an archway about fifty feet away that had a ramp that led downward and hurried on by.

There was a constant stream of people coming and going out of that archway and the mingled together sounds of hundreds of people conversing. I walked through the arch and went down.

The stone ramp led downward for what must have been about two floors. There wasn't any daylight down here. The lighting was provided by torches protruding from the walls at regular intervals and other small fires people had built wherever they felt like it.

These looked like the catacombs of Rome. Tunnels beneath the city where the dead were buried, the thing is the people in these tunnels were very much alive and kicking.

People had shops set up down there. People had homes set up down there. And down there, the streetwalkers were out in force. What I'd said before about the Romans being too shy to make daytime balling profitable, down there, they proved me wrong.

The whores below ground were sucking and fucking guys in any open space they could find, up against walls, right in the middle of the walkway, they didn't care. They'd just get that damn money and drop those drawers right where they were.

There were sex shows too. As if there wasn't enough of a show going on for free? There were tents up and guys shouting outside them that for a single denarius you could watch a virgin fuck a mastiff hunting dog or an experienced professional deep throat a horse. It was a case of either roll over Rover or let's give Mr. Ed something to talk about.

I've heard these kind of shows are still going on down in Mexico in the twentieth century. I didn't care to go down there to see that. I sure didn't want to see it here either. One thing was always going to be true about people, there always had been degenerates and there always would be.

I bypassed that and asked another guy where I could get a look at the fighters. He pointed me to a side tunnel.

*   *   *

The tunnels down here were as wide as narrow streets were on the surface. This was like a complete city beneath the city. Everything they had up top, they had down here except for the daylight.

Following the path I'd been pointed to, the road led upward then leveled off where I figured I must be at the same level as the arena floor.

I don't know how far I walked, a couple of hundred yards maybe before the tunnel came to an end. There were people standing at a fence made of iron bars. In front of them, in rows of cages just like the one I had been in in Micea were slaves that were waiting their turn to fight.

To the side of the tunnel there was a steel gate that opened out onto the arena floor. A lot of people were looking through the bars at the prisoners. Some of the guys on this side of the bars were betting on what slaves they thought would make it through the day.

I shouldered my way up to the bars of the fence and looked through, searching for Sherry. I could barely see her through the bars of six cages. She was standing up and looking out at the arena floor.

The beast hunt was in full swing now. Animals were being slaughtered left and right. Sherry watched this. She didn't look frightened but she didn't look very happy to be where she was either. Physically, Sherry St. Clair appeared to have handled her captivity well.

She was wearing the typical clothes for a slave girl. A short skirt with a loose tied at the waist toga top and lace up sandals. There were no visible bruises on Sherry so if she had taken some beatings the marks were already healed. Sherry's light cardboard colored brown skin still looked flawless. She was in a bad situation, but she was looking good.

Sherry might have been dressed like a slave but her posture, her entire body attitude told anyone who saw her that she could never be a slave. She would never be submissive to anyone unless she chose to. This was a strong woman, strong in mind. Being told she was owned by someone wouldn't change that.

I spotted at least four guards from where I was and this slave holding area was so large that I couldn't see where it ended. Calling out Sherry's name and yelling to her was out of the question.

A guard who was wearing a bad attitude walked close enough to the bars so that I could talk to him.

"Hey," I yelled, "I need to get in to see the fighters."

He ignored me.

"I'll pay you for a closer look," I shouted.

"No one gets in here," he shouted to me and everyone else against the bars.

"Come on," I said. "I was told that for a price we could get a close look. I want to make money on my wagers. Look, I'll give you a piece of what I win. I just got to see the fighters close up. I'm great at picking winners."

The guard stopped and looked at me directly.

"Last week Grondar was making money on the side doing exactly that," he said. "He was found out. This week he's in chains cracking rocks in the mines."

He walked away.

Well, that's fucking great, I thought. If I could have gotten on the other side of those bars at least I would have had a chance at surprising those guards and maybe letting a few slaves loose to help out and maybe pull this insane rescue off. I was so close to Sherry but from this side of the bars all I could do was watch her die.

The beast hunt was finishing up. The last animals were being cornered and chopped down.

The executions would come next. That wouldn't take very long. Then the caestus fights. After that Sherry St. Clair, a woman totally untrained in any combat would be handed a sword and be made to fight for her life.

She didn't stand a chance.

I had to figure a way to get her out of there and fast. Time was running out. The clock was ticking.

CHAPTER 47
The Smell of Rome

Trying to get to Sherry through this entrance was a dead end. I looked out through the bars that gave a view to the arena floor.

The executions were in progress. The announcer was listing the crimes of the accused and the victims were being dispatched. The people in the stands weren't even paying attention.

Most of the executions were a simple running through with a sword or having the throat cut. Only one of them was any different.

A guy was supposed to have burned his neighbor's house down with his neighbor and family inside. They stuck him inside a box with a hole for his head to stick out one end and his feet to stick out the other. Then they built a large fire and sat him on top of it.

His screams drew some light applause. Guess he won't be burning down any more houses.

I headed out in search of another way to try to get through another entrance to the slave holding area where Sherry was.

* * *

The ventilation down in the tunnels wasn't the best. With as many fires that were burning down here, I would have expected the smoke to be a real problem. But except for a slight burning of the nose, the smoke wasn't even noticeable. The thing that was bothering me about the ventilation down here as the day wore on was the way these rank sons of bitches smelled.

The day was getting warmer up top and more people were coming down to Sin City below the Coliseum. The more people that came down, the more it stank down here.

After a while it took on the smell of rotten milk and eggs mixed with piss and shit. People were crapping and pissing where ever the feeling hit them and to top it off so many whores were doing business that the air had a tinge of old cum to it.

It was a real nice place for a Saturday afternoon picnic.

After I'd run down a couple of side tunnels always trying to keep the arena floor to my left, I came back to another barred gate that lead onto arena floor.

This gate didn't have a side to it that lead into the slave holding area, only stone walls. Looking at it closely the gate didn't look like it had been used in a long time. It was rusted and kind of rickety.

The barbecuing of the guy in the box was over when I shouldered up to these bars. He was being dragged away and the fire was being put out.

I looked around and spotted two openings to the arena floor from the slave holding area where Sherry was.

The announcer started announcing the names of the pairs of fighters who were going to be fighting in the caestus matches. Five pairs were going to be fighting on the arena floor at the same time.

People were starting to gather in a crowd around me at the gate to watch the caestus fights. These must be popular contests with the people underground.

The combatants were coming out as they were introduced. It didn't surprise me a bit when they got to a pair that was fairly close to this gate and one of the fighters that ran out after being announced was Julio "Padre" Paez.

What did surprise me was that when the announcer had all the fighters turn and salute the people in the Royal box the one who sat in the large marble throne was the slim attractive lady who I'd seen in Micea when I'd fought there.

Sitting beside her, in his accustomed position of consort was none other than Caesar Lanista.

CHAPTER 48
Julio the Great

The caestus fights started and I didn't really have the time to just stand and watch Julio in his contest, even though I did want to see if he survived. Julio's opponent was a huge guy. He easily was over six foot four and weighed around two fifty.

A really big boy to be sure, he was announced as Saccus. What instantly worried me was that I knew what Julio's boxing style had been back in St. Louis. At his best, he was an aggressive wade in brawler that never backed up. He was a brave warrior.

Against an opponent with the size advantage as big as the one Saccus had over Julio, bravery will get you killed.

The guy came in swinging at Julio with punches designed to crush his skull. Julio surprised the hell out of me by slipping and dodging and landing a quick one-two, then moving away. Maybe Julio was learning a little bit in his old age, I thought.

He repeated this pattern of dodging, scoring and retreating three times.

After less than a minute and a half there were only two pairs of fighters still exchanging punches. Let's face it, most caestus fighters were idiots who didn't know what the fuck they were doing.

All three of the fights that were over ended the same way. The two guys ran at each other throwing wild ass punches. One shot connected, the fight was over. The loser got dragged away.

The match that was still going on besides Julio's was still in progress because those boys ended up on the ground wrestling. The way those guys were rolling around and clutching at each other and grunting I was beginning to wonder if they were trying to fuck instead of fight.

One got on top of the other guy and rained down three overhand blows that knocked his opponent unconscious. That romantic interlude was over.

Now the only pair left fighting was Julio and Saccus. The spectators in the stands were getting into this David and Goliath match-up and were cheering them on with gusto. The crowd around me was urging them on too.

I knew I had to get to figuring out another method to get to Sherry, but at the moment my options were limited. I just flat out did not have the time to explore all the underground passageways beneath the Coliseum.

The crowd gave a lusty cheer yet again when Saccus charged Julio and was skillfully fended off yet again and suddenly the tone of the audience changed.

I got to admit I was looking somewhere else trying to plan my next move when someone said, "I don't believe he just did that," and several other voices also expressed disbelief.

Julio had pointed to the bad cuts on Saccus's face and halted the action. Then he untied his own caestus and threw them off to the side in the dirt.

This was making Julio's David and Goliath match take on an epic feel. It was the same as if David had stopped his fight with Goliath after cracking him with that first rock and said, "Sorry about that. That wasn't really fair was it?" And threw away his sling and offered to start all over.

The crowd in the stands cheered Julio's incredible show of bravery and heart. The mob around me beat on the bars and chanted his name. Rust and dirt fell from where the bars were inlaid in the stone.

Julio acknowledged the cheers with but a polite nod of his head. I knew Julio didn't throw away his caestus as a grandstanding gesture. Julio genuinely didn't want to injure any opponent.

Julio is a nice guy. Too nice for this game.

The fight began again.

The pattern that Julio forced the fight into made me realize he wasn't as dumb as he'd always been acting. Saccus would come at him and he'd move, just a little, just a bit to the side, just enough so that Saccus couldn't have his feet set when Julio would stop and snap off some quick hooks to his ribs.

Whenever the openings were there, Julio would throw a quick flurry to the head just so Saccus never got used to where the punches would be going to next.

Julio was giving the much larger and stronger and younger Saccus a slow and methodical beating. It was a great exhibition of brains over brawn. This was the same game plan that Ray Leonard used to kick Marvin Hagler's ass.

Julio wasn't as skilled as Leonard, but he was making it work. And he was a huge hit with the mob in the stands and crowd around me.

After about twenty minutes of Julio raising knots all over Saccus's head, the audience started chanting his name.

Saccus was reduced to stumbling after Julio and eating pin-point counters by the time Julio scored his first knockdown.

When a guy has as good a left hook as Julio does, you don't dare miss a wild overhand right against him. Saccus threw a wild overhand right. Julio ducked it and came out of a crouch with a whistling left hook.

I could hear the loud pop from that punch even over the crowd's screams.

Saccus fell straight forward onto his face. Dirt flew up when he hit the ground.

He struggled to get to his feet. Blood ran from his nose and mouth.

"Please my friend," Julio said to him. "Do not get up. You have proved your bravery. You are a great warrior."

Saccus got up anyway.

When he lurched after Julio, he was dropped by a straight right that folded his legs up underneath him.

This time he lay on his back and spit blood into the air as the mass of people in the stands roared their approval.

This time Saccus would not be getting up.

Julio acknowledged the cheers and shouted for a doctor to be called.

Someone did come running out onto the field of death from a side door. It wasn't a doctor. It was a Roman soldier carrying an extra sword.

He stopped in front of Julio and handed him the sword.

The masses sounded like a rumbling title wave as Julio looked at the sword he clutched in his right fist.

His face expression showed confusion.

Then he understood and looked directly at the woman sitting on the throne in the royal box.

This was the same woman who ordered me to kill Torstan and I had refused. She stood with the red cloth in her hand having it wave in the wind. Julio shouted to her, "I will not kill this brave man."

Silence reined for a few very long heartbeats.

The slim attractive woman laughed. "I, Messalina, whose nephew is Caesar Caligula, decide what you do. You do not defy me!"

From the same door the soldier came from, four archers now marched out. They kneeled and took aim at Julio. Starting softly, then gradually gaining strength, the masses began chanting, "Pabow Paas...Pabow Paas...Pabow Paas..."

Messalina let the red cloth fall and Julio threw the sword in the dirt.

Julio raised his hands over his head and looked to the masses of blood crazed people. "A warrior does not have to be a killer," he shouted to them. "A man can be all things, merciful as well as strong."

The mob went wild cheering for Pablo. He was their hero, a gladiator warrior who actually thought for himself. Scattered shouts were mixed with the roar of the cheering.

"Julio the Great!" Someone shouted.

"Julio the Merciful!" Someone else shouted.

"Look at the bitch!" Came another yell. "She can't make him kill. Even in chains, he is free!"

The cheers were deafening. Never had a man stood as tall as when my short Mexican friend defied the Roman Royal family.

Messalina was white with rage at her order being ignored. One shout was heard above all others.

"Kill him!" Messalina screamed.

The archers let fly with a volley of arrows and Julio was shot clean through four times.

For a moment everything stopped.

Silence reigned.

Then all hell broke loose.

CHAPTER 49
Rioting Romans

Julio was dead, lying in the sand his blood mingled with all the others who died in this place of useless death. But his death would not be useless.

I yelled, "We've got to make her pay!" And grabbed the bars in front of me and shook them in a rage trying to tear them from their moorings. At that moment, I could have sworn that from all the way across the arena Caesar Lanista saw me. We locked eyes for an instant. By myself, even with the bars being rusted and old, I could never have ripped those bars loose, but the crowd around me was infuriated.

Everyone at the bars, at least twenty strong angry men took hold of the bars and started jerking them back and forth. Chunks of mortar fell where steel met stone.

Messalina's guard came out to protect her and Lanista. The mob started pelting them with rocks and garbage and anything they could get their hands on. The crowd erupted as a single screaming crazed mass and came down out of the stands and flooded into the killing field of the Coliseum's arena floor.

The bars in front of me ripped loose from the stone it was set in and with a loud clang fell forward onto the sand. We ran out onto the arena floor ready to kill anyone who stood in our way.

The masses attacked the four archers that killed Julio. The archers got off one more volley at the charging mob before they went down beneath them begging for mercy. They were shown the same kind of mercy Julio was given and were clubbed senseless, beaten until there was nothing left of them but broken dead corpses.

Messalina, Lanista and her guard retreated down a passageway out of the arena.

I headed directly for the nearest entrance to the slave holding area where Sherry was. The four guards in this area were at the gate to the underground. They were threatening and hacking at the rioting spectators on the other side of the iron bars that separated them.

Jamming my sword into the gate's latch where it kept the doors locked shut I wrenched with all my strength backward. I got to admit, the Romans did one thing really good. They made some good strong swords. The latch ripped loose and the gate came open.

I sprang into that slave holding area and confronted four desperate guards. They were between me and a wall of insane maniacs on the other side of that steel gate. Guess I didn't look as threatening as that wall of maniacs. A quick glance told me that Sherry St. Clair was watching me with wide eyed surprise. I think she couldn't believe who showed up to rescue her. In her shoes, I doubt I would have believed it either.

"Just throw me the keys," I yelled at the guards. "And you can get the fuck out of here. I got no fight with you, but I'm letting these people out."

Their answer to that was for all four of them to charge me. The strength of their charge drove me backward until my shoulders met the stone wall at the far end of the chamber. I was in there alone fighting four mean-ass guys. Just where the fuck was a crazed mob when you needed one anyway?

I was slicing and parrying and blocking, mostly blocking, when I got lucky and sliced one across the thigh and he backed off. Three to one now, but the way they were coming at me was designed to keep me working non-stop. They were taking turns attacking me conservatively and keeping a tight defense.

Things were not looking good because their intention was to tire me out and it was going to work unless something changed.

I was beginning to get winded when it did. The gate to the arena floor was thrown open and a single man charged the guards from behind.

The Black Avenger was back on the scene. Johnny ran one of the guards through before they knew they were under attack from behind.

The next two, like idiots backed against the front of cages and were grabbed from behind. I knew it wasn't very sporting for all four of them to charge me so I didn't feel bad when we ran them through with them being choked by slaves through the bars.

As we searched the guards to get the keys I said to Johnny, "What the hell are you doing here? I thought you went back to cry in your beer."

"Don't you know by now a brother can't resist a good riot," he said. "We smell them coming. I knew you couldn't finish this thing without me. So let's get Sherry and get home."

"I heard that," I told him.

*   *   *

Starting with Sherry's cell we unlocked all the slave cages. As the rest of the freed slaves flooded out through the gate and entered the fighting on the arena floor, Sherry came out and looked into my eyes deeply.

"You actually came for me," she said. "I'd given up all hope." She looked like she was going to break down and cry.

Johnny said, "Goddamn it, come on! We don't have time for no fuckin' cryin'. John'll come for any mother fuckin' woman, some farm animals too. Let's get the fuck out of here!"

We left the slave holding area and Sherry grabbed a sword from a dead guard. Everything around us was bedlam. The crowd was setting fire to anything that would burn. Johnny and me stayed on both sides of Sherry and hoisted her over the arena wall, then climbed it ourselves.

Anything that wasn't made of stone was starting to go up in flames. People were fighting and screaming and shouts were coming from everywhere. We fought our way to one of the main entrances with swirling insane masses of people around us fighting anything, and each other, in a mad destructive rage. We made our way to the archway where I came into the Coliseum.

The streets outside the Coliseum were even worse than what it had been inside. Things were just more spread out. The riot was in full swing out there.

Groups of people indiscriminately attacked shops and peddlers and merchants. The rioters set fire to everything. The collective consciousness was just to loot and destroy.

We kept close together and threatened anyone who came near us. Across an open space of violent chaos we headed to where I boarded my horse. Johnny saw the small stable where his horse had already been pulled down and the animals were gone. When we got to where my horse was boarded we saw that the owner was nailed to the door and the building was going up fast in flames. If anyone or anything was in there, they weren't getting out alive.

We set off on foot in the direction of the Temple of the Brothers of Isis.

CHAPTER 50
Through Flames

How long it took us to get to the temple is anybody's guess. It could have been one hour or it could have been five hours. It just seemed like it took us forever. I don't have a clue as to what goes through a man's mind when he's caught up in the frenzy that a riot is, but the people on the streets of Rome didn't seem like people anymore.

They were more like stampeding cattle, destroying anything in their path.

You would think that whoever was controlling the armies of Rome that were based in the city would send them out to restore order, but we saw no soldiers on the streets at all.

The riot spread swiftly ahead of us. The entire route we took back to the Temple of the Brothers of Isis was a battlefield.

*   *   *

When we got to the Temple it was being defended from looting and burning by Clovis and eight of the other Brothers who had bows and arrows. Theirs was the only building we'd seen that wasn't on fire.

We shouted who we were and waved. Clovis motioned us forward. We sprinted past their line of archers and Clovis took us into the temple. Once inside, we told Clovis all that happened since the night before and what had caused the outbreak of violence.

"It has happened before," he told us. "And for just about the same reasons. The mobs at the Coliseum cannot be controlled. Anything sets them off. The Legions are off conquering lands that Rome doesn't have the man power to control. They don't even have the man power to prevent anarchy in the streets."

"Thanks for the history lesson," I told Clovis. "Now we need to get this lady and ourselves back home."

He led us down the stairs into the chamber of the four portals. On the way down he reminded us that he had no idea where each of the portals went.

We stood in the room with the four humming portals and looked at each of them. They all looked the same to me. They were yawning doorways into other worlds.

Marius entered the room and shook our hands. "It has been a short friendship," he told us. "But I will miss you."

We told him we would miss him as well.

Since none of us knew where any of the portals lead I turned to Johnny and asked, "Does any of that Voodoo blood in your veins tell you which one of these gets us home?"

"My Voodoo blood don't tell me shit," he answered.

I asked Sherry, "Does your women's intuition tell you which one we should go through?"

She smiled. "My woman's intuition seems to be on vacation."

"All right," I told them and took Sherry's hand in mine. "Grab Johnny's hand." I told Sherry.

She did.

I pointed to the portal directly in front of us. "Let's go," I shouted and trailing them behind me took a running leap into the screaming vortex.

PART IV

In the dark backward and abysm of time…
-Shakespeare, The Tempest, I,2

Revenge is not sweet. It is bitter!
But then again, so is the strongest liquor.
-The Walker in Darkness

CHAPTER 51
Under a Blood Red Sky

We dove straight into the endless nothingness of the cold vastness of interstellar space and instantly burst into flames. The sensation was the same as before but I doubt if I took a leap through those vortexes a thousand times that I would ever get used to it. It was like being dipped in boiling oil.

I don't think that I'll ever eat freshly boiled lobster again because I know what kind of pain they went through just before they died. My skin felt like it was melting away and it seemed like it would go on forever.

The thought ran through my mind, what if the doorway wasn't open on the other end? Would we just career around the universe forever in pain? Then there was a doorway in front of us in the distance.

Something darker, a solid blackness stood out among the twinkling lights of the distant stars of the cosmos. It was coming closer, or we were flying toward it, three flaming comets in an eternal night.

The solid blackness was growing larger, more distinct against the celestial background. If this pitch blackness meant the doorway was shut then I knew we would blast ourselves to nothingness against it.

We flew through the doorway and skidded and rolled on hard dirt. I landed partially on my face like before. That was all right. Anything was better than feeling the skin frying from by bones.

But we were still in pitch blackness. That must have been why the doorway had been so black. It was darker than the bottom of a grave in there.

"Is everybody OK?" I asked,

Sherry answered first. "I seem to be all right. Where are we?"

"We in the dark, Goddamn it," Johnny said.

"We are there," I agreed.

The first thing I noticed before my eyes adjusted to the almost total absence of light was that where we were smelled strongly of ash. I can't explain it any other way. It was like you stuck your face in an ashtray and sucked in through your nose real hard. Not an appetizing smell, I can tell you.

Then my eyes did adjust and I was seeing what light there was to see. Ahead of us or in front of me anyway, were two lines of red light. They were a little in front and above us. I didn't know what it was but I wasn't going to sit there forever.

I told the others, "I'm going to find out what the hell that is."

"We're all coming," Johnny said. "In horror movies the black man always gets killed because he stays behind to do some stupid bull shit. I say fuck that."

"I wish this was a movie," Sherry said. "Then I could just leave the theatre."

Edging my way along, I felt on my side for the sword I had grown accustomed to hanging there. It was still at my side. I drew it now.

It wasn't but about five paces in the dark before my foot met a stone step.

I ran my left hand over the clothes I wore.

"Johnny," I said. "Do you realize we're still dressed as Romans?"

"Yeah, I noticed how I was dressed," he answered. "Wait a second, I'll run my hands over Sherry and tell you what she's wearing."

"Touch me, and I'll cut your hand off," Sherry said.

"Goddamn," Johnny answered. "Second time I get rejected in two mother fucking days. A goddamn fuckin' record."

"I'm betting we're not at home," I told them as I ascended the stairs with my left hand held out in front and above me.

After about eight or nine stairs my knuckles rang on a steel plate.

"I think I'm at a door," I told the others and pushed upward on the left hand side of it. Nothing gave. So I slid my hand to the other side and just before I got to the red line I pushed up.

With a loud groaning that only long rusted metal against metal makes, the door swung upward just about a foot before it stopped cold.

"Come on up here. I need some help," I told Johnny and Sherry stepped to the side.

Johnny got up beside me. "White man always gets the niggers to do the muscle work," he told me.

I kind of chuckled. "You're gonna be back to normal pretty soon," I told him. "I can tell. You'll bounce back."

"Yeah," he said and we put our shoulders to the door. "Like fuckin' never."

We pushed up with all the strength that our legs had. With a loud scream, the steel trap door above us came loose and we flung it wide open.

We were out in the open air, on the crest of a rounded hill. The sky was one we had never seen before. It was blood red, the color of deep scarlet thick blood.

Clouds flew past at dizzying speeds, black wispy clouds. They looked like enormous flying black veils. From the thicker clouds lightning bolts shot down and exploded sending sprays of dry dirt flying up into the air. And there was a lot of lightning hitting the ground. It seemed like hundreds of bolts were hitting the ground at once.

The land vibrated beneath our feet like a massive base drum was being pounded from under us.

Everything was ash and devastation. I could see no plants at all and no evidence that mankind had ever lived here.

"What the fuck is this?" I whispered and took a few steps away from the steel trap door.

The ground moved to my left. I glanced that way and a flap of Earth erupted up and "It" flew out at me too quick for the eye to track.

A shaggy thing the size of a horse only with eight legs, it was silvery, thickset, low to the ground, and knocked me from my feet before I even knew it was there.

Only one thing registered in my mind as it charged me as I lay on my side. "This is one big mother fucking spider!"

It grabbed me by the leg with some pincher things that came out of its mouth that felt like steel and started dragging me toward the hole it had hurtled out of.

Sherry screamed a blood curdling cry and that was probably what saved me. The thing froze in its tracks.

Thank god my sword was still in my hand. I managed to get a good swing at its head. It lifted one of its legs to block the swing and I cut that leg in half.

It screeched at me, a screech that sounded like a cross between a sea gull cry and a train braking.

Then Johnny was on it hacking and screaming, "You big ugly mother-fucking bug you! We need some fucking Raid!"

I got another good slice into the thing's side and got spurted all over my face with sticky green spider blood. Johnny jumped forward and hacked a straight slash right down on top of the spider's head that also splashed me with green blood by the bucket full.

The thing let go of me and skittered backward screeching at us. No doubt it was cussing us out.

We'd spoiled its dinner.

I stood up and wiped some of the spider slime from my eyes. Sherry moved up close to Johnny and me. We took a good slow look around us.

In hundreds of places we could see flaps of Earth lift up slightly and could see eight eyes peek out at us. They were all waiting for us to just take one step too close to their home, so they could spring on us and drag us down.

"What do you say we head back out the door we came in?" I told Sherry and Johnny.

"Smartest thing you said all fuckin' week," Johnny answered.

"On three," Sherry whispered.

"Yeah," The two of us agreed.

"Three!" Sherry yelled and we all ran back down the trapdoor and slammed it behind us.

We could hear the beating of spider feet on the steel door from above our heads.

"I don't even want to guess where we might be," I told them.

"It ain't Disneyland," Johnny said.

We took another running leap back into the vortex.

CHAPTER 52
November

The frying of the skin as we flew through hyperspace or outer space or cyber space or whatever the fucking kind of space it was wasn't any more pleasant than it had been before. This time I landed on my ass when the vortex farted us out onto the stone floor.

Johnny and Sherry came tumbling out of the vortex right after I did and landed on top of me nearly breaking my back. I guess sliding in on my face did have its advantages after all. At least I'd already be flattened out when someone else landed on me.

After we managed to untangle ourselves, and I've got to admit I didn't rush untangling from Sherry, we started to take a look around.

The portal we'd just been shit out of gave a loud pop like a cork being pulled from a big bottle. The stars in the center of the stone oval winked out. The loud humming that seemed to always accompany the vortex being active was gone. The light show from the glowing hieroglyphics carved in the stone was over. All that we saw in the center of this stone oval was clear air.

Behind the stone oval was a statue, an ugly statue. It was at least nine feet tall. It had the head of an elephant except that it had bull horns sticking out of its forehead. Its body was like a Mr. Universe contestant except that it had six arms and two of those ended in a sea creatures claws.

This was the statue of Asmodeus.

The same statue I'd seen in the chamber beneath the Masonic Lodge in Cahokia.

He was an ugly son of a bitch, but I was glad to see him.

*   *   *

Besides realizing where we were, the first thing we all noticed was we were back in the kind of clothes we had left the twentieth century in. My holster was back around me and the chrome plated 9 mm Johnny gave me was in it.

I checked the gun. It was loaded.

The gun felt better in my hand than that sword did. I like to do my killing from across the room where I can enjoy watching how they fall and flop around.

I took an inventory of what I had on me at that moment. In my back pocket was my wallet with all my current ID's from my life in East St. Louis. I don't know what I expected to find different in there, maybe a Martian ID or something like that.

In my front pocket I had the same roll of cash I'd left with. Thank god for that. I'd busted Roy Wilson's head to get a chunk of that money. I wanted to have as much fun spending that cash as I'd had getting it. There was also something extra in that pocket, four large Roman coins.

I don't know how they could have made the journey without changing into our money. I couldn't spend them now.

The chamber was torch lit, just like it was when Johnny and me left. It was a hell of a lot cleaner though. When we'd jumped through before there was a dead guy lying on the sacrificial alter with his chest carved open and his heart missing.

Now the whole place was positively sparkling, like the maid just finished cleaning up.

"Are we really back?" Sherry asked Johnny and me.

"Only one way to find out," I answered and we all went toward the iron door.

The corridors were all the same as I remembered them, damp with flickering torches the entire way.

Johnny's sawed-off shotgun had reappeared for him the same way the chrome nine millimeter had for me. He carried it out in front of him ready to blast anyone who was waiting for us.

We retraced our steps carefully, taking our time, making sure anybody waiting around a corner didn't get free shots before we could get shots off at them. No one was waiting for us.

Living in the Roman Empire in the time of Caligula had made us all paranoid. But you know what they say, just because you're paranoid doesn't mean someone's not out to get you.

We climbed up out of the trap door into the main office in the Masonic Lodge of Cahokia without being ambushed and phoned for a taxi back to Johnny's.

On the teak desk, along with other official Masonic lodge papers that needed to be signed or filed, was a businessman's day calendar. It was one of those that had a cute thought for the day along with the date and a place to write notes. The thought for the day was, "A boss is just like a diaper, on your ass and usually full of crap." I couldn't argue with that.

The date on the calendar was November 1st.

Almost five months had passed.

Christ! Time flies when you're having fun, don't it.

*   *   *

On the way to Johnny's with the three of us sharing the taxi's back seat, Sherry, sitting between us, turned to Johnny.

She touched him on the arm and looked into his eyes. "I'm sorry you lost Sushi," Sherry said in a whisper. "I know you really loved her."

Johnny turned his face and looked out the window. His face was like stone. "Fuck it," he said.

CHAPTER 53
Back Home

A freezing rain was coming down when we climbed out of the taxi and went into Johnny's Bar and Grill. The front door was unlocked. This didn't seem to surprise Johnny. The same way it didn't surprise him to find Jeanette was up and waiting for us.

If I haven't mentioned it till now, it was late in the night when we got back, sometime after midnight. Jeanette just seems to know things that the rest of us don't. I'm going to just have to get used to it.

Jeanette gave hugs to the three of us. When she was done hugging me, she slapped me a good one upside the head.

"What was that for?" I asked her.

She laughed. "I told you I would slap your jaws for you when you got back and I always keep my word."

"You don't forget a damn thing, do you?" I told her.

Jeanette turned to Sherry. "So this is the young lady you took your journey for." She looked her up and down like a drill sergeant doing an inspection. "You seemed to have come home in one piece," she told her.

Sherry answered, "If it wasn't for them, I wouldn't be alive."

Jeanette looked at Johnny. Quietly she asked, "Where is your young lady?"

Johnny walked to his bar and turned his back to us. The silence in Johnny's Bar and Grill suddenly seemed like a physical thing. He stood and stared at the rows of bottles stacked in front of the mirror behind the bar.

He whispered something that none of us could hear.

Jeanette went to him and touched him lightly on the back. "Are you OK, my grandson?" She asked.

Johnny hammered his right fist down onto the bar making the rows of bottles jump and clink together. They sounded like tiny Chinese bells.

"I said she wouldn't come with me!" He shouted. Quieter he added, "She wanted someone else."

His head dropped and he began sobbing.

Jeanette gathered him up in her arms and held him as only a loving grandmother could.

Softly she told him, "Someday the pain will stop. I know it will."

Johnny whispered back, "I don't think I want it to."

*   *   *

Sherry called for a car to come and pick her up. I told her that I'd taken her this far home I'd ride along and see her all the way.

Johnny didn't cry for very long. Maybe it was about ten minutes, I don't know. He did exceed the limit for what a bad mother fucker from East St. Louis is allowed though. So, for the next few months I'll be calling him my bitch. He'd do the same for me. That's what friends are for.

As soon as Jeanette was through mopping Johnny's eyes, he went up-stairs to his apartment.

I told Jeanette what happened to Julio "Padre" Paez and asked if she could give the four Roman coins I'd found in my pocket to Julio's wife.

"They might be worth something," I said.

She told me she would and as it turned out a few months later it was in the newspaper that Julio's wife had sold the coins to the St. Louis Museum of History for one hundred and fifty thousand dollars.

Shit! I don't mind giving to charity but if I would have known they was worth that much, I'd have kept them for myself.

Jeanette told me she'd been dropping by and paying my phone bill for me by using the spare key Johnny had in his cash register. The bill wasn't much. No one was making any calls.

"It is the least I could do," she said. "Since I knew you were going to bring my grandson home."

In the limo I asked Sherry if she knew for certain that her apartment would still be waiting for her. My arrangement with my landlord is that when he needs someone evicted, I do it for him and when I'm gone he lets the rent slide till I get back. This five months absence is a lot of sliding but I know he'll stick to it because he knows I'll break his neck if he doesn't.

"I don't have any problems with everything being in order for me," Sherry said. "My bank pays my bills for me and, I don't let it be widely known, but I own the lion's share of Patty's Kitten House. The other managers would run it as usual without me being around. There may have been a little dipping in the till, but nothing a good talking to won't cure."

We rode on to Sherry's place.

*   *   *

There was a new muscle-head guarding the front door to the Blaine Building when we arrived. We passed by him and pressed the button for the elevator. Something caught my eye about the guy.

I can't say what. There was just something about him that I didn't like. I walked back to him and jerked the 9 mm out of my holster.

He put his hands up.

"Your ID, out now!" I told him.

Sherry walked back to us as the guy slowly took out his wallet.

"Give them to her," I told the burly door man.

He did that.

Sherry looked at his driver's license and other IDs.

"Carl Jensen," she said, "From Belleville, Illinois. He even has a Belleville Area College ID and a Belleville library card."

She handed them back. I put my gun away.

"Sorry," Sherry said. "I'll explain later."

The elevator came. We entered and rode to Sherry's floor.

We stood outside Sherry's door and she unlocked her apartment. She opened her door and looked up into my eyes.

"Thanks," she said and I figured my moment had come, so I reached down, took her face in my hands, and bent to kiss her lips.

Sherry jerked and pulled away from me.

"I suppose I'll see you at work," Sherry stammered. "But of course if you need some days off, just let me know and I'll make arrangements." I could tell she was embarrassed by me coming on to her.

"Do you think I came after you because it was part of my job?" I asked her.

Her mouth dropped open. She clearly didn't know what to say.

To tell you the truth, neither did I.

"Well, fuck this," I told her. I turned to walk away and punched the button for the elevator. "I'll have to check my job description and see if it includes gladiator fights, killing mother fuckers and time travel."

I got on the elevator and rode down. Maybe I was being too hard on the woman. She'd been through a lot. And maybe I just didn't give a shit either.

CHAPTER 54
Going Home

The limo was waiting for me when I stepped back outside the Blaine Building. The driver got out and opened my door for me.

"What the fuck are you still here for?" I asked.

"When Miss St. Clair called, she said after I brought her here I was to wait, then take you anywhere you wanted to go," he answered.

Ain't that a bitch, I thought, Sherry never had any intention of doing the dance of the long dong tonight. Shit!

"Take me to mother fuckin' Mexico," I told the driver. "I want to suck down some cerveza's while a senorita is sucking down on me."

The driver smiled. "I've got a hundred mile radius," he said. "That's as far as I can take you. Sorry."

"Well, fuck it then. Take me home," I told him. "Go to the place where you picked us up. I live about a block from there."

* * *

I got out at Johnny's Bar and Grill and walked across the street. The freezing rain was pelting me in the face with bits of stinging gravel-like ice. The smell of the city of East St. Louis hit me like a bag of cement.

The smell of an American ghetto, discarded food left to rot, newspapers molding and the vague stench of street people's piss and shit and vomit. It was not a great smell, but it wasn't as eye-wateringly bad as the cities of Micea and Rome had been. At least we treated our sewage.

But this bad smell I could put up with because this was my city. East St. Louis is my home. It may not be paradise but it's pretty much where I belong.

I crossed the soggy slick street and watched the headlights of cars a block away create laser beams of white light off the wet pavement.

Four guys came around the building at the corner. They were slapping each other on the back and laughing at a joke or something else.

My hand went to my holster. I grabbed the pistol grip then thought, "What the fuck am I worried about. These are just some fucking idiots out getting a buzz, trying to get laid."

I dropped my hand to my side and stepped up the stairs that lead into my apartment building. I turned my back on the four guys as they passed behind me. The only person I should be worried about, I thought, is over a thousand years away from this time and place.

That was when two of them grabbed me by the arms and a third clamped his arm around my neck. The fourth shoved a rag wet soaked with a foul smelling chemical in my face.

I fought like hell but couldn't get loose.

Black spots danced in front of my eyes.

The last thought that went through my head was the old saying, "Just because you're paranoid, doesn't mean no one's out to get you."

I should have listened.

CHAPTER 55
Nostalgia

I came to as a fireball hurtling through the space between worlds. It's not my preferred way to wake up.

Two guys had me by my arms and another had me from behind by the hair of the head. I assumed the two guys were the same two that grabbed me outside my apartment building, but through the flames that enveloped all of us I couldn't tell who was who.

Someone was flying ahead of us toward our destination wherever the hell that was.

One thing was different about the way I was flying through space with these guys as opposed to the way me and Johnny and Sherry had been tumbling between the worlds. We weren't tumbling this time. We were just gliding along. Evidently these boys had this space jumping shit down pat.

We moved through space like we were on an escalator. Intergalactic tourists is what we were, just checking out the stars, gliding along smoothly.

The guy in front of us came to the black doorway and calmly stepped off into it and vanished. When we got there the two guys carrying me and the guy who had me by the hair did the same.

My ears popped as we left space and entered a huge torch lit chamber that was strewn with the bodies of sacrificial victims whose hearts had been ripped out.

The first thing I checked out about myself was what I was wearing. If I was anywhere but the twentieth century I would expect to be wearing the clothes of that time.

I still had on my same old East. St. Louis duds, so I figured we must still be in the same century.

The second thing I checked out was the four men who were waiting for us and were pointing what looked like M-16 rifles at me.

"Have any trouble?" A fifth man asked and he looked vaguely familiar but I couldn't immediately place where I'd seen him before. He looked to be in charge of this little gathering.

"No problem at all," the guy who'd come through in front of us answered. "They said this guy was a bad ass. Most women we snatch give us more trouble than he did."

I took a look around me and this ceremonial chamber was like a memory out of my past, but I just couldn't place it. The same way I couldn't place the face of the guy who seemed to be in charge.

The man in charge spoke to me then. "We're going to walk you up some stairs," he said. "You'll be covered the entire way. If you run, we'll kill you. If you don't, at least you'll have a fighting chance." He said to the guys on my sides and the one holding me by my hair, "Let him go."

They did. I was glad to have that damn hand out of my hair.

Behind me was the stone oval we came through. This one looked like it had been pieced back together and patched with cement. The statue behind it was missing one of its six arms and one of its horns.

They marched me to a large steel door.

When it opened, and I gazed up a long flight of stone stairs that led upward into darkness, I realized where I was. I was back in Viet Nam and the man who was in charge was none other than Colonial Ray Sharp.

It had been a long time since I'd been here and I'm not too keen on nostalgia. If there was a part of my Special Forces life I'd like to relive this wouldn't be it. Maybe fucking that Vietnamese nurse again would be all right. But they could keep this little adventure in the past.

*   *   *

They marched me up that long flight of stone stairs and when they pushed the trap door open we came out into bright sunlight. Back in East St. Louis a freezing rain was coming down. It was cold as hell there.

Here it was the exact opposite. It was hot, steaming hot, probably some-where around ninety-five or a hundred degrees. Maybe it wasn't that hot but it sure as hell felt like it was. The humidity in this jungle was off the scale.

The truth is that I really didn't care what the actual temperature was. It was fucking hot. It was about to get hotter.

A few of the huts that our guys burned down in my last visit here had been rebuilt. Most had not been. Twenty years had just left open spaces on the ground where either supply tents were pitched or tall grass had grown.

A group of soldiers that didn't look like they were a part of any particular army were outside and waiting for me to show up. These guys looked like mercenaries and cut throats.

The soldiers made a large circle and I was ordered to the center of that circle. Somebody ran to the rebuilt commander's hut and went inside.

A moment later, wearing combat fatigues and carrying his Roman short sword, Caesar Lanista came striding out.

Why did this not surprise me?

CHAPTER 56
Kill Me

Lanista shoved his way through the circle of men. He stood in front of me and smiled that evil grin of his.

"I told you once that you were mine and you still are," he said.

He was walking around and strutting for his men.

"Just fucking do it!" I told him.

"You do not give the orders here," he stated. "You are nothing but a simple annoyance that I will now remove."

"Just fucking do it!" I said again, this time I shouted it at him. I was getting tired of his entire fucking game. The way things had went for me I was at the point where it was either kill me or I go the fuck home and get drunk till I pass out.

"You didn't have the balls to fight me in Micea, in your own goddamned territory. So just use a gun, like the little fucking bitch coward that you are and fucking kill me. Big fucking gladiator warrior, my ass, you ain't shit!"

"You will not speak to me like this," Lanista roared at me.

"And there ain't shit you can do to stop me," I told him. "You ain't got the balls to fuck with someone like me."

I waved my hand at all the mercenaries around us, "You all do know your fearless leader here isn't really named Caesar right? There's some rich bitch back on Rome that leads him around like her fucking lap dog."

There was a snicker from a few of the mercenaries.

Lanista wheeled and pointed his sword at the spot where the snicker came from.

"One more sound," he said, "and I'll cut you in half!"

The two mercenaries who snickered smiled and cocked their rifles.

"Good job Bubba," I told Lanista. "Showed them who's boss. We're in the twentieth century now boy. Nobody is a slave any more. You're gonna have to prove you deserve to be the man."

"I will kill you," he said and stepped forward raising his blade.

I'd pissed this boy off just like I'd wanted to. Problem was I didn't have a sword to fight him with. Hell, I didn't even have a rock.

Now was when Colonial Ray Sharp stepped in. He held a hand gun. "All fights are equal," he told Lanista. "We fight here by the gladiator's code. Either we give him a sword or you drop yours."

"You do not order me," Lanista told him.

Sharp raised his pistol. "Make your choice," he said. "Drop it, or I drop you. We do this the right way."

Lanista smiled. "Of course," he said. "First I will kill Dark with my bare hands and then we will fight a second duel and I will kill you."

He threw his sword in the dirt.

CHAPTER 57
Serious Knuckle Dusting

Lanista came at me in a rush. He wanted to overwhelm me with his greater size and strength.

He damn near did it too.

He rushed in and caught me with a good hard jab and missed with an overhand right, then body blocked me and knocked me off my feet. Lanista actually body blocked me too well.

I flew for about four feet before I hit the ground so he had to chase me a couple of steps before he could dive on me. That gave me the time to roll and he missed his dive.

I got to my feet and was ready for his next rush.

When Lanista came at me the second time I moved to the side and caught him with my own sharp jab and moved away.

"Come on boy," I yelled at Lanista and even though I could tell I'd gotten underneath his skin, I knew he wasn't out of control. This was a seasoned warrior. He wasn't going to rattle easily.

He did come at me but this time it was more measured, more controlled. He used a pawing jab and did catch me with one of those but I paid him back with a counter right for his trouble.

We went on like this for a few minutes, just sparring. I quit taunting him because he was expecting it and I would just be wasting my breath.

One other thing was I was starting to tire fast. I hadn't even thought about it but this had been one hell of a long day for me. I'd been in a riot, fought the guards to get Sherry out, with Johnny and Sherry fought our way across the city of Rome, time hopped, fought a big ugly spider, time hopped again, got turned down by Sherry, (that would really have recharged my batteries having her blow my fuses), got drugged, time hopped or at least space hopped yet again and now I'm fighting again.

Shit, I should be hot tubing it with Sherry right now, soaking my tired-ass bones, not tangling with this Roman idiot. This is a fucked up life.

After Lanista made another move to try to tackle me, my foot slipped on a rock and to keep from being taken down I turned my back and skipped away. The lunge that Lanista made at me with my back turned was instinctive and I remembered something they tried to drill into us in that gladiators school, a basic belief of the Roman fighting man.

Never turn your back on your enemy. Turning your back means surrender. When your opponent turns his back, you can end the fight immediately by killing him.

I hadn't hurt Lanista with any of my punches. He'd eaten enough of them so he knew better than to just rush blindly at me. He came at me, but it wasn't very fast, so I started tossing in kicks to his left leg whenever he was close enough to even think about punching.

It worked like a charm. I was retreating while raising lumps on his lead leg.

Lanista got me with enough shots so that my nose was bleeding and my left eye was swollen and it was getting hard to see out of that side. Blood and swelling are no big deal to anyone who's spent much time in a boxing ring. It goes with the territory. What was worrying me was that I was breathing heavy and Lanista wasn't.

The time to make a move was now.

I pretended to stumble and turned my back on Lanista. He lunged in at me.

I bent over, chambered a kick, and without looking slammed it into his gut from behind.

The unexpected kick knocked the air from Lanista's lungs and put him on all fours where he was stunned and gasping for breath.

I leaped on his back then and, like I'd been taught in a Jiu-Jitsu class we took in the Special Forces, I applied a guillotine choke.

With my arm around Lanista's throat he fought like a madman. He stood up and dropped backward down on top of me. But I had my legs wrapped around his stomach and my arm around his throat and I wasn't letting go.

He was struggling like a pissed off bear trying to claw me off of him, then all at once, went limp. I knew he was out. His brain hadn't been getting oxygen for too long. He was gone.

I held the choke for an extra few seconds just to make sure. Then I let go, rolled him off of me and stood up.

As I was dusting myself off, Ray Sharp came out to me. "You are free to go," he told me. "The gateway will take you back to the same place you came from."

"What about him," I said pointing at the still unconscious Lanista.

"He'll probably come after you again," Sharp said. "I'd suggest you be ready."

I was lifting the trap door when Lanista came awake. He jumped up off of the ground, backhanded one of the mercenaries, and grabbed his rifle from him.

I was ready to dart down the stairs when Sharp drew on him and put his gun to Lanista's head.

"Put it down," Sharp told Lanista. "He won. You lost. It's over."

"I make the decisions and he dies!" Lanista shouted.

"Looks like it's time for me to take over the business," Sharp told Lanista and pulled the trigger, spraying Lanista's brains, blood, and chunks of his scalp into the air.

CHAPTER 58
Who's Worthy?

I took a taxi home from the Cahokia Masonic Lodge.

It'd been so long since I'd been home I was actually looking forward to it. Home is a place where at least you can rest. I sure as hell needed some rest.

At my place I unlocked the door and found that it was cleaner than I'd left it. Rosa must have kept coming by even though I didn't come home for quite a few months.

Christ! I was way behind on paying her. She'll probably want to kick my ass. Come to think of it, she always wants to kick my ass so it doesn't really make a difference.

The cat that showed up a day or two before I left for Never-Never Land was sitting up and licking his balls on my couch. He looked up at me as I entered.

"Don't let me bother you," I told him. "Make yourself at home. Now what the fuck is your name anyway?"

He didn't tell me.

"Oh yeah," I said. "I named you Tom. Who in the hell could forget that."

He went back to licking his balls.

"Go ahead," I told him. "If I could do it I would."

He gave me a strange look.

"I ain't saying I'd lick your balls, you little furry fuck-head," I told him. "I'd lick mine."

He went back to what he was doing before I'd so rudely interrupted him.

I went to the kitchen and looked in the fridge. I expected to find a jungle growing in there after I'd been gone so long. The ice box was cleaner than normal, mainly because there was hardly anything in it. But there was my bottle of Walker's Whisky in there. I carried it into the front room with me.

Next to the open window that Tom came in and out of was a litter box. It was fairly clean. Lined up a little farther down the wall was one of those plastic cat food and water bowl sets.

"Looks like you've been doing pretty good for yourself while I've been away," I told Tom. "You must be putting the moves on Rosa because somebody sure likes you."

It was getting light outside so without really thinking about it I sat on the couch, picked up the phone and dialed Julia's number. I knew she must have gotten home from work just a few minutes earlier.

Julia picked up on the third ring.

"Hello?"

"It's John," I said. "I'd like to see you."

She let her breath out in a long sigh. "I don't think so," Julia said. "You've been gone for so long without even a word. I can't go through that. Having a man in my life just up and vanish, that just don't work."

"Look, it wasn't my choice," I started.

She cut me off.

"I don't even want to hear the reasons," she said. "This isn't good for Felicia. It isn't good for me."

"Let me explain."

Julia cut me off again.

"No!" She said. "I've thought about this a long time. I wish you all the luck in the world, John. I really do. It's over."

She hung up.

I slammed the phone down.

Ain't that a son of a bitch! I thought.

*   *   *

I sat with my friend Hiram Walker and Tom sat beside me.

Tom got done licking his balls so he licked his ass some too.

"Good job boy," I told him. "Make sure you get it all."

He looked at me like he didn't appreciate the joke.

I turned on the TV and *Captain Kangaroo* was the only thing on that seemed half way interesting.

The whisky tasted horrible. That wasn't anything new.

Green Jeans was explaining to the Captain how to plow a field. Yeah, right. You two faggot mother fuckers have been plowing each other's fields for years. You don't need to explain it to him now.

The phone rang.

Out of habit, I picked it up.

"What do ya want?"

"John," it was Sherry. "Is that you?"

"Who the hell else would it be? What do ya want?"

"I got to thinking," She said. "There's no guarantee that Caesar Lanista won't come after me."

"What's that got to do with me?" I asked. "I'll be clocking in in a few days."

"Well, I was thinking, I could send a car by," she said. "And we could discuss this."

"You know how I am," I told her. "I'm not going to come by to just hold your hand 'cause you're nervous. I got a lot of important things to do today."

Tom looked at me, and I thought if you could talk I'd wring your fucking neck.

Sherry said, "John, you're not making this easy."

"Then just spit it out," I told her.

She said, "I've thought about it and have decided that if you are not worthy then no one is. Will you come if I send the car?"

"Let me think about this a while," I said. "OK, send the car. I guess I'll be finding out if you're worthy and I guarantee we'll both be coming in a little while."

I hung up.

Maybe I'll tell her after I get there that Caesar Lanista is dead, I thought.

Yeah, and maybe I'll wait a few months too.

It all depends on how worthy she is.

If she's really worthy, she may never find out.

AFTERWORD

Some of you people out there might want to be saying to me, "Hey, wake up! Don't you know that Caligula and Spartacus didn't live during the same time? Where do you get off telling us a story that had both of them in it?"

All right, I'm going to tell you a few things.

First of all, you have been getting your information from people (teachers, maybe even college professors) who never were there. Who got their information out of books written by people who (yes, you guessed it) never were there. So what do they know?

This is like getting a story from a friend, who knows a friend, who heard it from a friend, who probably got it from a friend, who wasn't your friend to begin with. That kind of information isn't worth anything.

Second, I never once said that the Rome John Dark went to was on the same Earth as the one I grew up on. I don't know where the Rome was that he went to. I do not know if he went to an alternate universe, another dimension, a counter Earth or if he just time traveled.

This is fiction, if you enjoyed the story that's what matters to me.

GREAT BOOKS

E-BOOKS

AUDIOBOOKS

&

MORE

Visit us today

www.speakingvolumes.us

VISIT

SPEAKING VOLUMES ONLINE

HUGO, NEBULA, EDGAR,

SHAMUS, ANTHONY MACAVITY,

AGATHA, CARL SANDBERG,

ELLERY QUEEN, OWEN WISTER,

SPUR & BRAM STOKER

AWARD-WINNING

USA TODAY & NEW YORK TIMES

BEST-SELLING AUTHORS

www.speakingvolumes.us

VISIT
SPEAKING VOLUMES ONLINE

National Best-Selling

&

Award Winning Authors

www.speakingvolumes.us